Angela Jariwala was born in West London to parents from Surat, India. She was a published author of two young adult novels, both published by Mantra Lingua Ltd, an award-winning publisher of multicultural and multilingual books for children and young people. Angela sadly passed away in December 2021 before finishing this novel.

ANGELA JARIWALA

THE
CAT
SHARE

**SIMON &
SCHUSTER**

London · New York · Amsterdam/Antwerp · Sydney/Melbourne · Toronto · New Delhi

First published in Great Britain by Simon & Schuster UK Ltd, 2025

Copyright © Angela Jariwala, 2025

The right of Angela Jariwala to be identified as author of this work
has been asserted in accordance with the Copyright, Designs and Patents Act, 1988.

1 3 5 7 9 10 8 6 4 2

Simon & Schuster UK Ltd, 1st Floor
222 Gray's Inn Road, London WC1X 8HB

Simon & Schuster Australia, Sydney
Simon & Schuster India, New Delhi

www.simonandschuster.co.uk
www.simonandschuster.com.au
www.simonandschuster.co.in

The authorised representative in the EEA is Simon & Schuster Netherlands BV,
Herculesplein 96, 3584 AA Utrecht, Netherlands. info@simonandschuster.nl

Simon & Schuster strongly believes in freedom of expression and stands against
censorship in all its forms. For more information, visit BooksBelong.com

A CIP catalogue record for this book is available from the British Library

Paperback ISBN: 978-1-3985-0454-7
eBook ISBN: 978-1-3985-0455-4
Audio ISBN: 978-1-3985-1385-3

This book is a work of fiction. Names, characters, places and incidents are either
a product of the author's imagination or are used fictitiously. Any resemblance
to actual people living or dead, events or locales is entirely coincidental.

Typeset in Bembo by M Rules

Printed and Bound in the UK using 100% Renewable Electricity at CPI Group (UK) Ltd

MIX
Paper | Supporting
responsible forestry
FSC
www.fsc.org
FSC® C013604

In memory of Angela.
And Dilly, the cat that inspired this story.

1

Jenni stood by the kitchen sink and filled up the kettle. The morning was quiet and cool, but sunlight filled the small flat with the promise of a beautiful day. Clicking the kettle onto its base, Jenni flicked the switch down and reached up to choose a mug from the shelf above. She picked her favourite – the one with a colourful pattern in a cheery yellow – and set about making herself a cup of tea.

Just then, a repetitive thudding coming from the direction of the back door made her look up with a smile. As was usual at this time in their morning routine, Oscar, Jenni's cat, was returning home from a night on the prowl. Also as was usual, the banging continued.

Jenni gave a sigh. 'Oscar, just push open the cat flap. We've been through this before. You don't need to keep hitting it with your paw.'

Oscar decided to give it a firm headbutt in reply.

Jenni walked over to the door and crouched down. She looked at the cat through the Perspex flap.

'Look. You are a cat. This is a *cat* flap, there's absolutely no reason why you can't enter the flat via this specially made portal.'

Oscar fixed her with a firm stare.

Rolling her eyes, Jenni stood up. They both knew what happened next in this charade, and there was no point pretending otherwise.

Jenni unlocked and opened the back door, stepping back to allow the small tabby to make his entrance.

Oscar, making it clear that he didn't know why they had to go through this farce every morning – *surely* she understood her role by now – strutted into the kitchen purring proudly and rubbing against Jenni's legs. Looking down, she saw he had something in his mouth: a faded Quavers crisp packet from the looks of things.

'Lovely. Thanks for this, Oscar,' she said, reaching down and taking it. She put it in the bin while Oscar, delighted to have done his bit for the environment, moved to phase two of their morning routine.

Knowing her place, Jenni set about getting him his breakfast, which he hungrily set about demolishing.

She often wondered how she had ended up with such an entitled cat, and realised it must have been something she'd done. Perhaps she'd given into his demands too easily and hadn't given him enough boundaries.

Jenni made a note to consider this more at a later point should she ever become a parent, although this really wasn't something she needed to worry about right now given her very single status. She hadn't been on a date for months and had no intention of reinstalling The Apps. She gave an involuntary shudder.

Tea made, she decided to sit outside to drink it, settling down on the rather rickety metal chair that stood next to the small table by her back door. Pushing aside various gardening tools, labels and bits of string, she balanced her cup on the corner of the table and adjusted her chair so that it didn't wobble on the uneven ground.

Jenni's garden was city-small, with a paved area near the house and a tiny rectangle of grass that left room – *just about* – for a shed wedged in the far corner. Flowerbeds lined the fences on either side of the square space and, as Jenni was lucky enough to live in a mid-terrace flat, she was surrounded on both sides by trees and shrubs, giving her – when the leaves came out – her own private haven, where she was hidden from the windows that looked down on her from the houses and the block of flats that backed on to hers.

At the moment, the garden didn't look like much, but spring was around the corner – all the signs were there. The fresh copper red leaves on the old rose bush were beginning to unfurl, the tips of the tulip bulbs were pushing through the cold soil and next door's cherry tree was lit with blossom.

Jenni loved her garden. When her ex-boyfriend Alex had left her, it had been what had saved her. And Oscar too, of course. She'd read somewhere that planting a garden was about hope: hope for the future, hope that life would go on, hope that you'd be there to see the flowers when they finally came into bloom, and that had been true for her.

After he'd gone and she'd been left alone in the flat that was meant to have been theirs, it had been the digging, cutting back and sowing seeds that had allowed her, quite literally, to put down her own roots, and had made the flat feel like somewhere she could live, rather than four walls that reminded her of failure.

Now, enjoying the slight breeze, she listened as her street came alive. She could hear that next door were up – windows were being opened, a radio was quietly playing – and on the other side she could hear Jo and Nick getting their bikes out ready to go for a ride. He was a keen cyclist, and although Jo said she enjoyed the fifty mile cycle out to Kent each weekend, Jenni wasn't convinced.

Leaning back with a contented sigh and feeling grateful she no longer had to go on the park run Alex was always so keen on doing first thing on a Saturday morning, she surveyed the garden. The ivy growing up the fence needed cutting back, and there was always weeding. She was going to give separating the hardy geraniums a go – Monty Don had made it look a breeze.

She decided not to dwell on the fact that her Friday night consisted of sitting on the sofa watching *Gardener's World*.

And, as her mum always said, the plants had two options – to live or die. A rather harsh take on the whole nature versus nurture business, but her mum's garden was stunning, so the tough love approach seemed to work – on the plants at least.

But for now, Jenni was content enjoying the feeling of calm. Weekends on her own had been hard to start with, but now she was used to filling the two empty days with activities that made her happy, although sometimes it was still hard.

This evening she was meeting her friend, Amy, but besides that she had no plans other than to wander to the street market to browse the stalls before heading back home.

The cat flap banged and Oscar appeared next to her, licking his lips, which, combined with the black patch of fur around his right eye, gave him a certain piratical appearance.

'Oh, so the flap's okay when you want to leave the house, is it?' she said, as Oscar jumped on the table next to her. She stroked his grey and black stripes, and he purred as he nuzzled into her hand. 'Ah, you're a big softy, aren't you, Oscar?'

Jenni gave him a last tickle under his chin before tucking a strand of her dark, curly hair behind her ear and standing up. 'Right, where are my secateurs? I'm going to sort out that ivy, it's gone bonkers and is growing over the shed window.'

Oscar stretched out in the sunshine, carefully lying on the secateurs that Jenni needed. He watched her lazily with one eye open as she searched for the missing object, and settled into a comfortable doze.

*

'Here you go. One G&T with horrible cucumber for you, and a double with a very normal slice of lemon for me.' Amy put the two glasses down on the table and flicked her blonde hair out of the way. 'Right, now tell me what you've been up to.'

Jenni took a long sip of her drink. Her trip to the market had been particularly successful as she'd managed to pick up some catnip as a treat for Oscar. He'd love rolling around on it in a blissful state.

'And then I got a big bag of popcorn from that really nice stall we like and headed home. Oh, I did have a quick look in Grace & Favour, but decided I really didn't need another cushion.'

'Impressive self-restraint, well done,' Amy replied. 'I'd love to just wander around the market, but sadly an accompanying toddler doesn't make for happy browsing.'

'No, especially when the toddler in question is George,' said Jenni. She loved her friend's little boy, but she had to admit it wasn't exactly restful looking around a shop full of breakable things with him in tow. 'I'm still scarred from our visit to that café. I don't know how he managed to reach the china on that shelf.'

Amy shuddered in reply. 'We've never gone back. We hurry past it now in shame. I felt awful.'

This evening, they'd chosen a booth on the right-hand side of the pub, but they'd had to move as they'd realised they were sitting under a speaker and couldn't hear each other over the music blaring out. They were now tucked away at a table at the back, not too far from the bar. The pub, the Dog & Duck, was an old favourite of theirs as it was a ten-minute walk from Jenni's house and near the train station for Amy, so she had an easy journey home too. The back of the pub was dimly lit, with small tea-lights on the bare wood tables, which were surrounded by mismatched wooden chairs. The navy blue walls, covered in displays of brightly coloured vintage plates and old photos, made it a cosy space, and the staff were friendly and happy to leave them chatting at the table so they didn't feel hassled.

'What did you get up today?' asked Jenni as she picked up the menus and handed one to Amy.

'We spent the day in soft play *hell*. Thoughts of this drink have been all that's got me through. And the joy of not having to do bath and bedtime.'

'Simon is on duty, is he?'

'Yes, and I'm allowed a lie-in tomorrow. Simon's going to do the morning shift, hence the double gin. Anyway, let's look at the menu and decide what to order.'

Jenni decided on the risotto as it was something she could never be bothered to cook for herself, while Amy went for the fish and chips. The waiter, Thomas, took their order and hurried back to the kitchen before dashing off to serve another group of people that had settled in at the table next to them.

'So tell me about work. How's life at Go Big?' said Amy. She and Jenni were both employed by the same company, a top-end outdoor clothing business. They both worked in marketing and had bonded over a particularly fraught campaign that had involved the launch of a range of walking gear. The words 'Wickaway fabric' still reduced both of them to hysterical laughter even three years later. Amy was currently on maternity leave as baby Tilly had recently joined brother George.

'Well, Clive's being a complete nightmare *again*. He's determined that we have to outperform Patagonia and has come over all ethical as he thinks we need to become a B Corp company too. I admire the sentiment, but he doesn't seem to understand that going green is not as simple as sticking "sustainable material" on our labels, and that a circular economy has nothing to do with cycle wear. It's all rather exhausting.'

Amy rolled her eyes in sympathy. 'What about Susan? How's she doing?'

'She's great, but even she gets frustrated with it all, and usually you can't tell what she's thinking.'

Susan was the new MD who had been brought in to manage Clive. A thankless task, but one she seemed more than equal to, although on this occasion explaining 'green-washing' to Clive had resulted in her having to go home for a lie down.

Jenni continued to fill Amy in on what was going on at work: who was sending passive aggressive emails to who, how Ryan had had a meltdown about the strength of the coffee and now no one dared refill the coffee machine, and how Lily, the new intern, was still in shock after seeing Clive model the new, very fitted, base layers.

Both Jenni and Amy agreed that Lily probably had grounds for some kind of legal action – no one needed to see Clive encased head to toe in just a thin layer of three-ply merino wool. Fortunately, Sandra in HR had come to the rescue and a costly lawsuit had been averted.

'Oh, and the other big news is that we're planning a massive photoshoot at a snowdome so we can get some really good images of the new ski-wear range. I'm in charge of coordinating it and it's going to be huge. I wish you were there to help. I've got to find five key influencers to come along – it's giving me sleepless nights!'

Jenni took a gulp of her drink.

'You'll be great,' said Amy, reassuringly. 'It always feels out of control when you start these things, but it will all come together.'

'Hmm.' Jenni felt doubtful, but she took comfort in her friend's confidence.

'I'll do some research for you when I'm doing the 2 am feed. If I see someone who looks a good fit for a brand collaboration, I'll let you know.'

'Thank you, that would be great. There's so much to do, I haven't really had time to give it a proper look. I don't want the obvious people and it needs to feel genuine. Anyway, you know all that, so let me know who you find.'

Just then, Thomas appeared with their food. After putting down the plates, he went off to find them knives and forks before reappearing with a small terracotta flowerpot filled with cutlery, paper napkins and various condiments. He headed back to the bar to get another round of drinks. G&Ts delivered, he left them to it and the friends tucked into their food.

Jenni loved her evenings out with Amy. She was a friend who she could just relax with and be herself, she didn't feel like she had to put on an act. Although they were at different stages in their lives – Amy was married with two children, while she was single, still recovering from her break-up with Alex – there was no competition between them, and Amy never made Jenni feel inadequate for being on her own, which some friends, however unintentionally, did. Jenni never went home feeling lonely after seeing Amy, and she enjoyed hearing stories about George and now Tilly, sharing Amy's enjoyment, and frustration sometimes, at life with young children.

'Oh this is delicious,' said Amy, swallowing a mouthful. 'Here. Try a chip, I've got loads.'

Jenni took a chip and dipped it into her risotto – nothing wrong with double carbs.

'So what are you up to tomorrow?' Amy asked.

Jenni, finishing her mouthful, was about to reply, and then broke off as the waiter came over to check they were happy with everything. As the waiting staff were obviously trained to do, he arrived when they both had their mouths full, so they had to nod enthusiastically, hoping this adequately conveyed their appreciation.

'I wish they wouldn't do that,' said Jenni, having swallowed and now able to speak.

'I know, they definitely do it on purpose so we can't say anything's wrong, it's so annoying. Anyway, where were we? Oh yes, what are you up to tomorrow?'

'Well, I really want to get into the shed and have a bit of a sort out. I'm going to try tie-dying some tote bags. Which reminds me, I've got a little present for Tilly.'

She handed Amy a tissue-wrapped present.

'I had some lovely natural dyes, so I tried them out on some sleepsuits and I wondered if Tilly could be a tester. If the colour holds, I thought I might do a few and see if I can sell them at the May Day craft fair.'

'Oh yes, that's a nice idea. I'll let you know, although I'm sure it's perfect. George loves his pyjama set.'

Jenni had studied textile design at college and had intended on a career making clothes, but the reality of finding a job in the fashion industry had soon put paid to those ambitions, and she was grateful when she'd got the job in marketing with Clive's start up, Go Big, even though selling someone else's clothes, particularly active wear given that she struggled to commit to even a yoga class, was not quite what she'd had in mind.

She'd always loved sewing and making things herself, but a small one-bedroom flat – and Alex's determination that the shed was for practical things like lawnmowers – meant that she hadn't had anywhere to experiment with her designs. One morning, a month after he'd left for good, she'd decided that the shed was now hers and she was going to use it. The lawnmower was Freecycled – Monty Don said lawns were now to be left to grow, so no need to cut it anymore – Alex's old bike was gifted to Nick next door for parts, and the fold-down table had been set up as a work station. The space reclaimed, Jenni had spent many happy hours in her shed, and her passion was tie-dying. There had been some unfortunate colour accidents, more distressed hippy than hip, but she'd got the hang of using more muted colour combinations, and Amy, who always mysteriously knew what the next trend would be at least six months before everyone else, had declared Jenni's creations a triumph and had encouraged her to branch out into babywear.

'What else are you thinking of selling?' asked Amy, eating her last chip and putting down her knife and fork.

'Perhaps some T-shirts, and I'm thinking socks as they are pretty easy to dye and have a good mark up,' Jenni said, taking the last mouthful of her risotto.

'What about printing some business cards to hand out?' Amy suggested. 'Have you got your website up and running?'

'Not yet, I mainly sell through Instagram, but that's a good idea. I've had some commissions for presents.'

'That sounds good. Pudding?'

Jenni, momentarily confused by the idea of a tie-dye pudding, shook her head. 'Oh. Umm. No, thanks. What about you?'

'I'm stuffed,' said Amy with a shake of her head. She glanced at the clock above the bar. 'In fact, I think I'd better head off soon. I know it's ridiculously early, but I'll have to get up in the night, so I don't want to be too late.'

Waiter summoned, bill paid, coats collected and Jenni's pink and green striped scarf finally located under a nearby chair, Jenni walked with Amy to the train station and then carried on the short walk home. There was still a bit of a chill in the air despite the lighter evenings.

As it was a Saturday evening, the high street was busy with people either heading home or only just setting out for the night. People spilled out of the pub, laughing and chatting, nursing pints of beer and balancing wine glasses. The Victoria was always really busy, which is why she and Amy had chosen the Dog & Duck further up the road, the one favoured by the locals, as it meant they could always get a seat and hear themselves talk.

Pausing at the zebra crossing for the cars to stop, she continued down the road, past the organic bakers, the general store – expensive but delicious – Rosie's vegan café and the very un-vegan local butchers that, come Saturday morning, always had a queue snaking around the corner. All the ingredients that made the area where she lived one of London's self-declared villages. Having grown up in a small rural community, Jenni knew the high street, which was full of life, people and bustle, was very much *not* a village, but she loved where she lived: and she loved that here you could choose your own community rather than having it forced upon you.

She remembered, just in time, that she had run out of cat biscuits, so she stopped at Barry's, the local grocery store, conveniently open 24/7.

Rather confusingly, both of the people who worked

there were called Barry. Smiley Barry was always friendly and happy to chat, while his co-worker, Grumpy Barry, would greet customers with a snarl — if they were lucky. Fortunately, Smiley Barry was on till duty that evening.

Biscuits bought, Jenni walked down the street, enjoying looking through the windows where the curtains or blinds had been left open, glimpsing snapshots of people's lives and marvelling at how the seemingly identical terraced houses, although all so similar in design and layout, each had their own quirks. Some had a wall knocked through here, a door added there, some were painted innocuous shades of cream and white, while others had chosen colours in bright, bold hues like magenta, aubergine and, surprisingly, a green that Jenni thought looked more Shrek than emerald.

Turning into Copestone Road, it was a short walk to her front door. Thinking about her flat felt slightly bittersweet — she knew she was lucky to own somewhere in London, but it had come at a cost. Although her dad had wanted her to use the money he had left her to buy out Alex, wanted her to have a secure future, she felt sad he wasn't here to share it with her.

Fumbling for the key, which, as usual, had hidden itself in the deepest recesses of her bag, she opened the front door and stepped into the shared hallway. Her upstairs neighbour was home, as evidenced by the fact that she could hear his TV blaring away as usual.

Over the sound of canned laughter, Jenni heard a loud meow. Oscar was obviously hungry.

Jenni opened her door and snapped on the light to see him sitting on the mat radiating a distinct, 'What time do you call this?' vibe.

Shrugging off her coat and scarf and hanging them on the peg in the hall, Jenni closed the door behind her and headed for the kitchen, Oscar weaving impatiently between her legs.

'I'm sorry, Oscar. Look, I've got biscuits. Let me take my shoes off and I'll feed you.'

Hearing the rattle of biscuits, Oscar collapsed dramatically on his back, paws in the air, purring. Obviously, all had been forgiven now and normal service had been resumed.

Jenni laughed as she shook the food into his bowl and watched as Oscar leapt up to get to his dinner. While he ate, Jenni retrieved her cup from the draining board and filled the kettle. She'd have herbal tea and watch some telly – perhaps whatever upstairs was enjoying – before going to bed.

The cat flap banged shut, signalling Oscar's exit and leaving Jenni alone in her kitchen. Nursing the hot cup between her hands, she tried not to picture Amy returning to her family, or Nick and Jo next door watching TV together. She knew she had friends and she'd see people at work, but sometimes trying to ignore the loneliness was exhausting.

This was not how she'd imagined her life in her late thirties.

Deciding not to think about the rest of the weekend stretching out ahead of her, she snapped off the kitchen light and headed for the distraction of Netflix.

2

Ben, pulling the front door shut behind him, glanced at his phone – he was running late. Fortunately, Pelham Fire Station was only a fifteen-minute walk from his house, so if he walked briskly he'd arrive on time.

People always assumed working nights must be difficult, but Ben, used to shifting his body clock between nights and days, enjoyed the feeling that his 'day' was just beginning when everyone else's was nearly over.

After getting home that morning, he'd had breakfast and then made himself go to bed. It was always tempting to keep going, but experience told him that he needed to sleep and would feel terrible if he ended up napping in the afternoon, waking feeling groggy and resentful. Everyone working in the fire service for any length of time eventually found what suited them best when it came to managing shifts, and for Ben it was definitely to get to bed as soon as he came home.

The hardest thing was the noise – trying to sleep when everyone else was up and about was difficult, and in the past it had driven him nuts to hear flatmates crashing around, neighbours slamming doors and people in the street talking loudly. In truth, he knew people weren't doing it on purpose, it just felt like they were when you were exhausted.

Fortunately, his current accommodation was in a block of flats built especially for key workers, so his neighbours all understood what it was like to work irregular hours and were always considerate as a result.

The builders working on a nearby house, however, not so much.

He'd lived in his small ground-floor flat for two years, but apart from the huge TV and Xbox, he hadn't done much to personalise it. The off-white walls were still bare, the shelf on the wall pretty much empty apart from a few books, and the houseplant his sister had given him in an attempt to 'brighten things up a bit' sat wilting on the windowsill. The flat looked like what it was: a place for him to sleep and store stuff. He didn't really think of it as home.

Sometimes, looking around his living room, which was lit only by the light of the TV, the image of another flat, another *time*, flashed into his mind: the warm glow of a lamp, cushions, framed photos on the mantlepiece, a vase of flowers on the coffee table. All the little touches that showed someone cared. But those touches – and the person who'd been responsible for them – were gone, and he'd promised himself that he wasn't going to get attached to any of that again.

Having managed to get a good seven hours of sleep in, Ben woke at five, giving him time to catch up on his washing, take care of some pressing chores, eat dinner and fit in a quick game before heading back to work.

Even after five years on the job, there was still something exciting about heading off into the night, unsure of what the darkness would bring; whether it would be a quiet night of admin and waiting around, or a call-out that saw them rushing to the engine, the noise of the siren and the blue lights cutting through the city streets, the very thing that gave him the buzz that made him want to go to work.

Although he hated to see the damage – to people or to buildings – he had to admit that a busy night went faster than a quiet one and, of course, the feeling of saving someone or something was one they all valued. It made the job worthwhile.

Turning left out of his road, Ben walked fast through the familiar streets towards Camberwick Road, where the station was based.

The massive red doors were thrown open, revealing the three engines parked within. The forecourt was currently empty, the painted yellow zigzag lines spilling out onto the road, warning pedestrians and vehicles to stay clear and take care.

Taz and Vick were already there, preparing for handover from the previous watch.

'Hey, Ben, how come you live the closest and you're always late?' Taz shouted as he spotted Ben's arrival.

'I know, I know, I can't even blame the traffic,' Ben replied, smiling.

'You need some young children. They'll help you get out the house in a hurry,' said Vick.

'Long day with the kids?' asked Ben.

Vick had two young children, and so her days were considerably busier than his, although her husband Brian, also a firefighter, had opposite shifts so they could cover childcare between them. She often joked that fighting fires was easier than dealing with toddlers.

'Yes, Max has a cold and couldn't go to nursery, so he's been at home with me. Dale convinced him to have a nap after lunch, thank God, so I managed to get a bit of sleep.'

'If we're quiet, you can always sleep later,' said Taz.

The station had its own sleeping quarters, which meant firefighters – much to the resentment and teasing of their colleagues in the police force who had no such provision – were able to sleep while on call.

At that moment, the watch commander appeared, and

other members of Ben's crew, Red Watch, moved into line, ready for the parade and inspection.

Ben hurried to throw his rucksack into his battered locker and head back smartish to fall in next to Vick.

'You don't half cut things fine,' she hissed at him out of the corner of her mouth.

His heart beating fast following his dash back from the common room, Ben vowed to leave home earlier in future.

3

Jenni gathered up her laptop, notebook and favourite pen and headed to the open-plan area of the office they jokingly called the 'arena' for the Monday Motivational Meet-Up. Clive, her boss, was keen on alliteration when it came to naming meetings – Jenni was sure some meetings had been invented simply because Clive had a great idea for wordplay: Friday Freeday came to mind.

The Go Big HQ had been designed to encourage 'collaboration, conversation and creative clashes', and so, at the far end of the office, away from the desks and the staff kitchen, was a semi-circular structure with tiered seating like in a Roman amphitheatre.

The idea was that, by breaking away from a traditional boardroom table, staff would be free to Go Big with their thinking and let their creative juices flow.

Personally speaking, Jenni found the wooden structure

had quite the opposite effect, and she dreaded having to haul herself up the awkwardly high steps and sit uncomfortably on a plyboard plank for hours on end.

After feeding Oscar earlier that morning, Jenni had rushed out of the house to catch the bus into town. Grateful that she worked for a company where trainers and jeans were acceptable attire, she was able to run the last few metres comfortably and caught the bus before it left the stop.

The rain had started falling in earnest as she'd left the house, and she could imagine Oscar's disdain should he put a paw outside. The day before had been equally wet, so she and Oscar had spent the day inside, and while she'd taken the opportunity to paint the bathroom in the warm yellow she'd been visualising for ages, Oscar curled up on the sofa and ignored her.

He was still cross with her for taking away Elsa.

Which, as she walked the length of the corridor, reminded her to message the street WhatsApp group to see if anyone had lost a small *Frozen* figurine – another of Oscar's 'presents' that she'd discovered waiting for her in the kitchen.

'Right, everyone, gather, gather. Let's get this meeting started.'

Clive was already in full flow when Jenni reached the arena and clambered into place. Today their esteemed leader was testing out their prototype cycling gear and was striding around in Lycra shorts and a half-zip short-sleeved T-shirt. A quick glance confirmed that the design team had taken the aerodynamic aspect of the brief to heart, and Clive's outfit was indecently tight.

Vowing not to look at her boss any lower than neck-height – and hoping that HR were on alert for further intern-shocking incidents – she braced herself to endure the next half hour.

Experienced at looking suitably motivated during Clive's talks, Jenni opened up her laptop to hide her notepad. Occasionally looking up to nod thoughtfully at appropriate intervals, she began making a list of materials she needed to prepare for her stall at the May Day fair, which she'd signed up to in a fit of enthusiasm ages ago. Now the date was getting closer, she was beginning to panic.

Clive walked manically around the stage, gesticulating wildly, and Jenni tuned in to hear him talking about the need for 'business leaders' to have agility and quick reactions. There was also something about pivoting.

Perhaps they should consider a range of activewear for entrepreneurs, Jenni thought, given that it seemed to require an awful lot of physical activity.

She looked up briefly to give a 'hmm, interesting' nod, and caught Barney in sales doing the same thing. They shared an eye roll before Jenni returned to her notepad. She was quite keen to add some extra detail to the handles of the tote bag she'd made, so she pondered getting one of those pompom makers she'd seen on the internet.

Clive had slowed down and come to a standstill, looking around at everyone. Thank goodness they were near the end now.

'So, what I want to see is more of the fantastic work you've all been doing. We need to make sure the new ski-wear range reaches the top-end of the market and that we establish Go Big as the brand everyone wants to be seen in. Jenni is leading the photo shoot and we can't wait to see the results.'

Jolted from her list, Jenni hurriedly looked up and gave a firm nod, aiming to convey complete control over the ski-wear situation and hoping beyond hope that Clive wouldn't call upon her to give a rundown on what was in place.

Thankfully, Susan took that moment to share some information about housekeeping – there was currently a coffee bean shortage and staff were being encouraged to use fewer scoops of coffee each time the machine was refilled, or to have tea instead.

Jenni noticed Ryan, who was notorious for his extra-strong espressos, was on the receiving end of some poisonous looks, but he stared defiantly ahead and, judging by the supportive glances of others in the finance team, it looked like the coffee wars were not going to be so easily resolved.

Climbing down from the third tier where she'd been

sitting, Jenni headed back to her desk, glad to be moving again as her bum had gone numb. She was on Sphere One, or as they privately called it, the third circle of hell, with Tim and Lucy and, currently, Will, who was covering for Amy. Their large circular desk – one of six in their area – was divided into four quarters by wire mesh dividers that were meant to provide privacy, but actually made them feel like prisoners.

Despite the modern, industrial-design vibe and gladiatorial arena, Jenni had to admit that the Go Big offices were quite swanky, and unlike many people who had not wanted to return to the office after the pandemic, she was happy to come into work three times a week.

Her portion of the desk faced the large, glass sliding doors that opened on to a roof terrace, and she could see that the earlier rain had now cleared and weak sunshine was filtering through the clouds. Behind Tim, book-filled shelves lined the partition between their department and the design team, and further down the open-plan space was the kitchen.

Jenni noted that Finance Person One was currently lurking in the doorway – presumably on lookout for Susan while Ryan added that extra scoop to the coffee filter.

Jenni decided that perhaps she'd wait before getting a cup of tea.

Plugging her laptop back in to her monitor, she typed in her password and opened up her email. Finding the one she was looking for, she reached for the phone and dialled the number of the photographer she wanted to book for the ski-wear shoot.

The morning passed quickly as Jenni worked her way through her to-do list: book photographer – tick; arrange model castings – tick; speak to the studio to arrange delivery of clothing – tick. There was also an email from Amy with some ideas for social media influencers, and Jenni made a note to speak to the comms team.

Her stomach rumbled and, looking at the clock, she real-ised it was past one – definitely time for lunch.

Jenni gathered up her coat and bag and stood up. 'Anyone want anything? she asked Tim and Lucy. Will had already disappeared.

'I'm fine, thanks,' said Lucy. 'I've brought in a tin of tomato soup, I need to save some money.'

'I'll come with you,' Tim said, standing up. 'I should be saving money too – the honeymoon cost a fortune – but I'm too lazy to plan my lunches in advance.'

He grabbed his coat and shoved his wallet into his pocket. Then decided to retrieve his scarf too. 'Right, ready.'

'So, how was Portugal?' Jenni asked as they headed down the stairs and out of the building onto the busy street below. Tim had recently got married and he and his now-husband Paul had had a week away honeymooning in the Algarve.

'Oh, just fantastic. The weather was lovely, warm enough

to sit by the pool and read a book, the hotel was amazing, we had our own little villa in the grounds, but you go up to the hotel and use all the facilities like the spa and restaurant. It was just so nice to do nothing.'

'That sounds amazing, and if you managed to get Paul to sit down and relax, that's a miracle!'

Jenni had met Paul on several social occasions. Whereas Tim was laid-back and never stressed – even when Clive was throwing ideas at him, demanding he produce a client-winning pitch on the tightest of deadlines – Paul was a whirlwind of activity, always with several projects on the go and constantly checking his phone. Jenni supposed it was a classic case of opposites attract, and while Tim did occasionally come into work moaning that he was exhausted, wishing they could have a quiet weekend, the two of them had obviously found a way to make their life together work.

'Well, he managed an hour on a sunbed on day one, but fortunately there were loads of activities so he went off and played tennis or windsurfed or whatever was running that day. It was wonderful. I ended up drinking G&Ts with all the parents who'd put their children in the kids' club. We all got drunk and had a marvellous time.'

Jenni laughed, imagining Paul arriving back, full of enthusiasm as he told Tim all about his day, just as the children were telling proud parents what they'd been up to in the sandpit or on the slides.

The street was busy, the pavements full of pedestrians and traffic crawling up to the lights at the end of the road. The greasy-looking paving slabs were slippery after the morning's rain, but the wind had dropped, and in the shelter of the tall red-brick buildings, it felt almost warm.

'I went to Porto with Alex once, but that was years ago now,' Jenni recalled, wistfully. 'We went around all the distilleries. It was just a long weekend but it was great. I'd love to go back.'

'Why don't you?' Tim asked, then stopping abruptly as the man walking in front of him suddenly stood still to look at his phone.

Tim tutted. 'Honestly, tourists. Don't people know that London pavements are like motorways – if you're going to walk slowly, walk on the inside lane, next to the shops,' he said, his voice rising as he directed the last bit at the man blocking the pavement.

Manoeuvring around the still-stationery man who was frowning at the map on his screen, Jenni and Tim carried on walking the last few metres and then turned into a sandwich shop.

In a long-practised routine, Tim joined the queue while Jenni grabbed an egg sandwich and salt and vinegar crisps for her, and a chicken sandwich and ready salted for Tim. Spotting his dark blue corduroy jacket nearing the counter, she joined him in line.

'Perfect timing,' he said with a smile as they paid and headed out.

Back at the office, they sat down in the kitchen to eat their lunch.

'Seriously, though, why don't you go on holiday? You've not had any time off for ages,' Tim said, picking up the conversation from earlier.

Jenni finished chewing before answering.

'I don't have anyone to go with. I know it shouldn't matter and I should be all independent and go on my own, but I just don't fancy it. And besides, I've got Oscar. Who'd look after him if I disappeared for a week?'

'I thought your neighbours fed him when you were away?'

Tim ate his final crisp and then meticulously straightened out the packet and folded it neatly, tucking the corner over into a little triangle. As ever, Jenni wondered what the point was of doing this: Tim said it was tidy, Jenni maintained it was the sign of a psychopath.

'Jo and Nick are great and they feed Oscar if I'm away for a weekend. If they had a pet, I could return the favour, but they don't so it feels a bit cheeky to ask them to do it for a whole week.'

Jenni brushed some crumbs off her lap. 'I suppose I could offer to wash their bikes or something in return,' she mused.

'Hmm, I think you're just making excuses,' Tim replied.

'You could come with me and Paul next time we go away. We could have a nice beach holiday somewhere hot.'

'That's very kind of you, but I really don't think colleagues should ever see each other in swimwear,' said Jenni. 'Besides, how weird would that be? Me, you and your husband – I'd feel such a gooseberry!'

'It could be sort of awks, but if you're not going to date anyone you need to start doing stuff like going on holiday on your own. Otherwise you really are the mad cat lady, living alone with just a fur baby for company.'

'Oi, enough of the mad, thank you very much.'

Tim grimaced. 'Uh-oh. Here comes Ryan. And Susan. Quick, let's go before we're caught in the crossfire.'

Gathering up their empty sandwich and crisp packets, they headed out of the kitchen, Jenni glancing back to see Susan casually-not-casually standing by the coffee machine, Ryan glowering by the sink waiting to see if she'd make a move.

Jenni fell into step beside Tim. 'Besides, I'm going to Somerset at the end of the month, which is now super trendy and full of media types, so all very glamorous.'

Tim stopped to look at her. 'Darling, going home to stay with your mum is not the same as a luxury mini-break at The Newt.'

He set off again at a brisk pace down the corridor, and Jenni, unable to disagree, pulled a face at his retreating back.

4

'Here you go, mate.' Taz handed over the pint of beer and sat down opposite Ben.

Ben took a long gulp. 'I needed that!'

'Oi, where are my crisps?' Dale asked, taking his pint from the tray Taz had put down in the centre of the table.

'They only had chilli flavoured and I know you can't handle anything spicy,' Taz said.

'Good point. Okay, I'll let you off.'

'I don't know why you've booked Tandoori Nights when you can't even manage a korma,' said Brian, elbowing Dale in the side.

'I can manage chips and curry sauce, I'll be fine. You worry about managing your beer. I don't want you puking your guts up again before we've even left the pub.'

'It was a stomach upset, I've told you.' Brian took a defiant gulp of his pint as if to prove his point. 'Either that or it was a bad pint.'

'Yeah, yeah, course it was. Shame Vick couldn't make it tonight – *she* can hold her drink,' Taz teased.

Dale, a tall and skinny south Londoner with a shaved head and a good heart, was married to Vick. Normally, they worked opposite shifts to take care of the kids, but Vick's mum was staying at the moment, which meant Dale could join 'the boys' for a rare night out.

Ben sat back, enjoying the chat. His watch were on day two of their four days off and had decided they were well overdue a pint and a curry. The problem with shift work was that Ben, like many others he worked with, often couldn't find convenient times to meet up with friends who worked more regular hours, and so it was often easier to plan a night out with those you knew would be off at the same time.

He'd spent the day in his flat, having been woken by his phone buzzing. Thinking it might be work, he'd jolted from sleep, but then he'd seen that it was a WhatsApp message asking if anyone had lost an Elsa figurine – their cat had returned home with it the previous evening. It had been forwarded to his street's message group from a neighbouring street.

Blessed with a niece who was a keen *Frozen* fan, and now with 'Let it Go' an earworm he couldn't shake, Ben had given up trying to sleep and, throwing back the covers, he'd sat up and swung himself off the bed.

Flipping the switch on the kettle, he'd made a cup of tea and opened the practically bare kitchen cupboard, searching for breakfast. He'd quickly realised he was out of bread, but he did have a box of cereal, which saved him a trip to the corner shop.

Shaking the suspiciously light carton of cornflakes, he'd poured the remaining cereal into a bowl – it was more dust than flakes – before sitting at the counter to eat while scrolling through his phone, liking some friends' posts on social media and reading the news headlines.

Suddenly, his phone had started ringing, causing him to jump and almost drop it into the milk left in the bowl.

Seeing his sister's number on the screen, he'd swiped to answer it, putting the phone on speaker so he could tidy up while he spoke to her.

'Hi, Pens.'

'Hey Benny Boo, how are you?'

Ben had winced at the use of his childhood nickname. 'I *was* fine. And if you don't want to be called Penny Poo, I'd drop the Benny Boo right now,' he'd said, squirting the pile of unwashed plates and cutlery in the sink with washing up liquid before running the hot water.

'Oh, no need to be like that. I'm just calling to see how you are.'

Ben had heard the concern in his sister's initial question, although she'd tried to keep it hidden beneath a deliberately breezy tone.

'I'm fine, Pen, honestly. You don't need to keep checking on me.'

'I do and I will,' she'd replied, and Ben had smiled at the fierceness in her voice.

His sister was two years younger than him, but since his breakdown – as the doctors had referred to it – their roles had reversed. She had been the one to find him in the flat that terrible night, had refused to let him stay there alone, and had instead taken him home with her, where she had looked after him and given him the time he needed to get back to himself; time spent sitting on the sofa, unable to do more than watch telly with his niece, Evie, hence his familiarity with Disney princesses and their signature theme tunes. Ben was pretty sure that, should he ever be on *Mastermind*, Disney's female leads would be his specialist subject.

Pen's voice had drawn him back to the conversation and he'd listened as she'd filled him in on what Evie was up to, and how they were planning a party for her seventh birthday next month. As she'd talked, he'd worked his way through the washing up.

'So put the date in the diary as Evie will be gutted if you can't come.'

No guilt, thought Ben.

'Mum and Dad will be down, so you can see them too. And stop pulling that face, I know you are.'

Ben had hastily rearranged his features. 'I wasn't, well, not much. But—'

'And don't use work as an excuse.'

Ben had sighed, reflecting, not for the first time, on how annoying it was to have a sister who knew what you were thinking.

'Okay, I'll see what I can do. But I think it's pretty low that you're using Evie's party as a way to make me spend time with Dad.'

'I'm—'

Ha. Penny wasn't the only one with superpowers. 'Yes, you are, Penelope James. But I do want to be there for Evie's birthday, so I'll see what I can do. Happy now?'

'Yes, I am,' said Penny, and Ben had heard the smile in her voice. 'Thank you, I know it's not easy with Dad, so I appreciate it.'

'I just hate the way he avoids talking to me now, like I let him down by being ill.'

Ben had felt the shame and anger wash over him as he'd remembered his dad's refusal to discuss why he hadn't been able to work.

'I know,' Pen said gently. 'He's just part of that generation where these things weren't discussed. He doesn't understand. I had to tell him off the other day for going on about people being sent to the funny farm. Thank God he's not on social media or we'd all be cancelled by association. So don't let it get to you.'

Ben had grimaced. It was more than not talking about. They both knew their dad had his own issues, which the family barely even acknowledged let alone talked about. But he hadn't wanted to get into a fight with Penny, so he'd let his sister chat away about a problem with a client who kept emailing her at all hours, demanding answers on the case she was working on.

Flinging the clean knives and forks back in the drawer, he'd noticed a movement in the garden outside. Thinking he'd imagined it, he'd turned back to the sink, until a small, black and grey striped object had hurtled out from under the bush and raced across the grass towards a squirrel.

Ben had watched as what he realised was a tabby cat had raced across the lawn before coming to an abrupt halt as the squirrel scuttled to safety up a nearby tree. Realising the chase was lost, the cat had nonchalantly sat back and, licking his paw, begun to clean his ears as if this had been the plan all along, and that he hadn't failed in any way to capture his prey.

The cat suddenly twisted into a low crouch, eyes narrowed. Wiggling its bum, it had hunkered down, ready to pounce.

And now the predator, focused on its next victim, prepares to attack, Ben imagined David Attenborough narrate in his head.

'Ben, are you even listening to me?' Penny demanded.

'Sorry, I was distracted by a cat in the garden,' Ben said, turning away from the scene. He'd glanced back out of the window, but the cat had gone, although the squirrel, sensing victory, was now scurrying along the fence.

'Well, fine, I'll go if looking out the window is more interesting than speaking to me,' said Penny with mock offence. 'Put Evie's birthday in the diary and let me know if you can make it,' she said.

'Okay, speak soon. Give Evie a hug from me.'

'Will do. Bye, Benny Boo!'

Before Ben could answer back, his sister had hung up.

The rest of the day passed as usual: shopping, a quick tour of duty on the Xbox and some telly before heading out to the pub. Now, surrounded by his workmates and feeling nicely blurred on his third pint, Ben felt himself relaxing.

'So did you hear what happened to Lewisdown crew?' Brian asked. The rest of the table shook their heads, so Brian proceeded to tell them how the crew had got a bollocking from the borough commander because they'd managed to get one of the engines wedged under a low railway bridge.

'The main road was blocked, so they had to go a different route. Fortunately, it wasn't an emergency call or they'd have really been in the shit. As it was, they were stuck for two hours. They had to halt the trains into London Bridge to give them time to sort it out. The local coppers had a field day.'

Publicly, they were all one big team, working together, but there was plenty of rivalry between the emergency services – particularly the police and the fire service, with the former thinking that all fire crews did was rescue cats stuck up trees and polish their big, red, shiny engines.

To be fair, there was an element of truth in the cat rescuing, on a quiet day, but just like their colleagues on the thin blue line, firefighters also saw their share of trauma and darkness. For Ben, his first road traffic accident was something he'd never forget.

'I can imagine they loved that!' Dale said, rolling his eyes.

Laughing, Ben downed the last of his pint.

'Right, drink up, lads. Time for one more and then let's order.'

5

It was Saturday morning, and Jenni opened her eyes to see the sun streaming through the faded Laura Ashley curtains, casting shadows on the pale pink striped wallpaper that she'd insisted upon as a nine-year-old, that had never been changed since. Old movie posters, exam timetables and postcards from friends had been taken down since she'd left home, but otherwise her old room was unchanged, and Jenni loved the familiarity of the space that had seen her through some tough times.

She'd caught the train from Waterloo the previous evening, and her mum had met her at the station, arriving in a cloud of black smoke created by Bertie, her mum's ancient red mini.

A thirty-minute drive later, turning the bend, the sight of the red brick and flint cottage, it's windows tucked up high beneath the slate roof, surrounded by fields and trees, had made Jenni's shoulders drop in relief, and she'd felt herself relax as she left behind the journey from London.

The peace that had greeted her, with just the birds singing as she'd opened the car door and climbed out, had added to her sense of calm. Growing up here, she'd taken her surroundings for granted – it was only now that she could see the beauty of the place. She loved London, and felt lucky to live in an area full of green spaces, but coming home made her appreciate the countryside in a way she hadn't when she was living there.

Dumping her bags in her room, her mum had made her a hot chocolate and they'd sat together on the old sofa in front of the fire before her mum had sent her off to bed. Shattered from a week at work that had involved some tense negotiations with the influencers Amy had identified as suitable brand ambassadors, and a rather fraught conversation with Clive to convince him reaching out to Wim Hof was not required, Jenni had fallen asleep pretty much as soon as her head hit the pillow.

Now, shifting so she could reach her phone and check the time, she saw she'd slept in later than usual and it was now ten. She could hear her mum moving around downstairs to the background mumblings of the ever-on Radio 4. Occasionally, she could hear her mum talking to herself, and she smiled as she imagined her searching for lost glasses amongst the piles of magazines and books stacked on the kitchen table.

Jenni's phone pinged, signalling a message and she swiped to read the text.

> Oscar grumpy that he had to use the cat flap
> but I've fed him and he's happy again now.
> Will pop back later. Hope you're having a nice
> time. X

Jenni sent a quick thank you back to her neighbour – Jo was familiar with Oscar's demands, but refused to indulge his more diva-like behaviour – then got out of bed and headed downstairs to the kitchen.

Her mum was seated at the end of the old pine table, the *Telegraph* crossword in front of her, battered thesaurus at the ready. Seeing her daughter, Annie took a long inhale on the cigarette she was smoking before hastily stubbing it out in the ashtray. Trying to hide the evidence underneath the newspaper while wafting smoke towards the open window, Annie dropped her pen on the floor, then managed to over-turn the – fortunately empty – mug on the table.

Jenni laughed. 'Mum, I can smell the smoke, you know. There's no pointing trying to hide it.'

'Oh, I know, love, but I know you don't like it. It's just my little treat.'

'Hmm,' muttered Jenni, disapprovingly.

Annie, tidying her short hair behind her ears, looked

slightly chastened, but didn't reply, deciding to ignore her daughter. Instead, she stood up and headed for the kettle to make herself another cup of tea – as was her want in any situation, good or bad.

'Tea, darling?'

'Yes, please.'

Jenni settled in the chair next to the warmth of the Rayburn, while her mum pulled out Jenni's old mug. Lifting the now-whistling kettle off the stove, she filled the cups with boiling water before adding milk – from a bottle not a plastic carton; the village still had a milkman and it was considered bad form if you didn't support the local farmer – then handed Jenni her drink.

'I'm going to patrol the borders. Are you going to come out?' Annie asked, picking up her cup.

Jenni glanced out of the window. The sun was, if not shining, then at least vaguely visible, so she decided to join her mum on her daily ritual – besides, tea in the garden would be rather nice.

'Yes, hold on, I'll just get my jumper.'

She left the kitchen and dashed up the stairs, instinctively stepping over the creaky third step from the bottom, and then ducking to avoid the beam at the top, muscle memory taking over.

Hooded jumper and thick socks on, Jenni joined Annie, who hastily stubbed out another cigarette, and they made their way down the winding gravel path to the wooden bench by the back wall, underneath the old pear tree that was just beginning to come into leaf.

Annie greeted each plant like a friend, glaring critically into the borders as they walked slowly along, occasionally reaching down to pluck an offending snail or slug from a forbidden leaf.

'Oh good, that one's survived, I thought the frost had got it.'

She bent over, examining one shrub more closely. The garden had always been her mother's domain. Her dad had been happy to let Annie oversee all the planting, only getting involved if a particularly large hole needed to be dug, or there was some difficult landscaping to be done that required some muscle. Annie had created a beautiful, sprawling cottage garden, where lupins, roses, foxgloves and granny bonnets intertwined to create an organised chaos of colour, which, however much she tried, Jenni could never replicate in her own small patch back in London.

Whereas the garden had stayed much the same since her dad's death, Jenni had begun to notice all the ways in which the house – more her dad's domain when he was alive – had changed in his absence. It had been a gradual process, but without her father there, slowly the balance had tipped in Annie's favour: plants everywhere, colour creeping in, stacks of books on any surface, topped off by a vase of flowers. It hadn't been a deliberate decision, but Jenni could see now how her mum had compromised – willingly and unconsciously – to accommodate the tastes of her husband. But she could also see how her dad had quietly restored order, and without him books were no longer returned to shelves, dead flowers were left in vases and the quiet, reliable order she remembered from her childhood had vanished.

She knew, though, that her dad would never be completely gone from the house. By unspoken agreement, the front room was rarely used and her mum's creative clutter hadn't spilled into it. It was the room her dad had used the most; his roll-top bureau was in there, and it was where he'd sat to do the paperwork – 'be quiet, your dad's Doing the Money' – as was his record player and speakers, perfectly aligned so he could sit in the precisely placed chair surrounded by the music he loved. And for some reason, Jenni could still sense him in the shed; the smell of the old canvas deckchairs and creosote somehow bringing him back to her.

Jenni reached the silvered wooden bench, the old brick wall behind it beginning to warm in the sun, and sat down to wait for her mum, who had been distracted by the sight of a rogue snail impinging on the hostas. Cupping the still-hot mug, she took in the familiar sounds, feeling the weight of calm. She could hear goldfinches instead of the paraquets that terrorised London's skies, and relaxed back against the bench.

Her friend Tim might have mocked her stay in Somerset, but she'd take this over a trip to Hauser and Wirth any day.

Satisfied that the all invertebrates had been vanquished, Jenni's mum joined her on the bench and took a loud slurp of her tea.

'That's better. Nothing like a cuppa to start the day,' she declared. 'Now, what do you want for lunch?'

'Mum, I hate it when you do this. I haven't even had breakfast yet, I've no idea what I want to eat later.'

'Well, you know I like to plan, and I'll need to go to Tesco's as we're out of butter, and then I need to swing by the plant stall . . .'

Jenni zoned out as her mum continued to outline the day ahead. She was happy to go along for the ride; to not have to think for a change. Relieved that, for once, she didn't have to find ways to fill the hours between Friday evening and Monday morning.

*

'Why have you been hanging out at the war memorial?' asked Jenni's mum with a faintly disapproving tone. As always when she returned to her childhood home, Jenni felt herself regress back to her early teens.

'Did Mrs Jones ring to tell you? That woman surely has better things to do!' Jennie replied. When she was younger, Mrs Jones, the village postmistress and local busybody, was always glaring out of her window at the teenagers in the village, even if all they were doing was talking. It was ten miles to the nearest youth club – what else were teenagers supposed to do?

'Of course Mrs Jones hasn't rung me. She's been dead for five years! I know she was all-seeing, but even she has her limits.'

Jenni's mum indicated her phone. 'You're on the village Facebook. Jane took a picture of you, look.'

Jenni glanced at her mum's screen and was horrified, first by the fact that someone had even set up a village page, and then to see a photo of her with the caption 'STRANGER?' written in 24-point font underneath – her mum was short-sighted and had enlarged the text on her phone.

She had to admit, she did look suspicious. In the picture, she was bent over and peering behind the bench, her hair covering most of her face, and she did have a somewhat furtive air about her. She'd been sent to the corner shop for flour and had, on a whim, decided to walk to the old memorial where she and her friends used to while away the hours when they were younger.

It was also where, years later, she and Alex had sat. Jenni's stomach had twisted uncomfortably when she'd remembered being there with him, through rain and shine, chatting, laughing, falling in love. She'd remembered that he'd carved their initials into the back of the bench – a project resulting in several splinters and a snapped yale key – and, just out of curiosity, she'd wanted to see if it was still there.

It had taken a bit of hunting, but eventually she'd found the outline of the 'J' and the 'A' both now faded and hard to read, the heart surrounding the initials gone – ironic, really, she'd thought.

She wondered whether, had they still been together, still in love, the carving would have looked fresh and strong, rather than worn away as it was now. Nostalgia was obviously getting to her.

This was the problem with coming home, all the earlier versions of yourself that you thought you'd left behind continued to live there, waiting for you to return.

'It's okay, you were recognised so you've been taken off the watchlist, and I was tagged,' continued her mother, pulling Jenni out of her thoughts of the past.

Watchlist? She hoped her mum was exaggerating, but had a horrible feeling such a thing probably existed in a village this small.

Her mother started to tap away at her phone, issuing a status update, not only regarding Jenni's return for the weekend, but also the state of her camellias, which, she thought people should know, didn't have as many buds as last year.

The butter, which had been left to warm up next to the Rayburn while Jenni went to buy flour, was now the perfect consistency, so Jenni, settled in the old wicker chair with the saggy bottom, watched the familiar sight of her mum creaming butter and sugar together, making it look effortless, even though Jenni knew from experience that it made your arm ache well before the mixture took on the perfect pale cream colour that signalled it was time to add the flour and eggs.

'I'm doing double the mixture and then you can take a cake home with you,' her mum said, dividing the batter between four tins.

'Thank you, I'll take it into work with me, everyone loves your sponges. Even Tim and he's off carbs. Actually, now he's had the honeymoon he might be back on them. Either way, it will be gratefully received.'

'How's work going?' Annie asked, looking at her daughter for clues, glad to see she looked less pinched around the face today and had a bit more colour in her cheeks.

'It's fine, just busy. You know, the usual.'

'No nice men, then?'

'No nice *single* men,' Jenni said, taking a sip of freshly made tea to prevent further questioning.

The kitchen filled with the smell of warm vanilla and sugar as Annie effortlessly multitasked, preparing the soup they were having for lunch, pulling out the perfectly risen sponges, turning them out onto the wire cooling rack, filling the sink with dirty dishes.

'Right, let's leave these to cool. I quite fancy a walk up the Tor before lunch.'

Out of habit, Jenni gave a groan. 'Do we have to?'

It was a long-established routine between mother and daughter, and although Jenni quite fancied a walk, she had to keep up her side of the bargain so that her mum could run through her lines, which invariably involved the need for stirring stumps and blowing away cobwebs.

But today, to her surprise, the script took a slightly different turn.

'Well, if you don't fancy it you can stay at home,' Annie said with false casualness.

Jenni stopped harrumphing her way through the anoraks hanging in the hall. *What was this?*

Seeing her daughter's surprised look, Annie continued, 'It's just I usually meet Alan at this time on a Saturday. You're welcome to come of course, but . . .'

Well, this was interesting, Jenni thought.

'Alan?' asked Jenni.

'Um, well, yes, he moved here from Bristol a while ago now. We kept bumping into each other when we were both out walking during lockdowns and decided to make it a da—a habit.'

Her mother corrected herself, but Jenni heard the unspoken 'date', and her curiosity was further piqued.

Before she could interrogate her mother further, Annie,

old waxed jacket on, a handful of toffees in the pocket, opened the back door and stepped out.

Turning back, she said, 'Why don't you finish off the cakes for me? The jam's in the larder.'

And before Jenni could reply, her mum had disappeared up the garden path without her.

6

Jenni laid in bed. It was late and she was tired, but she couldn't sleep. Her brain was busy going over the day, which had turned out to be quite surprising in the end.

Annie had returned from her non-date, her cheeks pink, with a lightness about her that Jenni hadn't seen for a long time. Certainly not since her dad died. After lunch, they'd gone out in Bertie to the farm shop. It was there, next to a particularly muddy 'field-fresh' bundle of carrots that her mum had casually said, 'Oh, I've invited Alan over for dinner tonight. I hope you don't mind?'

Jenni, marvelling at the many types of potatoes – why there were so many and what poor Charlotte must have looked like to inspire someone to name a spud after her – had turned to her mum.

'No, I don't mind at all. That sounds nice,' she'd added cautiously. Although, she hadn't been *entirely* sure she didn't mind, or that it sounded *remotely* nice. Who was this man taking her mother on walks? She supposed she was about to find out.

'Okay, lovely. I told him to come to us for seven-thirty. Now, I want to get some beef as he does like a nice roast.'

Jenni had felt annoyed. Why ask if she minded if he'd already been invited? And her mum was practically vegetarian and *hated* red meat – now she was buying beef!

But she'd known she was being unfair, maybe even a bit jealous, so summoning the best version of herself – and thanking Clive for that particular Monday Motivational gem – Jenni had helped Annie choose a choice cut of Longhorn beef and had debated the merits of the WI's offerings of lemon meringue pie over the apple tart, before finally choosing the bramble crumble.

Deciding to throw caution to the wind, they had also picked up a few local cheeses, crackers and two different chutneys before heading home to prepare for Alan's arrival.

Jenni, who'd been on alert for the knock at the front door, had been a bit put out when, instead, there was a brief tap on the *back* door and, before she could even get up, it had swung open with a hearty, 'Hello, only me!'

Annie, though, had showed no surprise at Alan letting himself in.

So, this is a regular thing, Jenni had thought, her eyes narrowing.

'Hello! Come on in.'

Annie had put down the tea towel she was holding to take the bottle Alan was proffering. 'Oh, lovely, thank you – you know I love this wine!'

Alan, who Jenni had to admit had a kind smile and a capable-looking face – she instinctively knew he was one of the cargo-short-wearing men who were good at mending things – handed over the bottle and gave Annie a quick peck on the cheek. He then turned to Jenni.

'Hello, I'm Alan. I've heard so much about you. Your mum's so proud of you.'

Instantly disarmed, Jenni had smiled back, uncertain how to reply given she'd only heard of him that morning, but she'd stood to shake his hand nonetheless. Upon sitting back down, Jenni had watched Alan reach inside the drawer where the corkscrew was kept and locate the wine glasses, with a familiar ease that had given her a pang. That and the easy companionship between him and her mum.

It had actually been a lovely evening, and Alan, who worked in social housing at Bristol council, was interesting and interested, sharing the frustrations of his work, but also the successes, and he'd enjoyed hearing about Jenni's job, too. He had two grown-up children: one in Manchester – a son, single, he hadn't hesitated to point out – and a daughter who had moved to New Zealand and who he was hoping to visit soon as they hadn't seen each other for over three years.

Jenni hadn't been able to help noticing that there was a quiet certainty to him that felt familiar: the way he moved around the kitchen, tidying away after Annie, washing up and restoring order, reminding her of her father. And she'd felt another jolt of loss as she'd realised that her mum had managed to find someone else; that it wouldn't be just the two of them anymore.

Jenni had left them to finish the tidying up and had gone to bed after saying goodnight.

As she'd climbed into bed, she had heard the back door quietly pulled shut, and she knew if she looked out of the window now she'd see the red dot of her mum's cigarette as she did her final check of the garden.

Jenni could hear a second voice, too – Alan was still there – and she listened to the sound of the two of them talking, their low voices accompanied by the occasional shared laughter as they walked the gravel paths.

Gosh, thought Jenni. *Unchaperoned walking in the garden after dark.*

She looked forward to seeing what the village Facebook page had to say about *that* tomorrow.

*

'Knob with your soup?' Annie asked, making her daughter look up in alarm.

Seeing the hard, round, baked biscuits – a Dorset delicacy – and suddenly understanding what her mother was on about, Jenni politely declined.

'Hmm, me neither, if I'm honest. No wonder they have that competition to see how far you can throw them each year. About all anyone wants to do with them.'

'Why did you buy them then?'

'Well, I like the big tin they come in, it's very useful for storing stuff. They caught my eye when I was in that nice deli in Sherdowne the other day, when Sheila and I ventured across the border.'

'Mum, you went for afternoon tea in a nice market town in the next county. You make it sound like you left the country.'

'Well, you say that, but the traffic on the A303 was so bad, we could have flown to Spain quicker.'

Jenni rolled her eyes and changed the subject. 'Alan was nice last night,' she said, casually, watching her mother closely.

'Hmm. Yes, it was a lovely evening, wasn't it?' her mum replied, dipping her spoon into her soup.

There was a pause and Jenni noticed Annie's cheeks redden slightly. 'He's asked me if I want to go to New Zealand with him. I'd like to, but I'm not sure I should leave the garden. I've got all the seeds in the greenhouse to water.'

'Mum, that's no excuse not to go. Jane would water for you. Do you want to go?'

'I do, I'd love to go – it's somewhere me and your dad always said we'd visit. Maybe that's why I feel a bit funny about saying yes.'

Jenni glanced up from her phone – Tim's WhatsApp message would have to wait – to see her mum looking at her intently.

'And I worry about how you will feel, darling,' she added. 'I don't like the idea of being so far from you.'

Jenni reached for her mum's hand. 'I know. I feel a bit odd about it too, if I'm being honest, but I'm glad you've found someone nice, and I'm glad you're not on your own. I think you should go.'

Annie smiled. 'Thank you. I'm quite content living on my own, but it is nice to have someone to share things with.' She looked at Jenni. 'What about you? I know splitting up from Alex has been difficult for you. Even if you're happy, it can be hard, can't it?"

'Yes,' admitted Jenni, finishing the last mouthful of soup and placing her spoon in the empty bowl. 'I don't know. I just can't imagine meeting anyone at the moment. All my friends are paired off, so no one knows any eligible men and I can't face the whole online dating thing. Besides, I'd rather be on my own than with someone for the sake of it.'

'You'll find the right person, give it time,' said Annie,

gathering up the empty bowls and stacking them in the sink.

'Yes, I'm sure my tall, dark stranger will appear any minute now.' Jenni tried to sound optimistic rather than sarcastic, if only to reassure her mum. But she wasn't so sure.

Her mum knew her too well, though, and gave her a kiss on the top of her head as she walked past her to get to the fridge.

'You will, but in the meantime go and get packed. You need to be at the station for half past and Bertie needs extra time to get up the big hill, so we need to leave in ten minutes.'

Jenni smiled, suddenly reluctant to leave the warmth of her mum's kitchen. But she stood up and headed for the stairs.

'I'll go and get my bags right now,' she said. 'And don't forget the cake – I'm not leaving here without it!'

7

Ben held on tight as the engine hurtled down the main road, lights flashing and siren blaring. Dale, Brian and Taz were seated around him, all quiet as they prepared for what the call would bring. Vick was driving and Ali was navigating, although nowadays the satnav showed the best route, changing in real time depending on road conditions and traffic build-ups.

Having carried out their engine and equipment checks and been debriefed, they had just settled into an hour of drills before the call had come in at half nine. Not entirely unexpectedly as Saturday nights were often busy.

Ben had been in the middle of a fifty-yard dash up a ladder, a coiled hose over his shoulder, when the alarm had sounded and Aisha, from Fire Control, had announced reports of a fire in a block of council-owned flats just over a mile away. Several residents had called to report smoke coming from the main stairwell.

Pulling on their beige fireproof trousers and jackets, Ben and the rest of his crew had climbed on board Engine A. Vick had started the motor and the engine had roared into life. She'd edged out through the huge doors onto the forecourt and then, checking that no one had illegally parked on the road outside – which happened surprisingly often – she'd pulled out onto the busy road. Cars had edged out of their way as they'd seen the engine coming, and Vick, focused only on the road in front of her, had pushed through the parting vehicles as fast as she safely could.

They were now five minutes out, but, having left the main road for residential streets, were slowed by the speed bumps that caused the crew to bounce in their seats, despite the engine's superior rear suspension. Ali, in touch with Aisha, was receiving more information and updating the crew: there'd been more 999 calls, reporting smoke, but no flames, and one call had mentioned that a group of teenagers had been seen fleeing the area. Housing officers from the council were on site and the building was being evacuated.

Fortunately, it was only four stories and, as it was a 1930s build, cladding was not an issue – news that caused the whole crew to breathe a little easier.

'The smoke is still dense so you'll need breathing apparatus and vision will be poor,' finished Ali.

In the time she had delivered the latest status report, they'd arrived on the scene. Ben could see residents in pyjamas and dressing gowns huddled at the designated fire assembly area. Babies, rudely awoken as parents snatched them from their cots, were crying, unhappy and feeling the cold, while a couple of older people were being helped slowly to the assembly point so that fire wardens could account for everyone. A woman, who introduced herself as the block's housing manager, approached them as they opened up the doors and started to prepare to tackle the incident.

'We think we've got everyone out. The fire wardens have banged on every door, cleared each floor and checked all corridors. We used the back stairwell to exit and no one has been back in.'

The woman, in her mid-forties with greying hair and a hi-vis jacket pulled on inside out over her cardigan, looked visibly relieved to be able to hand over the scene to the professionals.

Ben thanked her as she returned to help move residents to a nearby church hall, and carried on kitting up, pulling the protective helmet on last.

Suitably attired, he, Brian and Taz headed for the front stairwell. Vick and Ali stayed with the engine, along with Dale to assist with the hose.

The design of the building had created a wind tunnel, which was fanning any flames, and thick black smoke belched out of the third-floor window above them.

The main stairwell fire door was propped open – with a fire extinguisher, Ben noticed with irony.

Just great.

Fitted with a buzzer and entry system, the self-closing door was meant to remain shut at all times. But someone had obviously decided to leave it ajar, all the easier for the Deliveroo driver to reach them without them having to leave the comfort of their own sofa.

Ben turned to check the others were ready.

'Smells like rubber,' said Brian.

'Yeah, burning tyres,' added Taz.

'Ali said some teenagers had been spotted running away. Could be a bin fire?' Ben suggested.

'Yes, could be. Let's go.'

Breathing apparatus on, the three men cautiously entered the building to carry out an initial assessment.

The smoke, thick and black, meant they could see only a few centimetres in front of them. Guardedly, Ben edged forward into the space at the bottom of the stairs.

Fortunately, the crew were familiar with the layout of the building. They regularly visited homes in the local area, advising residents about fire safety, ensuring fire systems were up to date and working, and making sure that residents knew what to do in case of an emergency. Ben had visited just a few months ago, so he knew that the main entranceway to the block of flats had a room the size of a large cupboard that housed the fuse boxes for the electrics, and that it was used as a storage area for the cleaning crew. This was usually kept locked, but as Ben moved nearer to the door he could see through the thickening smoke that the door was cracked open.

'Hold on, guys, I think I've found the source of the fire. Possibly electrical.'

Brian relayed the information to the rest of the team at the engine – if it was the electrics, they'd need the CO2 extinguishers.

'We've got twenty more minutes left,' said Taz, noting the amount of oxygen remaining in the tanks.

'Hold on, it's not the electrics. There's a pile of something burning on the floor, looks like oily rags – I can see some syringes too, so be careful,' Ben warned the others. Blasting the pile of cloth with the extinguisher Brian passed to him, Ben put out the fire as Taz and Brian secured the area.

It was then that Ben heard a sound coming from inside the smoke-filled cupboard. He shuffled past the now-smouldering rags, trying to make out what the noise was. Crouched in the corner he spotted a boy, a scarf pulled up around his face, frightened eyes looking back at him.

'There's someone in here!' Ben radioed to the crew. 'Get an ambulance. Conscious, but smoke inhalation and possible burns.'

Reaching out, Ben pulled the teenager to his feet, taking

his weight as he stumbled. The boy coughed as he fought for breath.

'Coming out now,' Ben said, lifting the boy over his shoulder and exiting the small space.

Brian and Taz were waiting to help, and they all emerged from the building to the sound of the siren signalling the arrival of the paramedics.

With the young boy taken to be cared for and the fire safely extinguished, Red Watch were stood down. Back at the engine, Ben, Brian and Taz removed their breathing apparatus and the whole crew readied the engine for a return to the station.

'Well done, everyone, and good work, Ben,' called Vick, climbing up into the cab and settling behind the wheel.

'Buckle up, and we're good to go.'

The engine pulled away slowly, past a small cluster of people still waiting to be told where they would be sleeping that night.

'Go faster, Jay,' shouted Ali. 'Can't wait to get back to all that paperwork.'

Ben laughed. It was going to be a long night for them all, and he was anxious to know how the boy he'd saved was doing, but most of all he was relieved no one else had been harmed.

8

'Jenni, this is delicious,' said Tim, shoving another piece of cake into this mouth and brushing the crumbs from his hands.

'Okay, steady on, it's for everyone. I said you could help me by carrying it, not eating the entire thing.'

'Yes, well, I'm not sure Lucy deserves any, quite frankly.' Tim looked around dramatically. 'I'm not sure I can forgive her for what she did.'

'Is this about how she borrowed your favourite pen without asking?' Jenni said, gathering up some napkins, plates and a knife before balancing everything on a tray.

'Worse.' Tim lifted the cake and followed Jenni out of the kitchen and down the corridor, back to Circle Three. 'She used up all the staples in my stapler.'

'Oh God, he's not still going on about that, is he?' Lucy rolled her eyes as she joined them at the desk. 'I've apologised a billion times, and I bought you a muffin to say sorry,' she added, turning to Tim with a what-more-do-want look.

'You bought me triple chocolate muffin – the ones I *love* and cannot resist – just as I was getting beach ready. That was not a thoughtful gift, that was a gesture of pure evil.'

Jenni decided not to mention that he was already on his second slice of cake.

'Well, I thought it was delish,' said Will, who'd been given the offending muffin to polish off, helping to unload the plates from the tray and divvy up the cake. 'Quick, grab a slice before the others come over.'

Jenni made a mental note to tell her mum that her cake had been very popular, as more colleagues gravitated over to grab a slice, either chatting for a while or hurrying back to their desks muttering about deadlines.

Guiltily, Jenni thought about her own to-do list. The shoot was on Wednesday and she'd booked the models, lined up the samples, had a stylist in place and a photographer ready and waiting, but she still needed to coordinate the messaging with her influencers, finalise travel for everyone and book lunch. Argh, the list went on.

She'd arrived back at her flat just after ten last night. Bertie had triumphantly managed the hill in a cloud of exhaust fumes and she'd made it to the station on time. Her mum had waited for her to find a seat on the train before driving off, and Jenni had felt the usual pang of emotion: sadness at leaving her mum, but also relief to be returning to her own flat.

The train had slid through a landscape of green to grey, and upon arriving back in London, Jenni, juggling her bag and balancing a cake, had negotiated the busy concourse of Sunday-night returners, picking up her pace to match the speed of her fellow commuters, before catching the bus home.

Jo had texted to say that Oscar was fine, but Jenni had been anxious to get back and see him herself. He didn't approve of her going away and, sure enough, had made his feelings very clear by vomiting on the door mat.

Oscar had hunkered down on the work surface to watch as Jenni deposited the cake – which didn't look too battered, despite its journey – in the fridge, cleaned the door mat and hung it outside to dry, and then unpacked her overnight bag. Jobs done, she had thrown herself down on the sofa and flopped back into the cushions, at which point Oscar had deigned to join her. Peace made, the two of them had watched a few episodes of *Sewing Bee* before bed.

She'd obviously not been completely forgiven, though, as this morning, while she was getting ready for work, she'd noticed that Oscar had elected to go out early rather than join her for breakfast.

She'd buy some cat treats on the way home and shamelessly bribe her way back into his affections, she decided.

Her thoughts of Oscar were interrupted when Tim nudged her, nearly knocking the cake that was halfway to her mouth out of her hand.

'Uh-oh, here's Clive. Brace, brace.'

Jenni turned to find Clive bearing down on her, draped in some sort of waterproof fabric, despite the fact they were indoors. Even if he *had* gone outdoors, the current mild weather didn't merit him wearing what appeared to be a knee-length tent.

'Hello, hello, what's this. Refined carbs on the premises? You know my thoughts on the danger they present to the gut biome and the need for wholegrain flours.'

Jenni did indeed know far too much about Clive's thoughts on diet, and was in fact permanently scarred from the conversation about his quest for a healthy gut. No one needed to hear the words 'faecal transplant' during lunch. Or ever, in fact.

Deciding to cut him off before he began discussing beneficial bacteria again, she offered him the last slice of cake. 'It's been made with, um, fermented milk and the jam is unpasteurised – full of good bacteria,' she improvised wildly as Tim suppressed a snort of laughter.

'Oh, well, yes, that's very good,' Clive said taking a bite. Even a mouthful didn't stop him talking though and, spraying crumbs, he asked, 'You've got the snow shoot this week, haven't you?'

'Yes, everything's organised and we're good to go,' replied Jenni, mentally crossing her fingers.

'I've had an idea,' Clive said, filling Jenni with alarm. She desperately hoped he didn't want to come too. An hour and a half on the train with Clive and his gut microflora and fauna would be too much.

'This rain poncho has just come in. What do you think? It doubles as a picnic blanket, *and* you could sleep under it if you were bivouacking, so it's reuseable. And, of course, it's green, so very eco-friendly. Jenni, come with me and let's discuss it,' he ordered, plonking his empty plate down and striding back to his office.

Jenni shared a look of horror with Lucy before reluctantly following Clive.

She paused and turned back to hiss, 'Someone come and get me with something urgent if I'm not out in fifteen minutes.'

She spotted Clive beckoning from his office door.

'Actually, make that ten.'

*

'And then he made me try one on,' she said in a distressed voice. 'A—and the toggle got stuck where the poncho gathers around the neck. And . . . and I began to panic, and Clive kept shouting at me for tearing at the fabric. B—but I couldn't breathe, and then, *finally*, Tanya took pity on me and . . . and she cut me *out*,' finished Jenni, between heaving breaths, finally back at her desk.

Lucy and Tim made sympathetic noises as Will returned with a cup of coffee.

'Ryan's just made it, so it's nice and strong. Good for the shock,' Will said, placing the mug down.

Jenni took a sip and shuddered. Strong didn't adequately describe it, but the shot of caffeine seemed to be doing the trick so she braved another gulp.

'Oh love, that sounds hilariou—' Tim wiped his eyes and then, seeing Lucy's glare, hastily amended, 'Hideous! I mean *hideous*.'

'Apparently, he once made someone in sales try on a bala-clava, one from the Extreme Blizzard range that just has tiny slits for your eyes, and the poor guy was claustrophobic – he passed out in a panic!' Lucy nodded knowingly.

'Was that Tony, who mysteriously disappeared without saying goodbye and no one knew why?'

'Yes, apparently he got a pay-off on the condition he signed an NDA and didn't sue. Another one of HR's "deals".'

'Our HR department could work for a Mafia boss or something,' Will said with a note of awe in his voice. 'They're like fixers, tidying up after gangsters, making sure no one knows where the bodies are buried.'

'Maybe don't describe HR as being like the Mafia,' Lucy said. 'If they hear you, you might be next to be "fixed".'

'Yeah, I'll come in and find a horse's head on my desk.' Will seemed unnervingly excited about this idea, Jenni noticed.

Turning to Jenni, Tim said comfortingly, 'Well, you're okay now, and you can hardly see the rope burns on your neck.'

'Thank you, that's such a comfort,' Jenni glared at him crossly.

Tim decided to change the subject.

'You know what, why don't we call it a day? It's nearly five now, so let's go home.'

'Or better still, how about we pop across the road to the Red Lion for a medicinal drink?' suggested Lucy, already gathering up her stuff.

'Good idea,' said Jenni, pushing down the lid of her laptop and turning off her monitor. 'But no one is to mention the words "drawstring" or "toggle" in my presence ever again.' And with a shudder she left the office.

9

It was 8.30 in the morning and Jenni had travelled from London to Tamworth on the first train from Euston, pulling a wheelie suitcase of spare outfits – including the panic-attack-inducing rain poncho Clive had insisted she pack – safety pins, bull dog clips and other bits and pieces that might be needed on the shoot. The day of the snow-dome had dawned, and Jenni just hoped that all her planning would ensure everything ran smoothly.

The models and photographer would be meeting her at the venue, and the organiser, Julie, had confirmed that the outfits Jenni had sent in advance had arrived safely. She knew that she had checked and double-checked everything, and began to relax. Everything was on track – what could possibly go wrong?

She'd taken a taxi from Tamworth station to the snow-dome and introduced herself to the front desk. Julie, a petite woman in her twenties with bright red hair, had shown her to a storeroom to the side of the snowdome, which was where the outfits had been stored. There was a hanging rail in the corner and the ladies loo was down the corridor, which the models could use to get changed.

'We open at nine so you've got the place to yourself until then,' Julie explained.

'The dome is through the double doors on the right. It's real snow in there, so it's cold. I know that's obvious, but you'd be surprised how many people turn up in jeans and short-sleeved T-shirts. Make sure you put hats and gloves on before you go in. Although, you'll be fine as you've got all the kit.'

'Thanks, Julie. Yes, we're shooting our new ski-wear range today so everything's thermal and waterproof. We'll be fine,' Jenni reassured her as she started unpacking the boxes of clothes and sorting them in to piles for each model.

'I like that orange bobble hat,' said Julie, indicating the pile of fleecy items Jenni was stacking in one corner.

Jenni inwardly smiled at the thought of Clive's reaction if he ever heard the hat – in a bespoke colour called *burnt cinnamon,* which had been specially sourced at vast expense – described as plain old orange.

'When we've done the shoot you can have it,' she said. 'Remind me when we're leaving. It will look gorgeous with your hair.'

Julie ran a hand through her red curls. 'Oh yes, everyone would see me coming then, wouldn't they!' she laughed. 'Right, I'd better get back to the front desk. I'll send the others through when they arrive.'

Half an hour later, Jenni, clad in various mismatched items of sample-sized ski-wear, all too tight, stood in the vast warehouse-sized room that housed the ski slope. Barriers covered with blue and yellow hoardings lined the sides, a button ski-lift ran up one edge to take the more experienced skiers and snowboarders to the top of the undulating slope, while the more gentle incline starting from halfway up acted as a nursery slope for those still learning or lacking in confidence. The snow crunched under foot as she walked from the wooden scaffolding benches onto the white slope. Her two models, Amira and Ingrid, were dressed, and the photographer, Mickey, was happy with the lighting. They were ready to go.

They decided they'd start with base layers, have a break to warm up, and then shoot outer wear, ending with accessories. Satisfied with how everything was looking, Jenni stepped back to let Mickey get on with it.

While he did his thing, she took some snaps on her phone to share with the social media team – everyone loved a behind-the-scenes peek, and they'd use the pictures to start teasing the line before the main campaign dropped.

The next few hours passed in a blur of flashlights as Jenni

worked her way back and forth between the models, handing over jackets, removing fleeces, clipping Ingrid into the dreaded rain-poncho – fortunately, she managed to get her out of it again – and making sure all the items were photographed as she worked through her tick sheet.

Seeing Amira's teeth chattering, she reassured the two girls and Mickey that they were nearly finished. Just the burnt cinnamon accessories and they'd be done.

Dressed in hats, scarfs and gloves, Ingrid and Amira pretended they were having a snowball fight in the foothills of the Alps, while Mickey clicked away.

'Okay, lovely, and turn to the right slightly. We need playful and carefree. Perfect.'

Mickey took another few shots and then looked at the camera to check the images.

The snowdome, now open to the public, had begun to get busier as the morning had gone on. It was a weekday so it was still fairly quiet, but four professional-looking snowboarders had taken to the slope and Jenni found herself being covered in a fine spray of ice and snow as they whooshed past her, digging in the edge of their boards to slow themselves down as they reached the bottom of the run.

Afterwards, Jenni realised, somewhat ruefully, that if she'd only kept her focus on the shoot, rather than being distracted by Julie asking if they'd like hot chocolate, she wouldn't have ended up in A&E.

But as it was, she'd turned to accept the offer with a grateful smile at the exact moment a snowboarder shot past her. He'd swerved to avoid her as she'd stepped slightly into his path, but not enough, and he had clipped her shoulder as he'd sped past, spinning her around dramatically. Losing her footing, Jenni had hit the ice, landing awkwardly on her right arm, which she'd thrust out to try to save herself from falling face-down on the snow. The pile of clothes Jenni had been holding shot into the air, and as she'd landed hard on the ground, the last thing she saw was the burnt cinnamon arm warmers floating down to land gently next to her.

'Oh my God, Jenni, are you okay?' Mickey had shouted, as Julie rushed over and tried to help her back on to her feet, but Jenni, yelping in pain, had quickly realised that her leg wouldn't move.

'Don't worry, love, stay still. We need to get you to hospital.'

Jenni had been happy to comply. She could feel the ice melting and seeping through the layers of clothing, reaching her skin, and she had begun to shake with cold.

Julie had called an ambulance and, an hour later, still shouting instructions to her team, Jenni had found herself being stretchered out of the snowdome.

This was very much *not* how she'd envisioned the day would end.

10

Ben was perched on a stool at his kitchen counter eating breakfast. He'd propped his phone up against the cereal box and, while he ate, he read a newspaper report about the fire he'd attended at the weekend.

> Police and fire investigators have confirmed that the fire started in a service area. Evidence of drug use was found at the scene and it is suspected that the use of a naked flame resulted in an oil-covered cloth catching fire. Teenagers were seen fleeing the building and police are seeking assistance from local residents to help identify them.
>
> Taz Brynt, Operations Manager at Pelham Fire Station, said, 'Fortunately, firefighters arrived on the scene before the

blaze took hold and were able to extinguish it at source.' He went on to thank the onsite wardens for helping evacuate tenants, stressing the value of community work. 'More and more, it's about working with residents in their homes to make sure that, if the worst happens, they are able to get out safely and quickly. A special mention must go to Crew Manager Ben Walker, who rescued a fourteen-year-old boy from the scene.'

The boy's mother described Walker as 'a hero', adding that she'll be eternally grateful to him for saving her son's life. The boy, who cannot be named for legal reasons, is currently recovering in hospital.

The police are treating the incident as suspected arson.

Ben felt a flush of pride to see his name mentioned in the article, and thought about forwarding it to his parents. But he dismissed the idea and, instead, scrolled to the next article, fighting another yawn. Having just come off nights, his body was still out of sync and he'd had to force himself to get up and have breakfast. He was very tempted to just go back to bed.

A movement at the window caught his eye and, looking

up, he saw two green eyes glaring at him through the glass. Ben laughed as he realised that it was just a cat. In fact, the same cat he'd seen chasing a squirrel the other day. Standing up, he reached over to the window, opening it slightly, intending just to shoo it away. The little cat was grey with black stripes, and, up close, Ben noticed that he had a black patch over his right eye, making him look like a pirate – an impression that was enhanced when the cat took advantage of the open window, slid through the narrow gap and swaggered along the work surface before coming to a standstill and fixing Ben with a steely gaze.

'Um, get out of here, you!' Ben made wafting gestures towards the cat, trying to usher him back towards the window. 'You're not meant to be in here, go home!'

The cat, however, ignored him, looking around the kitchen as if assessing Ben's housekeeping. Ben almost apologised for not having done the washing up yet.

Instead, he clapped his hands at the cat and this time it moved, bolting back outside, although not before pausing to turn back and look at Ben with a look of reproach.

Ben watched as the cat disappeared into the shrubbery, slinking under the low branches before vanishing out of sight, its stripes helping to camouflage it completely. He wondered where it lived – he guessed it had a home since it looked healthy and well-fed.

Just then, the buzzer rang and Ben went to answer the

intercom. He was pleased to see a delivery man dropping off a package and went to the main front door to collect it.

Shouting a thank you, he carried his parcel back to his flat, giving it an experimental shake and, when it rattled, guessing it was the Lego he'd ordered for Evie's birthday present.

He'd had several texts from his sister reminding him of the forthcoming event, and he'd assured her that he'd be attending the party the following weekend.

His mum had texted saying she was looking forward to seeing him, and Ben was happy that she'd be there, it was just his dad that cast a shadow over proceedings.

Feeling a familiar heaviness begin to settle, Ben gave himself a shake. Deciding he needed to fight his tiredness and get out of the flat, Ben changed into his shorts and T-shirt, located his running shoes and, earbuds in, music on, headed out for a jog. He knew he needed to keep himself busy.

11

Jenni laid on her sofa, wrapped in her duvet, feeling sorry for herself. It had been a week since The Incident and, although her leg was hurting less, she was still in pain. She'd been signed off work until she could sit comfortably at a desk and had spent the last few days watching *Death in Paradise*. By now, she'd made it to series seven and she wasn't sure how much more she could take. She groaned at the ceiling in frustration.

The cat flap clacked open and shut, and a flump on the duvet indicated Oscar's arrival. Purring loudly and kneading the cushions, Oscar began preparations for an extended nap.

'I'm glad you're happy with this set-up,' Jenni grumbled.

Oscar seemed delighted to have Jenni at home, perhaps thinking that her presence indicated a more dedicated approach to his welfare, although he'd been displeased with Jenni's response times. Jenni had decided the constant mewing as she made her way slowly to the kitchen, hobbling on her crutches, was Oscar shouting encouragement, not him telling her to get a move on.

Being at home more had given her time to observe his habits and, although he was spending a lot of time with her, she had noticed he was gone for extended periods of time.

Perhaps I should fit him with an Airtag, or a cat cam, and see what he gets up to, she wondered idly. *At least if I can't go out, I can see what's going on via Oscar.*

She watched as the cat curled up into a tight comma and settled into sleep.

There was something very cosy about a dozing cat, Jenni thought. It made a house feel more like home.

Deciding she couldn't cope with any more paradise, however sunny the location, Jenni started flicking channels — how could there be so much stuff and nothing she wanted to watch?

Fortunately, she was saved by the doorbell. *Un*fortunately, that meant Jenni needed to move.

Pulling herself to standing, she tugged up her jogging bottoms and shook the crumbs from her hoodie before making her way laboriously to the door.

Upon opening the door, she discovered Amy and baby Tilly on the front step with a promising-looking cake tin.

'I thought you might need some sugar,' Amy said, following Jenni into the flat. 'How are you feeling?'

'Fed up! Everything's so difficult, I can't even sit up comfortably at the moment, although I'm being fitted with a boot thingy next week, which will make it easier. But it's just all really boring. Thank you for visiting.'

Jenni flumped back onto the sofa and Amy sat down more carefully, not wanting to wake up Tilly.

'I'm so sorry I haven't been over before, I was going to the park and Tilly fell asleep in the sling so I thought I'd pop in now and see how you're getting on.'

She adjusted the baby so she could sit down more comfortably.

'What actually happened? Your text made no sense at all. Something about being attacked by a snowboarder and being smothered in knitwear. I've been so worried.'

'Sorry about that – the painkillers were strong, and they gave me morphine at the hospital too, so I was a bit confused.'

Jenni explained what had happened and Amy nodded sympathetically as Jenni described how she'd had to be carried off the slopes, accompanied by the two models and the photographer. Getting back to London by train would have been a nightmare, but fortunately Go Big's insurance had covered her journey in a private ambulance.

'And after all that, Tim emailed me to say that Clive's favourite photo of the entire shoot is the one the photographer took just as I got knocked to the ground.

Apparently, there's a fantastic shot of me flying through the air, surrounded by the burnt cinnamon knitwear range. He described it as "playful but unconventional", and says it defines the Go Big brand, so now I'm part of the campaign,' Jenni grumbled.

Amy smothered a laugh. 'Surely a broken leg is a small price to pay for a new career in modelling?'

'*Hmph*, hardly, but at least they're being good about me having time off.'

Just then a small cry erupted from Tilly.

'Uh-oh, someone's woken up hungry,' Amy said, unbuttoning the sling so she could lift Tilly out. 'Here, can you hold her for me while I go and sort her bottle out. I'll make us some tea at the same time.'

Handing her daughter to Jenni, Amy stood up and headed for the kitchen, gathering her bag up as she went. Jenni watched in envy at the speed with which she moved.

Tilly, furious at being removed from her warm cocoon and unimpressed at being handed to Jenni, began to cry harder. 'Hold on, Tilly, I'll be back in a minute,' shouted Amy from the kitchen. 'I'll just put the kettle on while I'm here!'

Jenni tried bouncing Tilly up and down a bit while looking around for something to distract her with. 'Look, Tilly, say hello to Oscar.'

Oscar, having been rudely awoken from his sleep, opened

one eye. Twitching his tail in obvious disapproval, he glared at Jenni before standing up to give a disdainful stretch.

Fortunately, the movement was enough to fascinate Tilly, who stopped crying and looked at the cat.

'Come here, Oscar, come and say hello,' Jenni said, stretching out her free hand to him. Oscar, ignoring the gesture completely, jumped off the back of the sofa and stalked out the room.

Tilly began to cry again.

'Great, thanks for that, Oscar. Desert me in my hour of need,' muttered Jenni, frantically bouncing Tilly again as the baby's sobs increased in volume. How could such a small child make so much noise?

Fortunately, Amy returned at that moment carrying a tray with two mugs of tea, Tilly's bottle, a couple of plates and a knife, which she put on the coffee table. Reaching over, she took Tilly from Jenni and offered the bottle to the baby who took it greedily, her crying stopping instantly.

'Right, that's better.' Amy settled back into the chair with the baby tucked against her. 'Are you okay to cut the cake?'

'It'd take more than a broken leg to keep me from cake,' Jenni replied, opening the cake tin to discover her favourite coffee and walnut.

'Delicious! Although, I need to stop eating so much. I can't do any exercise at the moment and I'll be the size of a house once I'm out of plaster.'

'Oh, rubbish, you could do with putting some weight on, you got too skinny after breaking up with Alex. You need a happy stomach.'

'A what now?' Jenni spluttered on a mouthful of cake.

'My mum has a theory that the weight you put on when you're in a relationship is a "happy stomach".' Amy took another bite of cake. 'You've been sad, and it's a scientific fact that misery burns calories faster than joy – it's time for you to get a happy stomach.'

'Right, okay, thanks for your top medical diagnosis, Doctor, that doesn't sound at all made up. And I'm not un-happy, I'm just . . .' Jenni paused.

She wasn't sure how she felt anymore. She wasn't miserable – she was used to being without Alex now – but since she'd seen her mum with Alan, she had to admit that she'd felt, not sad exactly, but . . .

'I'm just a bit lonely sometimes.'

The truth hit her and she put down her plate and looked at Amy.

'It's hard being on my own all the time, keeping busy, worrying if I should be out, that if I stay home I'll never meet anyone. Having to tell people on Monday that I've had a good weekend, pretending I've been doing stuff so they don't feel sorry for me. And breaking my leg . . . it's made me realise that if anything happens, there's literally no one else I can lean on.'

'Oh, Jenni – you can always come and hang out with us, you don't have to be on your own all the time.'

'I know that, and thank you, but it's not the same as just being at home, with someone else who is happy to be home too.'

Seeing Amy's concerned face, Jenni tried to lighten the situation. 'It's fine, I have a very dedicated companion who brings me dead rodents and bits of litter, so I'm really very well provided for. And look, I'm having another slice, so lots of work going into the happy stomach.'

Jenni cut another chunk of cake and took a big bite.

Smiling, Amy reached over and took another piece too. 'I'll support you on this important mission. If your happiness requires me to eat more cake, then you can count on me!'

12

Ben hadn't realised quite how noisy a group of seven-year-olds could be. Currently, he was backed into a corner clutching a warm beer while several of Evie's friends ran around in circles waving foam swords.

You walk into burning buildings, you save lives. Wherever there is danger, you are there. A children's party is nothing to be scared of!

He tried giving himself a talking to, but really, feral children fuelled by sugar were terrifying.

He'd arrived half an hour ago, his sense of foreboding increasing as he'd walked towards his sister and her husband Antony's house. Not just because he was going to have to talk to his parents, well, his dad, but because he could hear the noise getting louder with every step. And as he'd reached number 218, if the screams of delight coming from within weren't enough to tell him that he'd reached his destination, the helium balloons festooning the gate did the trick.

Steeling himself, he'd pressed the doorbell and waited on the step.

'Hello, Evie, happy birthday!'

'Uncle Ben!' Evie jumped up at him to give him a hug, pleased to see him. 'Come in and join my party. Did you bring me a present?'

'Evie, that's very rude, you don't ask if people have brought you gifts.' Penny had appeared from the sitting room looking slightly flushed. 'Hello, Ben. Evie, why don't you go and join in with musical chairs? Daddy's just getting everyone organised.'

Pulling the door shut behind her, Penny dragged Ben into the kitchen.

'Oh my God, it's chaos. I don't know why I said yes to having a party here, we should have done this in the park and let them all run wild, or somewhere I wouldn't care if they threw up on things.'

Ben looked around the normally pristine kitchen. Discarded wrapping paper was gathered in drifts along the wall, bunting hung crookedly from light fittings, various tiny shoes had been abandoned wherever they were most likely to be a trip hazard, jelly handprints adorned the glass bi-fold doors and Ben hoped that the brown stains mashed into the rug were chocolate cake and not something infinitely worse. Muffled sobbing could be heard coming from the other room.

'Oh dear, now Reuben's crying again. I should have thought of a game where no-one would have to be out. Negotiating with the EU is easier than getting him to accept that he *did* move during musical statues.'

'I did think pirates and princesses was a brave theme,' Ben pointed out, lowering himself gingerly onto a chair having removed the jammy dodger stuck to the seat.

'Well, I thought Evie would want to be a Disney princess, but then she decided she wanted to be a pirate and, of course, everyone decided they wanted to be pirates too, even if they were originally a princess, so there's a lot more swashbuckling that I'd originally planned. Here, have a drink. God knows I need one, but I have to stay sober as I'm in charge. Hahaha!' Penny's laugh had a hysterical edge to it as she thrust a beer at Ben, the contents slopping over the sides.

'Thanks, Pen,' he said, taking a long gulp. Dutch courage and all that.

Penny ran a hand through her dishevelled hair, removing a streamer in the process. She straightened her shoulders and took a deep breath. 'Right, I'm going back in.'

She cast a nervous glance towards the living room where the noise levels had increased. 'Go and talk to Mum and Dad. They're hiding in the garden. Dad's doing the barbecue.'

'I don't really—'

'It's either that or you have to go in there and manage

pass the parcel. It's your choice.' Penny interrupted him, an unhinged look in her eyes.

A loud bang from the other room, followed by a scream, then the sound of another child bursting into tears made the decision slightly easier.

'I'll go and talk to Mum and Dad,' said Ben, taking another gulp of beer and heading for the garden.

Pushing open the glass doors, Ben headed up the path, making his way from one Yorkshire stone paver to the next. Penny had just had the garden redesigned to accommodate Antony's home office and Evie's trampoline. Low, white-rendered raised beds lined the slate-black fencing, and olive trees — which were artfully underlit as soon as dusk arrived — stood to attention at regular intervals, disguising the plastic ducting that ran electrics and Wi-Fi to what Antony called his work pod and what Penny called *the shed*.

As he walked through a rose-covered arch, his mum said, 'Benjamin, hello! We were wondering where you'd got to.'

Ben's mum, her blonde hair now streaked with grey piled into a bun, stood up for a hug as he joined them. Ben smiled and leant down to wrap his arms around her.

'I was on duty last night so I had a bit of late start today.'

Antony was a keen barbecuer and, as something big in the City, he'd used his latest annual bonus to create, not only the work pod/garden room/shed, but also to furnish the raised decking area with a micro-concrete outdoor kitchen specially designed to fit around his Green Egg. Situated far too close to the wooden pergola for Ben's professional liking – did they not know how many domestic fires were caused by incorrectly sited barbecues, not to mention the carbon monoxide poisoning, each year? – Ben had to admit it was a pretty smart set up.

'How's Dad getting on?' he asked his mum in a low voice, looking over towards his father, who was bent over the barbecue.

As Antony had been roped into helping to manage the party games, Ben's parents had been allocated cooking duties, and as Ben's mum buttered bread rolls, his dad, charged with grilling burgers, could be heard muttering furiously as he glared at the temperature gauge.

'Well, yes, he's got the lid off now,' said his mother diplomatically. 'Why don't you go and see if you can help?'

Taking another fortifying gulp of beer, Ben headed over to his father. 'Hi, Dad, how are you?'

His dad glanced up to glare at him. 'I'd be fine if it wasn't for this stupid thing. Honestly, what's wrong with a good old-fashioned grill? I don't know why he insists on this ridiculous contraption. More money and trouble than it's worth.'

'Ian, I do wish you'd just calm down.' Ben's mum joined them. 'Let Ben look at it, he knows about fire. You come and help with me the rolls.'

Ben reached for the tongs, ready to assist, but before he could his father snatched them away.

'Ben knows nothing about *starting* fires, Mary, he only knows how to put them out. He'll be no help whatsoever.'

Ian turned back to the grill, his shoulders set.

Ben rolled his eyes. Typical.

'Dad, I think I can manage to cook some burgers. Why don't you sit down with Mum?' He tried again and went to lift the domed lid of the barbecue, but his dad pushed it firmly back down.

'I can cope, thank you very much. Just let me get on with it.'

Sighing heavily, Ben walked back to the table and sat down next to his mum, his jaw tightly clenched.

His mother reached out a soothing hand.

'Just ignore him, you know how he gets,' she said gently.

'Yes,' said Ben through clenched teeth. 'Unbearable. I don't know why he won't let me help, he's obviously stressed.'

'I know, I know, but he thinks needing help is a sign of weakness. He . . . he just can't, you know that.'

Ben looked at his mum's anxious face and let his anger go. He had seen first-hand what had happened when his dad had needed help. But Ben had learnt that asking for help came from strength not weakness, and he wished his dad, an ex-policeman, could discover the same.

Following his breakdown, Ben had thought his dad might have been able to understand, but instead he'd told him he needed to pull himself together. Ian's refusal to admit that he'd ever experienced anything similar had left Ben angry and hurt. As his counsellor kept telling him, it was something Ben needed to talk to his dad about.

Hell will freeze over before I feel ready for that conversation, Ben thought angrily, staring at his father's rigid back as he banged the lid shut on the barbecue and flung the tongs down in frustration.

In the meantime, Mary and Penny were stuck in the middle, trying to bridge the gap between the men in the family. Ben knew that their patience with the tension was running out.

'Why don't you pop back indoors and give your sister a hand?' Mary suggested, seeing the look of disappointment on Ben's face. 'We'll be ready to eat in about ten minutes, so she'll need some help getting everyone ready.'

Ben looked over at his dad again. He was exuding impatience and disapproval as he continued to wrestle with the barbecue, and Ben heard him mutter something about how it was fine for others to just give up and walk off.

Ben's heart hardened.

Deciding, upon reflection, that a house of seven-year-olds seemed a lot less effort to deal with, he picked up his drink and walked away.

*

'Thank God that's over for another year.'

Penny fell back into the dark-green velvet sofa and stuck her feet up on the coffee table. She'd changed into leggings and a long cashmere jumper and, her slim shoulders finally relaxing, reached for her glass and took a large gulp of wine.

Ben, sitting next to her, smiled. 'You did a great job. Evie had a fantastic time.'

'She did, didn't she?' Penny looked pleased. 'I love it really, especially when it's all over and the house has been de-caked! Thank you for helping.'

'No problem, it was fun.'

Penny threw Ben a questioning look, and he laughed.

'Okay, perhaps not fun exactly, but I'm happy to help.'

Once the games were finished and the burgers eaten, parents had started to arrive to collect their children and, one by one, Evie's friends had been dispatched, some more easily than others, clutching party bags and covered in chocolate. Antony had taken charge of bath time while Ben and Penny tidied the house, relocating sofa cushions, wiping down surfaces and putting toys back into cupboards. Now, eating leftover cocktail sausages – organic, of course – and an entire cheese and pineapple hedgehog – for some reason the children had shunned this culinary delicacy from Penny's childhood – they were happily slumped on the sofa.

'Another beer?' Penny asked, standing up to head to the fridge so she could top up her wine glass.

'Yes, please, that would be great.' Ben slid another cube of cheddar and pineapple off its stick and into his mouth.

Penny returned with their drinks, curling her legs under her on the sofa.

'Why don't you stay over? You've still got some of your things here. Saves you having to get home.'

'That's a good idea. I'll get up with Evie tomorrow morning. I promised her we could make her Lego castle while we watch *Frozen* again.'

'Ooh, yes, that sounds good. I can have a lie in. Thank you, Uncle Ben.'

The two sat in silence for a moment, enjoying the quiet after the earlier noise. Light filtered in through the slatted shutters and the candles on the mantlepiece threw a cosy glow over the room. From upstairs came the sound of water running and Antony coaxing Evie through the bedtime routine.

Penny turned to look at Ben. 'Saw you chatting to Dad, was he okay?'

Ben shrugged. 'He was a nightmare earlier when he was doing the barbecue, but I asked how his journey was so he started telling me about how bad the traffic had been. I made the mistake of asking what route he'd taken and he went off on one about the merits of the south circular versus the M25 onto the A3. He was quite animated for Dad!'

'At least Mum didn't chime in about how she won't use

the satnav on her phone because then "they" will be tracking her!'

Ben conceded that that was a small mercy. His mum was great in nearly all respects but she was deeply suspicious about modern technology. They'd only just persuaded her to get a mobile phone for emergencies.

'At least you and Dad spent a bit of time together, I know it's hard for you.'

Ben didn't reply. He joked, but the fact his dad could happily discuss, at length, the best route to get to Wandsworth from Winchester, but not how his son was, or what he was doing, upset him. And he felt like a coward for not confronting his dad about it, but he didn't want to make things hard for his mum. Penny, seeing his frowning face, changed the subject.

'It wasn't just dad I saw you chatting to,' she said, teasingly. 'You and Kieran's mum were getting along rather well.'

'Sami? Yeh, she was asking me about fire blankets for the kitchen,' Ben replied, looking surprised. 'She wanted to know where she should get them from.'

'Hmm, I don't think that's why she was giving you her mobile number, though.'

Penny took another gulp of wine and pushed a strand of hair behind her ear. 'She's asked me several times if you're single, and she's not the only mum-friend who's been interested in finding out more about you. Some of them aren't even single!'

'Well, I'm certainly not interested in the married ones!' Ben said, shocked.

'I know, I'm just teasing,' she said, before adding more carefully, 'But what about Sami? She's lovely. Why don't you give her a call and ask her out?'

Ben didn't answer straight away.

'I don't know. I just don't feel ready for all of that, and besides, my work doesn't make it easy to date people. I've tried, and it's no fun when I'm not around for evenings and nights, and can't do weekends. It annoys people.'

'It annoyed Luisa, you mean.' Penny grimaced. She'd never been a fan of Ben's ex-girlfriend.

'Not just Luisa. Milly wasn't keen either. '

'You went on *one* date. I hardly think that counts.'

Penny looked across at her brother as he studiously stared into his glass, ignoring her.

Penny softened. 'Look, I know the whole thing with Luisa hit you hard, and it's fine to be by yourself if that's what you want. But I just want you to be happy, and to know there are lots of women interested in you if you *do* want to find someone. I can't keep fending off the single girls in the PTA forever, you know.'

Ben cracked a smile. 'Thanks, Pen. I'm just getting used to being by myself again. I'm not sure I'm ready for all the stuff that comes with being with someone else right now, but I'll let you know when I am.'

'Okay, well, when you *are* I can auction you off as a prize in the school raffle. Tall and handsome, a firefighter – you're a catch, you know. I'm in charge of raising funds for the school roof this year, so if I have to sell my brother to the highest bidder, then so be it.'

Ben, catching her look of determination, was alarmed to see that she didn't appear to be joking.

13

'Hello, darling, how are you?'

Jenni heard the metal flick of a lighter, followed by an inhale of breath that indicated her mum had just lit a cigarette. She pictured her mum, perched on the stool next to the Rayburn, Benson and Hedges on the table next to her, and rolled her eyes affectionately. Followed quickly by a jolt of grief as she pictured her dad there too, quietly pushing an ashtray towards Annie before taking the phone to say hello himself. Perhaps that feeling would never go away.

Jenni filled her mum in on how she was – leg healing and in a boot, she could move around much more easily now. She was still working from home, but felt so much better now she could pop out for a pint of milk – or snacks, more to the point – without having to text Jo or Nick next door and ask them. It didn't feel right revealing that her most meaningful relationships at the moment were with Cadbury's and Walkers crisps.

Work had been great and had sent her a hamper full of posh food and treats, which she'd been working her way through — although not the kimchi, despite Clive's note urging her to try it for the love of her gut health.

She was so looking forward to getting back to the office to catch up on all the gossip. Tim had tried to fill her in on what was going on, but he had become paranoid that IT was monitoring his email, and she'd been unable to crack his cryptic codes. Fortunately, Lucy was less into conspiracy theories and had simply called her for a chat.

Her mum also had news.

'So ...' There was a pause, another inhale followed by a longer exhale. 'I've decided to go to New Zealand with Alan.' Before adding, 'What do you think?'

'I think that's great news. When are you going?' Jenni said, before realising with relief that she really did in fact feel pleased for her mum and wasn't just saying it.

Another exhale. 'Oh, darling, I'm so pleased you're okay with it. I have to admit to feeling a bit nervous about it all. But, you know, the whole thing with your dad, it's just made me think I need to live a little, we never know what will happen.'

'Don't say that! You're going to live forever!' Jenni couldn't imagine life without her mum as well as her dad. 'But you're right, you should definitely go for it.'

'We've booked to go next month, and we're going for three weeks. It's such a long time to be away, but we want to have some time to explore on our own after visiting Alan's daughter. Will you be okay? I worry about you being on your own all the time.'

'Of course I'll be okay, I'll be fine. I wish you'd stop worrying about me. And we can always FaceTime – you got quite good at it during lockdown.'

'That's true, I embraced the technology, I was rather proud. And when I'm back, perhaps we could do something together? I know, I know, you're fine on your own,' her mother added hastily. 'I just mean it would be nice to see you when I'm back.'

Jenni, who'd begun to bristle, softened. 'That would be lovely. Just don't be tempted to move out there, I couldn't cope with that!'

'Don't worry, darling. I have no plans to relocate to the other side of the world. Besides, there's far too much going on here.'

Annie moved on to village gossip, while Jenni made sympathetic noises, agreeing with her mother that angering the WI was a recipe for disaster and that the keep fit woman should have known better than to take their slot on the village hall rota. But really she was only half listening, thinking instead about what she'd said to her mum. It was fine she was on her own, wasn't it? She didn't need anyone else to spend her days with. She had plenty to be getting on with . . . didn't she?

Her mum finally said goodbye and ended the call leaving Jenni in silence.

She looked around her flat, suddenly deflated. Even her mum, who lived in a remote village with fewer than five hundred people, had managed to find someone new, but here Jenni was. Alone. Again.

The cardboard box by the door caught her eye. She'd ordered a bunch of plain white garments with the intention of getting ready for the May fair, which was now only weeks away.

Pleased to have something to distract her, Jenni decided to spend the day tie-dying, preparing stock for her stall. See, she was very busy and had plenty of things to do.

She was keen to get started, but Oscar had other ideas. While she'd been talking to her mum, he'd been alternately scrabbling at her legs or nibbling her toes, and now he saw she was heading towards the kitchen, he began in earnest his campaign for more food.

'I'm just a walking snack dispenser to you, aren't I?' Jenni grumbled as she hobbled into the kitchen. She paused a moment to look out of the window, trying to decide whether it was too cold to work in the shed. If she worked in the house she'd have to be careful not to make a mess. Before she could decide a sharp nip on her ankle caused her to jump. Oscar was in no mood to wait.

'Ow! I really shouldn't be rewarding you for biting me,' Jenni grumbled, lifting down the jar that contained Oscar's snacks. Prising off the lid, Jenni shook a few of the cat treats into a bowl for Oscar, who settled down to hoover them all up. Shaking a few extra out for him – Jenni knew he'd want more – she put the jar back on the shelf and decided the shed would be better as she planned to have several buckets of dye on the go at once and didn't want to risk staining the bathroom.

Gathering up the turmeric and onion skins she'd been saving, she unlocked the back door and stepped out into the garden.

Oscar, snacks finished, stalked past her, jumped up on the garden wall that separated her from the family next door, and began licking himself.

Two strides – well, hops – took her to the shed and she let herself in, breathing in the smell of wood, acrylic paint and white spirit. Her neighbour had been giving away some old paint for free, which Jenni had gratefully taken off his hands, so one wall of her shed was a rather fetching blush pink, another olive green, while the remaining two were a pale blue. And although none of them *should* have worked together, Jenni was rather pleased with the mismatched result. It gave her workspace a cosy, creative feel, so different from the white walls that Alex had favoured.

Painting the shed had been her first rebellion; a reclaiming of her space. Alex had always talked her out of the ideas she'd wanted to try, preferring a more restrained mid-century minimalism that was certainly stylish, but had never felt like *her*. The fact that she'd used the money her dad had left her to buy out Alex made the flat extra special, as she felt it connected her to her dad.

Here, in the colourful muddle of her shed, Jenni could lose herself. Twisting sections of fabric and securing them with rubber bands and lengths of string, knotting sleeves, experimenting with twine to create different patterns and effects, before plunging them into carefully mixed buckets of dye, then pegging the items out on her makeshift washing line.

Hours later, with small sleepsuits, toddler-sized T-shirts, leggings and socks of various sizes dangling colourfully from the line strung from one end of the shed to the other, Jenni headed back to the house for a cup of tea.

Oscar, asleep on the garden table, flattened an ear as she passed. She stopped to stroke him, the black pirate patch around his eye just visible from behind his tail, which he'd coiled around him.

Jenni smiled at him. She hadn't realised how long she'd been occupied, and now the late spring light was darkening and shadows were stretching across the garden and up the garden fence.

Jenni looked around, seeing more signs of nature

springing back to life after the long winter. She took a deep breath in and felt a moment of contentment.

This was fine, she thought. She was okay on her own. She could manage like this, just her and Oscar.

She didn't need anyone else.

14

Ben lay awake, unable to sleep. Exhausted from worry, his thoughts ranged from what he'd do if he was made redundant to global warming, always circling back to his dad, wondering if they'd ever manage to reclaim the feeling of ease they'd once shared.

Finally giving up trying to sleep, he threw back the duvet cover and got out of bed. Tugging on an old Metallica T-shirt that clashed with his checked pyjama bottoms, and pushing his hair off his face, he turned on the hall light and headed for the kitchen.

Having become used to the constant noise generated by a family with a young child while staying at his sister's house, his flat felt eerily quiet in comparison. Even a distant siren and the rumble of a car idling outside didn't make him feel less alone in the world.

Why did this always happen to me?

Catching himself catastrophising, as his therapist had taught him to recognise, he took a depth breath. He'd been doing really well – one sleepless night didn't mean the dreaded insomnia had returned. He just needed to sit quietly in the kitchen for a bit, calm down, and then go back to bed.

Following his own advice, he made himself a Boy Scout hot chocolate, as his dad used to call it when he and Penny were small: cocoa and sugar stirred together instead of drinking chocolate. He put the radio on, just to have some noise in the room with him.

Ben put the mug in the microwave and waited for the ping to signal it was hot enough, before moving to sit at the breakfast counter. His hand reached for his phone before acknowledging that doomscrolling probably wouldn't help.

Under a stack of junk mail, takeaway menus and random till receipts, he pulled out the fire service quarterly magazine he'd brought home from work – articles on new regulations and threats to pensions should send him to sleep if nothing else did.

He was halfway through an opinion piece about the best new smoke alarms when the hairs on the back of his neck began to prickle.

He was being watched.

He shook his head to get rid of the sensation, fighting the urge to look around the room. Of course, there was no one there. He was just being paranoid.

He tried to plough on with the piece he was reading, sipping again at his cocoa, but the feeling wouldn't go away.

Rolling his eyes at his own stupidity, he looked up and glanced around the kitchen to reassure himself that he was alone.

There, see, just being silly, there's no one looking at—

His caught his breath as he saw a face at the window.

Bright green eyes were staring at him, sharp teeth on display as the creature opened its mouth, it's fluffy ears flattened against—

Wait, *fluffy* ears? Gradually, logic took over and Ben realised that the terrifying monster at the window was not, in fact, his worst nightmare made real, but instead a cat. The same small cat that had visited him previously.

Laughing at himself and feeling somewhat embarrassed – though his heart was still pounding – Ben approached the window.

'Hello, little fellow. You gave me the fright of my life! What are you doing here?'

There was a muffled yowl through the glass.

'Hold on. I'll open the window.'

Although he knew it was a cat, Ben wanted to make sure his eyes weren't playing tricks on him. In the morning, he'd laugh about this with his mates, but right now he felt the need to be certain. And, truthfully, he would welcome the company.

Ben gingerly lifted the latch and pushed the window

open a fraction, half expecting the cat to disappear. Instead, defying all laws of physics, it somehow oozed through the narrow gap and into the kitchen.

The cat began purr, nudging at Ben's still outstretched arm. Shrugging to himself, he closed the window to shut out the cool night air and gave in, stroking the cat's mackerel-striped fur.

'Well, you're very friendly, aren't you? What are you doing outside at this time of night?'

The cat – obviously – didn't answer. Instead, it dropped onto its side with its paws lifted so Ben could rub its tummy.

Ben felt strangely honoured. He was sure he'd read something about how cats would only reveal their tummies if they were comfortable with you, and he felt flattered that he'd gained this little cat's trust so quickly. He gently went to stroke the exposed fur, but as soon as his hand made contact, it wrapped it's front paws around his forearm and began thumping its back legs against its 'prey'.

'Ouch!' Ben extracted his arm, examining his hand for scratches. 'That was a trap!'

The cat, seemingly satisfied that Ben understood the pecking order, jumped off the draining board, strolled over to the breakfast bar, jumped up on Ben's stool and looked expectantly at him.

The cheek of it, Ben thought. The cat had not only broken in, lulled him into a false sense of security and then attacked him, it had now nicked his seat and seemed to be expecting a slap-up meal.

'Come here.' Ben tapped the other stool.

The cat just stared at him.

Not yet feeling brave enough to put his hands on the cat again – not without one of those special leather gauntlet things used to train birds of prey – he sat down in the spare – less comfy if he was honest – seat, picked up his hot chocolate and carried on reading.

The cat hunched down on the chair next to him, paws tucked neatly beneath its body. It seemed happy enough, so Ben continued flipping through the magazine while he finished his drink. Calmer now, he was beginning to feel tired again. He'd just get to the end of this article then he'd go back to bed.

As if sensing time was up, the cat suddenly jumped down from the stool, leapt back up to the sink and waited by the window. It turned back to Ben and gave a small meow.

'Okay, little chap, hold on and I'll let you out.'

The cat paused to give Ben's hand a quick nudge then squeezed back through the window. Ben heard a slight flump as it dropped from the windowsill and its paws hit the ground. Then silence.

Smiling to himself Ben closed the window, turned out the light and headed back to bed.

Strangely, he was no longer feeling quite so alone.

15

The last few weeks had been a blur for Jenni. A check-up back at the hospital had confirmed that her leg was on the mend, so now, boot- and crutches-free, she had practically skipped into work, delighted to leave the confines of her flat. While she loved working from home, it was less of a pleasure if it was from necessity rather than choice.

Even Oscar seemed fed up with her, she thought. He was disappearing for longer spells, slinking out early and returning home later each night. Perhaps they were entering the teenage years, although at three perhaps he was past the teens now – did cat years work the same as dog years?

Her first day back in the office had been a bit of a shock. Excited to be returning, Jenni had picked up coffees from her favourite café to celebrate. However, as she'd pushed through the revolving door at Go Big HQ, balancing the cardboard tray containing the drinks for the team in one hand, she'd been surprised to find Lucy and Tim waiting for her.

'Surprise! Hello, love, we thought we'd come and greet you!' Tim practically shouted, jiggling up and down on the spot.

'Um, hello, yes, lovely to see you both, but I really didn't need a welcome committee,' Jenni said, catching Lucy glaring at Tim and mouthing 'Act normal!' before calling, 'Oh, it's no trouble, we just thought it would be a nice surprise.'

'Yes, nice, nice to see you, and to, um, help,' said Tim, grabbing the coffees from Jenni who was now feeling distinctly suspicious. What was going on?

'It's honestly fine, I don't need any help—' Jenni tried to protest, but Lucy interrupted.

'Here, let's get you up to the office.'

Lucy put her arm around Jenni's shoulder and began to steer her towards the stairs.

'The doctor said I need to take it easy for a bit longer, so I'll take the lift. I'll meet you up there if you want to walk up?'

'I told you,' Jenni heard Tim hiss to Lucy, who tutted, but when Jenni turned to look at them both, their faces snapped into wide smiles.

'Of course, no problem, let's take the lift,' Tim said, striding towards the bank of lifts and jabbing the 'up' button.

Lucy rushed ahead to join Tim, the two of them

whispering intensely while leaving Jenni to make her way more slowly to join them. As she drew alongside them, they stopped talking abruptly and, again, plastered slightly manic grins on their faces.

'Okay. What's going on with you two? Has something happened? Oh, you're not throwing a welcome back party for me, are you? Do I need to look surp—'

'We are *not* throwing you a party,' interrupted Lucy, as the lift doors pinged open and she ushered Jenni into the lift. 'But, well, there is something, and, um . . .' she sighed dramatically. 'Tim, you explain.'

Tim pushed the button for the sixth floor and the lift – much like Jenni's feeling of alarm – began to rise.

'What's happened? Am I fired? Is Clive getting rid of me? What's going on? You have to tell me.'

Tim turned to Jenni. 'Okay, calm down! It's none of that. The opposite, in fact. You could see it as more of a *celebration* of you . . . perhaps.'

'Just tell me!' Jenni's alarm was now turning to frustration.

'Okay, okay. It's just, the decor has been updated and we thought you might be a bit . . . we thought you might not like . . . it.' He trailed off.

'Is that it? Why won't I like it? How bad can it be?' Jenni said, puzzled. 'I mean, I do have strong views on orange these days, but I'm sure it can't be that awful.'

The lift shuddered to a stop. Lucy turned to face Jenni

and grabbed her by the shoulders. 'It's worse than orange,' she said solemnly.

'Yes,' Tim added, his face serious. 'You need to prepare yourself. And know that we tried to stop him.'

With a jolt, the doors opened at the Go Big reception area.

'Oh. My. God.' Jenni gasped, frozen to the spot. 'What the fuck is this?'

'Don't panic,' said Lucy. 'It's just in here. And the kitchen. And a little bit in the break-out area. But other than that, hardly noticeable.'

'Fuck,' whispered Jenni again, ignoring Lucy's attempt to reassure her. It was suddenly clear why they'd been so keen for her to take the back stairs, avoiding reception and the giant photos of her. *Everywhere.*

'I mean, I knew he'd used them for the campaign, but I didn't think Clive would do *this*,' Jenni said weakly.

Framed photos of her, depicting the moment her feet were swept from beneath her, the armful of colourful knit-wear flying through the air, and if you didn't know what happened next, the look on her face seemed one of happy surprise rather than horror, were displayed on every wall, some so large every pore on her nose was visible.

Jenni shuddered.

Tim patted her consolingly on the shoulder. 'Your hair looks great though, nice swish as you're, um, falling.'

Before Jenni could formulate a response, the internal door

to the office swung open and Clive strode through with a grin so wide he looked like the Joker.

'Jenni! Our star! You're back! Wonderful. I see you're admiring the campaign shoot – your colleagues here tried to suggest I go with different shots, but this picture says playful abandon to me and I'm just loving this direction for us, aren't you?'

Taking Jenni's inability to speak as agreement, he continued, 'I can tell you're as chuffed as I am! Jolly good. Right, see you in the Monday Motivational in fifteen minutes.'

He disappeared into the loo before any of them could reply.

'Don't worry, love, we've covered as many as we can with mental health awareness posters. You'll hardly notice them after a while . . .' Tim said, as he dumped the now-cold coffees on the reception desk, ignoring the tut from Fran who took the clear desk policy very seriously.

Taking Jenni's arm and speaking quietly, as if calming a startled animal, Lucy guided her towards their desks.

*

'And they're *everywhere*, Amy, I can't even go to the loo without seeing my fall of shame. I've a good mind to go to HR. It's the very definition of employee harassment, surely.'

Amy, now crying with laughter, was unable to speak.

'How would you like it if when you come back from

maternity leave, Clive had enlarged that photo of you flashing your Spanx at the Christmas party and stuck it in reception, hmm? Imagine that plastered around the office, staring down at you while you're trying to work?'

This sobering thought gave Amy pause and she pulled herself together, wiping the tears from her eyes.

'Oh, Jenni, I'm sorry. It must be awful, but, you know, the campaign has done really well already, and you said that the other images, the ones with the models in, are scheduled to feed out soon, so you'll quickly become digital chip paper. And you know Clive likes to change the office "energy" every few months. They'll all be taken down soon.'

'Well, I'm working on trek-wear next so perhaps some nice tropical parrots might get me off the walls.'

'That's the spirit! And talking of walls, I need your help with something,' Amy said. 'But let's have another coffee first.'

Jenni settled back on the bright red sofa while Amy, the sleeves of her striped top rolled up beneath black dungarees, walked over to flick the switch on the kettle. Amy and her family lived a bus ride away and, still enjoying the novelty of being able to leave her flat, Jenni had been happy to make the short journey to visit her friend. While Tilly, George and Simon were at the park, she and Amy could enjoy an uninterrupted catch-up.

Amy's rental house was meant to be temporary while they

found somewhere to buy, but with babies, and Simon's job looking uncertain, they'd decided to stay put for a while, even though the tall, narrow house wasn't ideal for a young family with pushchairs. The kitchen and living room, where they were currently sitting, worked well in theory as Amy could cook and keep an eye on the children sat at the table at the same time, but it was on the first floor, which meant walking up and down the stairs with babies and bags of shopping ten times a day .

Amy came back with mugs of coffee, and as they drank them, Jenni showed her pictures of the stock she was going to sell at the fair in a couple of weeks.

'Oh, I like that one – that's lovely,' Amy said, pointing at a cotton bag dyed a bright pink.

'Well, you can have it if you can help me on the stall for a couple hours,' Jenni said, looking beseechingly at her friend. 'Just so I can go and look around the other stalls and see what the competition is. And I'll need a loo break.'

'I'm sure I can, I'll check with Simon to see if he can look after the kids.'

'Thank you – it will be much more fun if you're there. I'm feeling a bit nervous, to be honest,' Jenni confessed, now that she realised just how much work was involved and that the fair was so close.

'You've got some great stuff, you'll be fine. Now, have you finished your tea?'

Jenni took a last hasty gulp and nodded.

'Right, follow me.'

Amy led the way up the stairs to the top floor where her and Simon's bedroom at the front of the house was adjoined by a smaller room at the back. Tilly had been in a cot in her parents' bedroom up until now, but was going to join George in the back bedroom next week.

'I've cleared this corner for her cot and I need some help putting these fairy lights up, just to make Tilly's corner a bit cuter, and the light will be softer when I have to come in for night feeds.'

'That's a nice idea. What do you want me to do?'

'If I stand on this chair, can you feed the lights up to me so I don't get in a tangle?'

As Amy reached up to snag the cable over hooks along the wall, Jenni carefully passed her each section to hang. Eventually, all in place, Amy stepped down and plugged in the lights.

'Ta-dah!'

The little lights, trailing across the bedroom wall above the cot, cast a gentle glow on the woodland animal design of Tilly's duvet, making the space look magical.

'Gorgeous,' said Jenni. 'Lucky Tilly!'

'Hopefully she'll sleep okay in here and then it will be lucky Mummy, too!'

Just then, the sound of the front door opening reached

them, followed by thumps on the stairs, indicating that George, Simon and Tilly were heading up to the sitting room.

'Oh well,' said Amy. 'That's the end of any peace and quiet. Come on, I know George will want to show you his dinosaurs.'

Jenni tried to look enthusiastic as, after taking one last look at the pretty bedroom, she followed Amy downstairs to ooh and ahh over George's latest obsession.

16

'I haven't got any cat treats, you know.'

The cat stared at Ben.

'This is coffee. Cats can't have coffee.'

The cat blinked slowly and Ben weakened.

'Well, I might have something in the fridge, maybe. I'm not sure I should be feeding you, though. You must have breakfast waiting for you at home?'

This was met by an unblinking stare.

'I suppose a bit of chicken won't hurt.'

Ben opened the fridge door. He'd been planning to use up the leftover chicken for his own lunch, but hey. He pulled a corner off a slice and took it over to the cat on a saucer. 'Here you go, Fred.'

Since the cat's first visit a few weeks ago, Fred, as Ben now called him – after Frederick Fawcett, his commanding officer – had become a frequent visitor and this morning, when Ben arrived home, he'd found him sitting outside on the windowsill, ears pressed to his head, and he'd felt guilty that the poor little chap had been waiting for him in such horrid weather. Ben decided the least he could do was give him some chicken.

Fred looked well cared for and was obviously being fed somewhere, but he didn't want the little cat to go hungry.

'Here you go, then,' he said, as he put the saucer on the floor. Fred ignored it before jumping on the stool, looking expectantly at Ben.

'I can't believe I'm doing this,' grumbled Ben, picking up the saucer and placing it on the breakfast bar. Fred bent his head and sniffed at it, before picking delicately at the chicken pieces.

Unbelievable, thought Ben. 'You wait until I tell the crew at work. They think it's weird I've let you in, let alone allowed you to nick my favourite chair. And now you're actually sitting at my table eating my lunch!'

Ben had told Taz and the gang about his midnight visit from Fred and, as expected, they'd taken the piss royally. Taz, in particular, had enjoyed teasing Ben about how scared he was at the sight of a cute, fluffy kitten.

But as Fred's visits continued, they'd all laughed hearing about his demands and how he was now dictating what Ben watched on TV – anything with police and detectives and Fred purred loudly and curled up on his lap. But old war films and he'd start yowling and stalk out of the room if Ben didn't change channel immediately. Which was annoying as Ben much preferred the latter.

But Ben enjoyed the cat's company either way and particularly liked it when Fred joined him on mornings like this. When he got home after a busy night shift, it was hard to settle down, and the presence of the cat helped him adjust. And although he didn't want to encourage him too much, he *had* thrown a packet of Lick-e-Lix yoghurt snacks into his shopping basket when he'd last gone to the supermarket.

His guilt at feeding Fred was offset by how happy the foul-smelling, liquidised, liver-flavoured treat had made the cat, who barely drew breath gobbling it up.

Ben smiled now as he watched Fred, food finished, lick his paw and rub it over his ear before curling up on the stool for a snooze.

Making sure the window was open so the cat could get out whenever he wanted to, Ben decided it was time for him to do the same, and headed to bed to catch up on some sleep before he needed to get back to the station for the start of another night shift.

Fred, now fast asleep, didn't even notice that Ben had gone.

17

'Argh. Why won't you work?' Jenni shook her laptop in frustration. 'Why are you looking for the printer? It's *right here*.'

Unable to face the pictures of shame, and knowing that Tim and Lucy weren't going in to the office that day, Jenni had decided to work from home too. She'd got up at her normal time, fed Oscar, who had been waiting for her in the kitchen pretending he was starved, had a cup of tea, then changed into leggings and fleece and gone for a quick walk around the park. Her physio had told her to make sure she did some exercise every day, and Jenni had started to enjoy her new routine.

The mornings were getting lighter, and each day the leaves on the trees were that bit greener, the plants a little taller, the flower-buds less tightly furled.

As well as the change in the season, Jenni also enjoyed seeing a new cast of characters on her walks: parents hurrying their children to school, a group of older women powerwalking around the park – Jenni would say hello to them by the gate and then again by the café as they embarked on their second lap – dog walkers in a tangle of leads, and cyclists on their commute.

It was a snapshot of her neighbourhood that she usually missed while travelling to the office, and somehow seeing the same people out and about each morning made her feel a bit more connected. A smile from Mum in Red Coat or a nod of recognition from Man with Naughty Labradoodle made her day a bit brighter.

She'd returned to an empty flat. Oscar had gone out again and, after breakfast, she'd fired up her laptop to start work.

Stopping only for lunch, Jenni had steadily worked through her to-do list, checking items off and adding new things on, as well as answering emails, until the day came to an end. She'd had just one more thing to do – print off a label – and then she'd call it a day. But the printer and the computer had fallen out and she had no idea how to get them talking again.

Giving the computer another shake, she was about to start randomly pressing buttons when the doorbell rang. Glad to be interrupted, Jenni shut her laptop and headed for the door, careful to make sure she had her keys with her so her front door didn't swing shut behind her, leaving her trapped in the communal hall.

Hastily checking that her leggings weren't the baggy ones with holes in – sartorial standards when working at home were pretty low – Jenni opened the door to find a delivery man on the doorstep. Muttering about traffic and roadworks, he handed her a padded envelope and a small parcel before stomping off back down the path to his van.

Jenni tore open the jiffy bag. *Aha*, just what she'd been waiting for.

There had been several posts concerning missing cats on the street WhatsApp lately, and so, even though she knew he'd hate it, she'd ordered Oscar a lovely, bright green collar so that it was obvious he wasn't a stray. But first, she actually had to get it on him

As if by magic, the rattle of the cat flap announced Oscar's return from wherever he'd been hanging out that day.

'Perfect timing!' Jenni said. 'Right, you, stay there.'

Distracting him with a large bowl of his favourite food, Jenni shut the kitchen door and locked the cat flap.

There was no escape now.

Moving calmly so as not to alarm him, she stretched open the green collar and knelt next to him. Gently, holding the collar wide, she reached over, securing it around his neck and quickly pushing the clasp together.

Oscar looked up at her and shook his head, momentarily distracted by the thing now around his neck.

'That's it, just keep eating, nothing to see here,' Jenni

soothed, tapping a few biscuits into another bowl. 'Here you go. Have some Dreamies.'

Oscar, eyeing her suspiciously, but unable to resist, started crunching through the biscuits. Running a finger between the collar and his fur, and satisfied that it wasn't too tight, Jenni stood up.

Oscar might not like it much, but if he did stray too far from home, at least it was clear now that he belonged to someone.

With Oscar sorted, Jenni turned her attention to the other package that had arrived. Sliding the blade of a small kitchen knife through the excessive amount of tape used to seal the parcel, she was pleased to discover that the business cards she'd ordered were finally here. She'd designed them herself and they were printed using eco dyes on untreated card.

Initially unable to think of a name for her business, Jenni had been inspired by the sight of Oscar clambering to the top of a pile of neatly folded T-shirts in the corner of the shed, and decided on 'House of Oscar'. And so, along with her contact details, the card was decorated with a small silhouette of a cat climbing from the 'o' to the 'f', which she'd drawn.

One less thing to worry about, she thought, although that didn't reduce by much her list of things she needed to prepare. With the fair looming next weekend, she still had lots to get done, and now she'd finished the day job she needed to get back in the shed to re-fold and pack her stock.

She also needed to call Amy to check she could definitely help out on the day, pick up the wallpaper table from next door, which Jo and Nick were generously allowing her to use, print out a price list – she'd have to leave this for now, given the printer's refusal to co-operate – and she also needed to get her float sorted. The organisers had advised her to make sure she had plenty of small coins on the day, and she also wondered whether she should get one of those portable card readers.

Was she mad for assuming she'd sell anything at all? Jenni tried to quash the rising feeling of panic.

At the beginning of the year, she'd made a resolution to be more creative. Her years with Alex had meant that, over time, she'd ended up neglecting her own interests. It wasn't that he'd stopped her from crafting or drawing, it was more that there were other things he preferred to do, like going out for the day, or staying in bed together watching telly, or meeting up with other couples for brunch, and she'd gone along with it.

When he'd left, all these things had stopped, leaving Jenni uncertain as to who she was anymore. She'd had so many questions: what did she *used* to like to do? How *did* she want to spend her time? She was better now at knowing how she wanted to fill her spare hours, but, when she'd seen the advert asking for stallholders at the fair, she'd felt fired up for the first time in a long time. It had seemed a good idea to put down the deposit, but now she was regretting New-Year-New-You-Jenni's decision.

Jenni looked at the clock on the oven. She had a couple of hours before her mum was due to call – they'd arranged to speak when Annie arrived in Wellington – so she decided to nip to the shops to get something for dinner before heading out to her shed. As she pulled on her trainers and stuffed a bag for life into her coat pocket, Jenni found herself wishing that someone was heading home to her, carrying the shopping they'd picked up on the way, ready to cook and ask about her day while she drank a glass of wine.

She shook herself. There was no point thinking about all that. It was just her now and she was *fine*, she could *cope*.

But the feeling of longing lingered as she walked around the supermarket, finally throwing a single baked potato and a family bag of Giant Buttons into her basket.

18

It was something Vick had said that had got Ben thinking. She was telling him about dropping off her daughter at school earlier that day; about how all the other parents were so fed up of having to wait outside in the rain for the gates to open, that they'd decided to petition the headteacher for a covered shelter. They were tired of starting their days soaking wet, waiting for Denise, the surly caretaker who refused to let anyone other than teachers onto the grounds before 8.50am.

And God help you if you dared to buzz the reception desk.

As Vick described everyone huddled up in the rain, Ben couldn't help but picture Fred, ears pressed flat, hunkered low on the windowsill, waiting to be let in.

He knew he was being soppy – for goodness' sake, Fred wasn't even his cat – but perhaps it wouldn't hurt to create a little house for him, or any other waifs and strays – a hedge-hog, maybe, or more likely a squirrel – to shelter in.

Today, he was out in the community, advising on fitting smoke alarms and checking homes were fire safe, a job he enjoyed, although it broke his heart to see the conditions some of the old folk were living in. But in between appointments, he'd had time to think and so by the time he got back to the station, he'd decided he was going to build Fred a shelter where he could hang out while he waited for Ben to come home.

As he called into Barry's on his way home, to pick up some sausages and potatoes for his dinner, Ben began to picture the shelter – maybe a seventy-by-fifty-centimetre frame, some marine ply for the sides so it didn't warp in wet weather, and he could cut an arch into the front piece of board so Fred would feel cosy and could get in and out easily. Maybe a pitched roof, and some felt to make the whole structure watertight.

Occupied with these thoughts, the journey home passed quickly and he was soon on his doorstep, searching for his keys. He said hello to Maisie, the woman who lived next door, who was in her front garden putting the rubbish out, then headed indoors.

Slinging the bag of shopping down on the counter, he turned on the oven, letting it heat up while he had a quick shower.

He glanced out of the window – no sign of Fred yet.

Later, comfy in his grey joggers and hooded top with a

belly full of sausage and mash, he tidied up the kitchen – he'd never been particularly worried about washing up or keeping the place tidy before his breakdown, but one thing he'd learnt during counselling was that the little things helped. Even if it was only pulling the sheets straight, you'd made the bed – you could say you'd achieved something for the day – and that was a start.

Pouring himself an alcohol-free lager, he sat in the living room with some paper and a not-too-blunt pencil and began to sketch out a design for Fred's house.

He'd nearly finished, and was just writing down the list of materials he'd need – that DT GSCE had not been wasted – when his phone rang, interrupting his concentration.

He'd left it in the kitchen where it was vibrating itself across the worktop; one more ring and it would hurl itself to the floor. Catching it just in time, Ben picked it up and swiped to answer.

'Hi, Mum, how are you?'

'How did you know it was me?' his mum answered, sounding suspicious.

'I've told you before, your name comes up when you ring me.'

Ben rolled his eyes towards the ceiling. *Honestly.* Every. Single. Time.

'What if you get hacked? Then they'll have my number and steal my identity.'

Ben took a deep breath. He loved his mum, of course he did, but he did find her distrust, and seemingly deliberate misunderstanding, of technology frustrating sometimes.

Although it would make life so much easier for her – and everyone else – Mary wouldn't shop online because she didn't trust it, and she downright refused to even contemplate online banking. In fact, she much preferred to pay for things in cash. Even though Ben kept telling her she was making herself more of a target by walking around with hundreds of pounds in her purse, he couldn't change her mind.

Ben decided now was the time to interrupt before she moved on to her thoughts about doorbells with cameras.

'So how are you, Mum? All okay?'

'Yes, dear, absolutely fine. In fact, I was just ringing to see if you were free the weekend after next. Penelope and family are going to come and stay for the May bank holiday and it would be lovely to see you too.'

Ben pulled a face, but if he was going to have to spend the weekend at his parents, it would be better to do it when Penny was there and he had Evie to divert attention away from the inevitable awkwardness with his dad.

'Hold on, I just need to check.' Ben pulled his rota out of his backpack. 'Yes, that's fine. I can't come until Sunday, though, as I'm on duty on Saturday. It's the local fair and we've been asked to take the engine so the kids can see it.'

Ben always liked this part of the job, remembering the excitement he'd felt when the fire engine had come to his school and had parked in the playground. He still remembered clambering up into the driver's seat and pretending to steer.

'What time is Pen getting to you?' Ben asked, so he could make sure he arrived after his sister.

'Please don't call her that.' He could hear his mother shudder down the phone. 'It's bad enough that you've shortened your name to Ben without your sister's name being reduced to a writing implement.'

Ben rolled his eyes again.

Apparently, it hadn't occurred to Mary when naming her children Benjamin and Penelope, that people would shorten their names. Ben and Penny were bad enough, as far as she was concerned, but Ben and Pen – so common!

His mother sniffed, then said, 'She's coming for eleven on the Saturday. What time will you be here?'

The next few minutes were spent discussing the various transport options available to him, and Ben let his mother work her way through the logistics of travelling from London to Winchester. Ben wasn't sure what was finally concluded, but when his mum came to an end, a question mark sounding on her final sentence, Ben just replied, 'Sounds great!' and left it at that.

He was about to say goodbye when a thought occurred to him. 'Hold on, Mum. Can I speak to Dad quickly?'

There was a silence. 'Your dad?' his mum said, surprise sounding in her voice. 'Um, yes, of course. Hold on, I'll get him.'

Ben, now regretting his impetuous decision, waited, hearing his mum in the background, his dad saying, 'Why does he want to speak to me?'

There was a clank as the receiver – his parents were still on a landline, the beige handset connected with a long curl of wire – was picked up, and his dad's voice came on the line.

'Ben? Are you okay?'

'Hi, Dad, yes, I'm fine. I wanted to ask you a favour.'

'Hmmm,' his dad replied cautiously.

'There's this cat that keeps visiting me and I thought I'd make it a shelter for when I'm not here. So it doesn't have to sit out in the cold. I've drawn up a plan and was wondering if I could use some wood from your workshop maybe . . .' Ben trailed off, waiting for his dad to say something. 'Anyway, could I have a look?' he finished.

After a long pause, his father replied. 'Yes. I'll see you when you're down.'

'Um, great, thanks.'

More silence.

'Bye then.'

'Bye.' And his dad hung up the phone.

Ben wondered why he'd just done that. He supposed he'd been caught up in planning Fred's house, and the idea of using some of his dad's leftover supplies had just come to him while he was talking to his mum. Before his breakdown, his dad had been a keen woodworker and loved nothing more than spending a day in his garage, sawing and sanding, gluing and painting, which was one of the reasons why his parents had moved to the detached house outside Winchester, with its outbuildings and no close neighbours to disturb with the noise from a circular saw.

When he and Penny were little, his dad had made them all sorts of things – Penny's favourite was her dolls' house, while Ben had always loved the truck with the coloured bricks stacked on top. But that had all stopped when his dad became ill, not that they were allowed to mention it.

Ben's memories afterwards were of his dad sitting in his chair, watching the snooker while Ben's mum spoke too much, talking without listening, just to fill the silence that descended on the house like a cloud.

Oh well, he'd asked now, and there wasn't room in his flat to swing a cat – not that he would; poor Fred! – let alone the workbench he'd need to do a DIY project.

With any luck, his dad would just leave him to it, and if he could spend a few hours locked away in the workshop, by the end of the weekend Fred would have a house.

19

Jenni was asleep, wrapped in the floral duvet that Alex had always hated – he preferred plain white Egyptian cotton – dreaming peacefully, when the phone rang. The shrill noise jerked her awake and she fumbled to reach it, dislodging Oscar – who, for once, wasn't out on the prowl – from his comfortable position in the crook of her legs. Stretching his back into a perfect arch, he shook himself and jumped lightly from the bed, the hollow sound of the cat flap banging shut seconds later.

It took Jenni a few seconds to focus on the name glowing on the screen: Amy. Hurriedly, she swiped to answer.

'Amy. What's happened? Are you okay?'

But Amy was already talking frantically. Jenni caught the words 'Fire' and her heart jolted.

'Amy, start again. What's happened?'

Jenni heard her take a gulp, trying to regulate her breathing.

'The fairy lights caught fire. The ones we put above Tilly's cot—'

'Oh my God, Amy, is she . . . are you—'

'We're fine. We're all fine, but can you come over? I'm on my own with the kids and the fire brigade are here. Simon is away and . . .'

Amy broke off, sounding tearful and Jenni heard her whisper . 'It's okay, sweetheart, Mummy's okay, I'm just talking to Auntie Jenni.'

'I'll get a Uber and be with you as soon as I can. I'll text you when I'm on my way.'

Hands shaking, Jenni opened the app, ordered a taxi, and had just enough time to pull on some clothes in the minutes it took for the car to get to her. Once in and on her way, she texted Amy and fifteen minutes later she was pulling up outside her house.

Even though Amy had said they were all fine, Jenni felt a clutch of fear when she saw the fire engine parked outside, blue lights flashing, uniformed officers moving purposefully in and out of the front door. There were no signs of smoke or flames, much to Jenni's relief, and, thanking the driver, Jenni clambered out of the car and slammed the door shut behind her.

'Oh my God, are you okay?' Jenni said, finding Amy sitting shivering on the next door neighbour's wall and hugging her. She could feel her shaking.

Amy, in Ugg boots with a coat over her pyjamas, nodded.

'Yes, we're all fine. It was such a shock, though. The alarm went off and I didn't know what to do, if I should have tried to put it out, or what. Simon is away so both the kids were in with me, thank goodness, otherwise I can't bear to think about what might have happened—' Amy's voice broke.

'But they were with you and you are all okay,' Jenni said soothingly, giving her friend's hand a squeeze. 'Where are they now?'

'Next door with my neighbour, Abbey. I'm waiting to speak to one of the firefighters. They've been really good – they're sure it was the fairy lights. It's quite common apparently, the wire gets twisted or something and they can ignite. There's some smoke damage, so we're going to stay with Simon's mum. He's going to meet us there.'

Amy took a breath and stepped back to let a firefighter pass, who was carrying bits of equipment back to the engine. Another came over to them.

'We're heading off now,' he said, removing his helmet and running a hand through his curly hair.

An unusual shade of blond, thought Jenni. She was sure that colour had a particular name, but she couldn't for the life of her remember.

'Are you okay?' the firefighter asked Amy. 'I heard you say your husband is on his way back home?'

Amy nodded. 'Yes, we're fine. Thank you. My friend's here now.'

The firefighter looked over at Jenni and nodded. 'Great, good you're here.'

'No problem, good to be here. Well, not good, obviously, everyone might have burnt to death, but they didn't so, um, well, yes. I'm here.' Jenni finished, flustered.

The firefighter smiled awkwardly in return, turning back to Amy. 'Have you got somewhere to stay?'

As Amy replied, Jenni felt confused.

What on earth was that about? She knew plenty of men with broad shoulders and nice blue eyes, well, eyes at least, and she didn't normally have a problem stringing a sentence together.

I must be in shock, she thought. *Yes, that's it. Nothing to do with his tousled good looks at all.*

Distracted by her thoughts, she tuned back in to hear Amy saying, 'I'll get the kids and go to my mother-in-law's for now. Am I okay to go in and grab some bits?'

'Yes, of course,' he replied. 'It's upsetting, I know, but it's all secure in there now.'

He nodded again to Jenni before joining his colleagues who were climbing into the engine.

Jenni and Amy watched the vehicle pull away and drive carefully down the street.

'George is loving this,' said Amy with a shaky smile. She pointed next door where George was looking out of Abbey's sitting-room window, waving as the engine went past.

'He was so excited when they turned up – he loves the blue flashing lights. I'd promised I'd take him to see a fire engine – this isn't quite what I had in mind though.'

Jenni gave her friend a sympathetic smile as Amy turned to look at her.

'And don't think I didn't notice that weird thing you said either. Flustered by the sight of the fit fireman, much?' asked Amy with a beady gleam in her eye.

'I don't know what you're on about,' said Jenni. 'You must be in shock.'

Amy gave an annoyingly knowing smile. 'Hmm. Maybe.'

'Come on then, let's go. What do you need?' Jenni changed the subject and was relieved when Amy led the way into the house, heading to the kitchen first and filling a bag with beakers, bottles and biscuits for Tilly and George.

'Can you get some clothes for the kids?' Amy asked Jenni. 'I'll grab some stuff for me and Simon from the laundry pile. '

'Of course.'

Jenni grabbed a carrier bag from the kitchen and headed up the stairs towards their bedroom.

The smell of smoke was stronger up here, but other than the dark smudges of soot on the primrose yellow wall above the cot, the room seemed remarkably intact.

Thank goodness the alarm had sounded, thought Jenni with a shudder. *And that the kids hadn't been in their own beds.*

As the reality of what could have happened sunk in, Jenni felt anxious to get out of the small room. She pulled open the wardrobe door and tipped a pile of Tilly's clothes from the top shelf into the bag, then did the same with a pile of George's on the next shelf. Amy would have to give them all a wash to get rid of the smell of smoke, but at least they'd have enough clothes for a few days.

Carrying the bags – why did children need so much stuff? – they went next door where Tilly and George were glued to CBeebies. Abbey made them a cup of tea, while Amy rang Simon again and booked a cab to take them to his mother's house.

Jenni's head was beginning to pound now from lack of sleep. Perhaps she could have a quick power nap before going in to work.

As she took a sip of tea and waited for Amy to finish her call, her thoughts wandered back to her earlier encounter with the good-looking firefighter: strawberry blond – that was the colour of his hair.

*

'I can't believe it. Poor Amy,' Tim said again, stuffing the last bit of chicken sandwich in his mouth. They were having lunch in the staff kitchen and Jenni was grateful to see that Clive had updated the décor. Thank goodness all the photos of her had now been replaced.

Jenni, stealing a crisp, agreed. The whole thing had knocked Amy for six. 'She says she won't go home until all traces of the fire have gone. I can tell she's haunted by the thought of what might have happened if the kids hadn't been in with her. It was only because Simon was away and she'd promised them they could have a sleepover with her . . .'

'When's the house going to be ready?'

'Their landlord is going to get it repainted this week and Simon's taking some time off so he can get it put back to normal. His mum's going to have the kids this Saturday while Amy's helping me at the fair, and Simon's promised it will be ready when she's finished.'

'That's good,' Tim said, slapping Jenni's hand away as she reached for another of his crisps.

'Ow!'

'Get your own, madam. I'd forgotten you had the fair this weekend – are you ready?'

Jenni, rubbing her hand, pulled a face. 'Sort of,' she replied, not looking Tim in the eye.

Tim sighed. 'So that's a no!'

'I'm nervous that no one's going to actually buy anything. I just need a few finishing touches, like a tablecloth, and I thought a little bunch of flowers would look nice.'

Jenni had spent the previous evening sorting through her stock, refolding everything, again, according to Marie Kondo's strict instructions, even the socks – thank you,

YouTube – and had packed it all carefully into a crate so she could carry it down to the Green where the fair was being held.

Inspired by the way the sleepsuits and T-shirts had looked drying in the shed, she'd bought a couple of poles, some old-fashioned wooden pegs and a length of washing line so she could hang some of them up, hopefully creating an eye-catching display. Everything else would be laid out flat. Nick and Jo next door were going to carry the table down for her, and her card reader had arrived.

She was good to go.

She just had to stop imagining herself standing alone, her carefully created wares untouched while the surrounding stalls thronged with punters eager to purchase more interesting gifts.

Jenni shook her head to clear it of negative thoughts and reminded herself she was at least doing something creative. If nothing else, she could get to the end of the year and know that she had tried.

She became aware that Tim had been talking and had now stopped, a question mark hanging in the air. He was obviously waiting for her answer.

'Um. Yeeesss?' she replied cautiously, not entirely sure if this was an appropriate response to whatever Tim had been saying.

Her caution turned to alarm when he shrieked with joy.

'Yes!' He punched the air. 'I know you always say you're useless at quizzes, but we'll have the best time. It's not until next month, so you've got plenty of time to revise. We don't want another incident like last time.'

Oh God. Too late, Jenni realised she'd agree to go to Tim's local pub quiz. Tim spoke of it as if it was a light-hearted fun-filled evening, but having been once before, Jenni knew the very opposite was true.

Tim's teammates – the Petit Fours, named for a reason known only to themselves – were hideously competitive and things had got nasty when Jenni had incorrectly identified a Fleetwood Mac album cover. She still had flashbacks when she heard *Rumours* playing.

Hoping she could come up with an excuse nearer the time, she asked Tim how he was getting on with his new health regime. Deciding they'd overindulged on their honeymoon, Tim and Paul had taken up Nordic walking. Jenni was just grateful that she lived in a different part of London – she wasn't sure she could cope with bumping into Tim and his husband, striding through the park brandishing their ski poles.

Tim had explained how it was much more complicated than it looked and was most definitely not just 'walking with sticks', as Jenni dismissively seemed to think. Apparently, all the East End hipsters were at it, although Jenni was yet to be convinced.

As was usual when Tim got into a new hobby, he was very keen on purchasing all the kit, so he and Paul had spent hundreds of pounds on special gloves and the lightest, most aerodynamic poles. He'd even convinced Clive that there was a gap in the market and R&D were currently working on a bespoke walking range.

'We usually go out on Saturday morning, so I have just had the best idea,' said Tim excitedly. 'How about you stay over after the quiz night and then you can come with us? Nothing like striding through Victoria Park at seven-thirty to get the blood flowing. And before you say anything,' he began, seeing Jenni's look of horror, 'no, it's not just for old people, I'll have you know. Only Janice has a free bus pass, the rest of us are very sprightly. And besides, you could do with some exercise after a month on your arse.'

'Excuse me, I had an injured leg,' said Jenni indignantly. 'And you're making me sound like I need winching from the sofa by the emergency services. I go for a walk every morning, thank you very much.'

Tim looked at her questioningly. 'Do you now?'

'Well, not quite *every* morning currently, sort of once a week, maybe. But I'm still very mobile, I'll have you know.'

Jenni stood up energetically to demonstrate just how active she was, scooped up the rubbish, including Tim's crisp packet, neatly folded into the psychopathic triangle as per usual, and deposited it in the bin.

Tim got up too, brushing the crumbs from his Uniqlo merino wool knit. He turned to Jenni.

'I'm just saying, love, Janice is seventy-two and she could walk you out of the park.'

Before she could reply, Tim strode briskly out of the kitchen and Jenni hurriedly followed him, breaking into a skip-run to catch up.

'See?' Tim said, as she drew up breathlessly beside him. 'Proving my point.'

20

Ben pushed open the kitchen door, hearing the plaintive meowing before he saw the shadow at the window.

'I know, I know, I'm late. Hold on a minute,' he said, marching to the window and opening it. Fred pushed his head against Ben's arm in greeting as he slid into the kitchen, giving another rebuking meow.

As Ben stroked the cat, running his hand over the smooth fur, he noticed Fred was wearing a collar. Was Fred's owner sending a message? Had they noticed that their cat was spending more time away from home?

He wondered if there was a tag with any information on it and reached for the collar, but Fred had other ideas and dropped to the floor with another, louder, more pointed meow.

Ben, aware he was being told off, hastily rummaged in the cupboard and grabbed a tin of tuna.

'Look, mate, I shouldn't be feeding you at all, but here you go.'

Ben mashed the tuna onto the plate before putting it on the floor. Fred looked at in disgust, then jumped up onto his stool.

Sighing, Ben lifted the plate onto the breakfast bar, where Fred daintily started picking at the tuna, purring contentedly.

Ben hadn't seen the cat for a while, and he'd missed him. But perhaps Fred had just got fed up waiting for him on the windowsill while he was at work, which made Ben more determined to make the cat house he had planned.

Since talking to his dad about it, he'd been making more detailed drawings and was actually looking forward to getting started, even if it did mean spending a day with his father, he thought ruefully.

Work had been busy and intense. The week had begun with a house fire involving a young family; thankfully, though, no one was hurt. He was looking forward to the May fair on the Green tomorrow. He loved events like these, seeing the children's eyes light up as they spotted the big red vehicle, helping them climb into the cab, press the button to turn the lights on. Even the older children, who weren't impressed by anything, would sidle up and ask questions.

Fred, plate emptied, jumped down from the breakfast bar and headed for the window.

'Oh, that's my lot, is it?' said Ben. 'Eat and leave, why don't you? You're treating this house like it's a hotel!'

Shaking his head as Fred disappeared into the darkness, Ben realised he'd been looking forward to the cat's company.

Maybe Penny was right and he did need to get out more, rather than spending Friday nights in with someone else's cat. The trouble was, he just couldn't face sitting in bars or restaurants, awkwardly making conversation, or trying to wittily reply to WhatsApp messages, all the while knowing that it wasn't going to go anywhere.

His feeling of dread was interrupted as the phone rang: Taz – perfect timing.

Two hours later, Taz arrived carrying a bag of food and his Xbox controller. Soon they were both immersed in a game, half-empty takeaway cartons lying on the coffee table.

*

It was the morning of the fair and Ben clambered on board, slammed the door shut and the engine rumbled out of the station. Vick was driving and Taz made up the third member of the team. They'd arrived for roll-call at eight and had spent the previous few hours preparing the engine. Ben had gathered up the promotional material they took with them to community events – everyone loved a sticker – and then, after a final safety check, they'd left for the Green, near the main shopping street, to set up in time for the fair to start at 11am.

They'd been told to park near to the main gates, so setting up was easy once they'd arrived. All the doors and hatches on the engine were opened, a table was unfolded for the leaflets about joining the service. And as it was never too soon to start recruiting, for the kids they'd brought a box of dressing-up clothes: miniature high-vis jackets, waterproof trousers with fluorescent stripes taped around the legs and small bright yellow helmets.

Ben had just finished laying out the pens and badges when Taz joined him. 'Here you go, mate: flat white, no sugar,' he said, handing Ben the paper cup.

The fair was already buzzing with activity. Vans and cars, their doors and boots flung open, had parked next to trestle tables and were being unpacked, bunting had been strung between tree branches and two women were wrestling with a bell tent, which was advertised as the chill-out zone, something they would be in desperate need of once they'd succeeded in putting it up. Ben could also see a huge bouncy castle slowly rising at the far end of the Green, and a generator had been hauled over to a low wooden platform where the PA system was being set up for a band that had been booked for later in the day.

'Thanks, mate,' Ben said, taking a grateful sip of coffee. 'Ended up being a late night.'

'I know, we shouldn't have got started on another game after we'd eaten. And I had to wait ages for the bus,' said Taz, shaking his head.

'Couldn't let you go until we'd taken down the enemy.'

'I hope you're talking about that game you've been play-ing?' asked Vick, joining them with bacon and egg butties. 'It's very unnerving to hear you go on about battles and power struggles. Given the current state of affairs, I never know if it's for real or not.'

'Excuse me,' Taz said indignantly as he took a butty from Vick. 'It's based on real-life theatres of war and de-mands high-level tactical decisions to implement military strategies—'

'La, la, la, I'm not listening,' Vick interrupted. 'I already have to hear all about *Fortnite* thanks to my kids, I don't need any more gaming chat, thank you very much. So, are we ready to go?'

She turned to Ben, ignoring the wounded look he and Taz shared. 'Gates open in an hour and, if we're all set up, I'll have a wander around now. I need a few presents and' –pointing to the nearest stall – 'that looks perfect. Who doesn't love a bar of organic soap for their birthday?'

Vick, again, chose to ignore the look Ben and Taz exchanged.

'Yeah, we're all sorted, you go and we'll hang around here,' Ben said, wiping egg from his mouth with a paper towel. 'But make sure you're back for midday. That's when the local reporter's coming around.'

Vick sighed. 'You know, I'm all for promoting the service, but it really gets on my nerves that it's still considered an unusual job for a woman. But sure, I'll be back in time to – what was it that last article said? – "fight fires and stereotypes". See you later.'

As Vick headed off to browse the stalls, Ben and Taz returned to their discussion. 'It's a high-level game of strategy where you can change the course of history,' Taz said.

'Yeah, and *Fortnite* is not to be underestimated either. I just don't think she gets it.'

Taz looked at his watch. 'Right. We've got an hour before she gets back, let's talk tactics.'

21

'Here you go, let me just wrap it for you.' Jenni deftly folded pale cream tissue paper around the small T-shirt and handed it over to the woman standing on the other side of her stall.

'Thanks, love. Good luck today, you've got some lovely stuff.'

Jenni smiled gratefully as another satisfied customer headed off. To her side, Amy was helping a young woman with a small baby choose sleepsuits hanging from the washing line. Having picked one with a soft pink and purple pattern – made using red onion skins to create the warm colours – Amy packaged it up while Jenni took the payment. The woman picked up one of Jenni's cards displayed at the front of the stall and headed off with a cheery goodbye.

'It's going well!' Amy squeezed her friends arm enthusiastically.

Jenni smiled. 'I'm relieved people are actually buying things, I was so worried!'

'You're doing brilliantly. We're nearly out of the tote bags and there are only a few T-shirts left, and loads of people have taken your card.'

Jenni looked around at the depleted stall and gave another smile.

The day had started in a panic. Arriving early with Jo and Nick, she had been unable to find the organisers and so had spent the first fifteen minutes frantically trying to find someone who knew where her pitch was meant to be. Finally, she'd managed to locate a harassed-looking woman called Fiona, who'd consulted her map and directed her to a spot right in the middle of a row of other stalls selling handmade crafts.

Heading back to Jo and Nick, who'd stayed put to keep an eye on the bags and boxes Jenni had brought with her, they'd helped Jenni carry everything over to her designated place. Table deposited, her neighbours had set off home and Jenni had started unpacking her wares.

Glancing around her, she'd noted anxiously that the other stands were already set up and the stallholders were either standing around sipping hot drinks, or calmly rearranging the odd item or two. Frantically clipping the legs of the table into place, Jenni had flung a striped tablecloth over the shabby top to hide its worn surface and had begun to lay out the items she'd spent months preparing.

It was a beautiful bright day, thank goodness, and as Jenni had made the finishing touches to her stall she'd felt the warmth from the sun on her back. The other stallholders in her row were a friendly bunch, and some of them seemed to know each other, perhaps from other events they'd done together. Doug, selling stained-glass pictures, had seen Jenni struggling with the poles for her washing line and had come over to give her a hand, pushing them into the ground and steadying them while she strung the line between the props. In return, she'd been happy to help him put up the bunting he was using to decorate the gazebo covering his stand.

The Green, a space used for the annual fair, was bordered on one side by a main road and a line of handsome three-storey Georgian houses on the other. At the far end was a small children's playground, already busy even though it was only ten in the morning, fathers standing next to empty pushchairs, mothers pushing toddlers on swings, while at the opposite end was a parade of independent shops. A path ran diagonally through the grass, and mature London plane trees, their pompom seedheads still dangling like baubles, stretched out overhead, buds beginning to unfurl into leaf. Hooped-top black metal fencing edged the Green and a wildflower meadow, left unmown, added a jumble of jewel-like colour across the grass.

The area was popular with dog walkers and used for after-school picnics, but today all the usual activities had been cast aside and replaced with the annual May Day fete. Food stalls were arranged in a semi-circle at the shop end of the park, and Jenni could see vans promising everything from candy floss to artisan sourdough doughnuts to burgers and Korean fried chicken. Another cluster of stalls offered tombola prizes, games to play and things to win, and beyond that was a vintage carousel, bouncy castle, inflatable slide and a coconut shy.

Near the main entrance, Jenni could see a fire engine, the firefighters' florescent yellow helmets visible too. The sight of it took her back to the morning of Amy's fire, watching the crew dashing in and out of her house.

Poor Amy. She gave a shudder thinking again how lucky they'd all been.

Her thoughts were interrupted by her friend's arrival. Jenni had given the stall a final once-over, checked the card reader was working and then, before she'd had time to panic again, the gates had opened and people had started arriving.

There had been a steady stream of punters all day, but now, nearing the end of the fair, the organisers were pulling out the winning tombola numbers while parents began extracting over-sugared children – the doughnut stall had run out of their fluffy, still-warm treats hours ago – from the bouncy castle with the promise of an ice cream for the way home.

'I think we could start packing up now. What do you think?' Jenni said to Amy.

'Yeah, let's take the washing line down first. How are you getting the table home?'

'Jo and Nick are coming back to help carry it.'

'Okay, that's good. I'm going to meet Simon at the house at four, so I'll head off in a bit.'

'How are you feeling about going back?'

'I'm actually okay. It's all been repainted and the fairy lights are gone, so there are no horrid reminders of the fire. And if I'm honest, after staying at Simon's mum's, I can't wait to have our own space again. She's been great, but I think she's ready for us to go now too!'

'That sounds fair. It will be nice for you all to be home again. Which reminds me,' Jenni pulled a bag out from under the table, 'here's a few welcome home goodies to thank you for helping today.'

'Oh! Lovely, thank you.' Amy smiled, pulling the bottle of wine out of the bag.

'I thought you could save that for when I visit!'

'I'll save this for you instead,' Amy said, holding out the Play-Doh Jenni had included for Tilly.

'Hello, sorry to interrupt, am I too late to buy something?'

Jenni looked up and, with a sudden shock of recognition, realised it was the firefighter with the very blue eyes that had attended the fire at Amy's house, and her cheeks flushed crimson as she remembered their previous encounter.

'Oh, I remember you,' he said, making her blush deepen.

'Croft Park? Faulty lights? How are you all doing?' he asked, turning to Amy.

'We're all fine now, thank you. My son wants to send you a card but I'm afraid I completely forgot your name. He wants to be a firefighter now!'

'It's Ben Walker,' said Ben with a smile, 'and honestly, you're welcome. I'm just glad you're all OK. But I'm looking for something for my niece, she's seven. Have you got anything that might fit her?'

'Definitely, Jenni can help you find something,' said Amy, nudging her friend in the ribs, while Jenni searched through the items they'd already started packing away. She knew she had a few top and legging sets for older children, and upon finding the packages she was looking for she put them out on the stall. 'Here you go, would any of these be any good?'

Ben took his time looking through the different sets, finally settling on a blue and green combination. 'I think she'd like these.'

'An excellent choice for the discerning seven-year-old.' Jenni said. 'You have impeccable taste.'

'Well, I hope my niece agrees, she's a total nightmare if she doesn't like something.'

'I can always swap it if she wants a different colour. Here's my card with all my socials on it, you can get hold of me any time.'

Seeing Ben's eyebrow raise slightly, Jenni felt herself blush again. 'I mean, contact me,' she amended hastily. 'All strictly professional,' she gabbled nervously.

Ben took one of her business cards, along with the now-wrapped present.

'Thanks,' he said, the corner of his mouth lifting into another smile. 'I'm sure she'll be very happy with them, but it's good to know where I can find you.'

Cringing, and ignoring Amy's giggling, Jenni watched as he walked away, an unexpectedly fluttery feeling in her tummy.

22

Fred was waiting for Ben when he finally got home. His visits were getting more frequent and Ben was feeling slightly guilty – he didn't want to be accused of cat-napping and he hoped the owner wasn't feeling too annoyed by the amount of time Fred was away from home. There'd been a piece on the news the other night about a woman who'd been accused of stealing someone's cat, but how could he resist that little face glaring in at him from the window?

Ben opened it and Fred entered the kitchen with a piercing meow, before looking expectantly towards the cupboard – he'd quickly learnt this was where his snacks were kept. Ben rolled his eyes and grabbed a handful.

It had been a long day, but a fun one, helping the children climb into the cab of the engine, chatting to anyone who dropped by, handing out leaflets and safety information – he hoped people had read them before they got dropped into a recycling bin.

It had been good to hang out with Vick and Taz, too, and he'd enjoyed looking around the stalls. He'd even managed to buy a scented candle to take to his mum's tomorrow, and he bought something for Evie after Vick had recommended the tie-dye clothing stall.

It was always strange to bump into someone he'd met on a call, so it had taken him aback at first, but he was pleased to hear she was doing okay. And her friend. Ben smiled as he thought of the woman with the long, dark curls, her face serious as she concentrated on wrapping the gift, her obvious pride in her work as he'd picked out the present for Evie.

Vick and Taz had teased him when he'd told them he'd taken her card. 'You should definitely message her, mate,' Taz said. 'What have you got to lose?'

'She said to contact her if I needed to exchange them for another colour. She wasn't asking me on a date,' Ben replied.

'But it *could* be a date,' said Vick, clambering up behind the wheel. 'I know that what's-her-face hurt you, but you need to start dating again. Unless you're still hung up on her?'

'No,' Ben said shortly. Then, 'I'm just busy, that's all. Anyway, I'm fine, I keep telling you.'

'There's *fine*, and there's *happy*,' said Vick, turning on the engine and checking the mirrors before slowly guiding the fire engine across the grass towards the exit.

'You're as bad as my sister,' grumbled Ben. 'She's planning to auction me off to the highest bidder if I don't get a date soon.'

Taz laughed. 'Hope she's not expecting to raise much money.'

Ben gave him a half-gentle punch to the upper arm in reply.

'What about Kate, the woman who's just joined Blue Watch?' Vick asked, lifting a hand to wave to the organisers as they headed through the gate and out onto the main road.

'I don't want to date someone at work, we know that ends in trouble. Ouch. Present company excepted,' he amended hastily as Vick elbowed him in the ribs.

'Oi, Brian and I are very happy, thanks very much.'

Ben smiled. 'You are, but you're very much the exception to the rule. Most times it's a disaster.

It was true, he thought. Dating someone at work was a bad idea, and it was particularly hard if you split up and had to continue working together, especially in professions like the emergency services. It wasn't worth the risk, as far as Ben was concerned.

He turned to Taz. 'What about you? You're always pushing me start dating again, but you're still single.'

'Yeah, but I'm *happily* single. You're not. You're a much better human when you're going out with someone. And sure, women are throwing their business cards at you right now, but you're not getting any younger, are you?'

'Thanks, Taz, great pep talk.'

Vick snorted with laughter. 'He's right, though. Not just the getting any younger bit. Women know they have to get a move on if they want kids. Men can afford to wait, but life will pass you by before you know it. You're never going to meet someone and have a family if you don't put yourself out there.'

Ben was about to protest, but deep down he knew they were right. He'd thought he would have a partner by now, perhaps a child. He'd imagined a little boy who would play with Evie. When Luisa had finally left, his whole future had gone with her, and he didn't know if he could put himself through that again. Far safer to stay as he was than risk being hurt again.

Taz offered to go to a bar with him the next time they were off, and Ben had agreed, mainly to stop them going on at him. But now he was home, alone once more, the conversation from earlier came back to him.

And strangely, when he thought about a possible new future, he pictured the woman with long dark curls handing him her business card, which he realised he hadn't thrown away.

23

Jenni flopped down on the sofa, kicking off her trainers. She was shattered, but happy. Her phone beeped and she looked down to see a message from her mum: a big thumbs up and a love heart in reply to the pictures of the stall Jenni had sent her earlier that day, followed by another message:

> So proud of you. And your dad would have
> been too. Well done, sweetie. Xxx

Tears pricked Jenni's eyes. She wished she could have called her dad now; told him about the day, that she'd almost sold out and the organisers had asked if she'd do another event with them. He'd been her biggest cheerleader, the one who'd told her she could do it, that she'd be okay no matter what. He'd been there whenever she'd needed help after Alex had left, happily showing her how to put up a shelf or moving something too heavy for her to manage on her own.

Blinking, she stood up. This was the trouble with grief. You thought you'd got it sorted, paid off the debt, but it could creep up on you again at any time, demanding another instalment.

The unwelcome visitor that comes and goes is how she'd heard it described.

She caught sight of the photo of her with her parents that she displayed on the bookshelf. Her family.

But now her mum was with someone new, on the trip of a lifetime the other side of the world, while Jenni was home alone on a Saturday night.

She shook herself. Enough with the pity, it wasn't helping, it was just making her sad.

She went into the kitchen and made herself some tea and toast, realising Oscar wasn't home, *again*.

He was out more and more lately. Feeling abandoned – even her own cat didn't want to spend time with her – she went back to the living room with her tea and sat on the sofa, flicking through the TV channels for something to distract her.

Just then, she heard the cat flap slam, and seconds later Oscar stalked into the room. He must have sensed her thinking about him, she thought, as he jumped up on the end of the sofa and began kneading at the blanket, purring, before turning around three times and settling down.

'What time do you call this, young man?' Jenni addressed the cat.

Oscar stared back, before blinking slowly.

'It's not like you to not want dinner, either. Where have you been?'

Oscar gave another slow blink. Then, as if bored with the interrogation, tucked his head down, curled his tail around him and went to sleep.

Something is going on, Jenni thought. *He's definitely going somewhere.*

And, as she looked at him more closely, she saw that he was plumper than he used to be.

But for now, she was just happy to have him home, curled up next to her, as she settled in for another evening alone, but she was going to have to work out where he was going and what he was up to.

24

Ben looked around at his family, who were sitting at the dark, mahogany dining table, which had been extended specially for the day. Although he hadn't grown up in this house, there was so much that was familiar from his childhood – not just the table, but the photos on the sideboard, the green floral curtains that Penny had told him, somehow, were fashionable again; even the cream plates rimmed in gold, which were part of a set that his parents had received as a wedding present.

Ben found it comforting, or claustrophobic, depending on his mood, and today he was edging towards the latter, each item provoking memories of old arguments and tensions: the chipped gravy jug was certainly not sparking joy, as he remembered the trouble he'd been in for knocking it off the work surface. He supposed, in retrospect, throwing a roast potato at his sister wasn't the best idea, but at the time she'd deserved it. Shame she'd ducked at the last minute.

He shook himself and made an effort to break out of his gloomy mood. He focused on Evie, giggling away, and Penny sharing a joke with his mum, Antony happily helping himself to another slice of roast beef. He glanced at his dad, who was staring contentedly enough into the middle distance.

Ben's train had arrived a bit later than expected, due to inevitable Sunday engineering works. Antony had collected him from the station, and he'd enjoyed the journey to his parents' house, leaving behind the city and heading down the country lanes, listening as his brother-in-law told him about his new garden project – an outdoor cold-water bath. Ben, who'd been caught enough times in a jet of cold water from a hose, did *not* share Antony's beliefs in the benefits of freezing water, and silently predicted that this was yet another fad, and that the bath would soon be joining the Peloton, which he knew Penny was currently trying to sell on eBay, despite her husband's protests that he'd be back in the saddle any day now.

Ben's mother had greeted him enthusiastically when they'd arrived, and Evie had jumped up to be carried as soon as he'd stepped through the door. Penny put the kettle on, chatting away, but his dad, as usual, had barely looked up from his chair by the fire where he was reading the newspaper.

Ben now realised that this was when he'd felt his mood dip.

Why had he even asked for his dad's help to make the

house for Fred? He could have spent a nice afternoon with his mum and sister, but now he'd be stuck in the garage for hours with his monosyllabic father.

'Right, has everyone finished?' his mum asked, pushing back her chair and standing up.

Ben and Penny helped clear the table, carrying the dirty plates through to the kitchen where Mary efficiently began scraping leftover food into the compost bin and stacking the plates by the sink. The good china wasn't allowed in the dishwasher.

'I've made a crumble and the custard's on the hob. Ben, take those bowls, and, Penny, can you pour the custard into that jug?'

Seeing Penny sneaking a spoonful of the pudding, Mary flapped the tea towel she was holding at her daughter. 'Don't do that. I've told you a hundred times not to steal the topping.'

'Ben made me do it.'

'I did not!' Ben answered indignantly. 'Why do always blame me?'

Penny rolled her eyes. 'Because you're the one who attacked me with potatoes and broke Mum's jug.'

'That was fifteen years ago. And what's that got to do with you eating the crumble?'

Mary, practised at breaking up their bickering, interrupted. 'Stop it, both of you.' She pointed the wooden spoon she was holding at each of her children in turn. 'Bowls. Custard. *Go!*'

Orders issued, Mary pulled on her oven gloves and, picking up the crumble, headed to the dining room.

Perhaps, Ben wondered, if he started a fight with his sister, he'd be sent to his room like a naughty schoolboy – then he wouldn't have to spend the afternoon in a cold garage with his father.

*

'Not like that. Here, give it to me.' Ian took the two pieces of wood that Ben was holding and began pulling them apart. 'Hand me that chisel.'

Ben sheepishly passed it over.

'Sorry, I forgot which bit was meant to go where and stuck it back to front.'

'Hmm, yes, well you did a good job of getting it wrong,' his father muttered distractedly, inserting the edge of the sharpened blade between what was meant to be the base and an upright of the cat house.

'Hammer,' demanded his dad, staring at the wood. Ben dutifully passed the nearest one. 'No, the *claw* one.'

Ben reached into the tool box to grab the right hammer, the action taking him back to other fraught times he'd been his dad's apprentice.

After the crumble had been polished off and dishes tidied

away, Penny had suggested that they all go for a walk. Ian hadn't mentioned anything about starting the DIY project, so Ben had stood up to go with them, but Mary, who'd declared she was going to have a quiet ten minutes listening to the radio, had despatched Ben and his dad, somewhat awkwardly, to the shed.

It hadn't started well.

When Ben had unfurled his drawings, Ian had spent ten minutes picking apart the measurements, tutting loudly. But as the afternoon progressed, Ben had to admit his dad had been right – he'd been too ambitious – and the two of them had settled into something of a companionable rhythm.

The frame had taken shape, the correct nails used and Ben had been surprised that he was actually quite enjoying spending time with his dad. The smell of the planed wood, the glue in the green squeezy bottle, the noise of the saw, had transported him back to his childhood, and in a good way this time. He'd also felt his dad relax too, the familiar environment where he felt in control seeming to reduce the distance and tension between them.

'Who does this cat belong to anyway?' Ian asked, finally pulling the wood apart and then refixing it the correct way around.

'I don't know, to be honest,' Ben said. 'Must be a neighbour. He just started popping round. He's a funny little thing. Very demanding, but good company.'

'You'd better be careful. People get upset if you start feeding their cat. Do you remember that moggy near our old house?'

Ben laughed at the memory. 'Yes, the one that had 'DO NOT FEED ME' written on his collar!'

Ian smiled. 'That cat used to go up and down the street begging for food. His owner got so fed up with people feeding him, he posted a note through everyone's doors explaining that the cat did, in fact, get fed three times a day at home, and encouraging them not to be fooled. He worked out that, one day, the cat had eaten *twelve* different dinners!'

Ben laughed again.

'I miss that old house,' his dad said suddenly.

'Why? I thought you liked it here?' Ben felt slightly alarmed. Their conversation never usually strayed to the past.

'This one is fine, and it makes your mum happy, she wanted a change. But we had some good times in that old house. It was the first one me and your mum bought – it was three thousand pounds.'

Ben made a spluttering noise.

'It was a lot of money in those days,' his dad added, 'but we could just about afford the mortgage when I got promoted. Flat-headed screwdriver.' His father stretched out a hand, not looking up from what he was doing.

'Three grand – that's just two month's rent for me,' Ben said grumpily, passing over the tool, slightly thrown by the fact his dad was talking about any of this with him. They never talked about *before* anymore.

'They were happy times, easier. You have it harder in lots of ways.' His father straightened up.

Ben was too startled by this comment to respond, and before he could think what to reply, his dad said, 'Right, there we go. All done. We'll leave the clamps on the joints overnight and then tomorrow we can paint it. I've got some Ronseal leftover from when we did the fence.'

Ben was shocked. His father had never acknowledged that things might be hard for him or his generation. He'd always felt the opposite in fact – that his dad thought his life was a doddle in comparison, so there was no excuse when he *had* found it difficult to cope.

Ben opened his mouth to say something, but Ian was already heading out of the garage.

'See, I've always said you were projecting your own feelings on to him, imagining that he thought you were a failure because that's how *you* felt.'

Penny wrapped her hands around the mug of hot chocolate she'd just made.

Their parents' house was an oak-beamed barn conversion with all the rooms on one level and a huge double-height living area. A corridor stretched from the large sitting room to the snug at the other end of the house, with bedrooms opening onto a pretty courtyard at the back. Mary had loved the sandblasted wooden beams and, on a more practical level, the fact that it would be better for when they were old and couldn't manage stairs, which Ben and Penny both thought was a depressing reason to buy a house.

In the background, they could hear clattering from the kitchen as their mum finished drying the last of the dishes – their offer to help had been politely rebuffed – and did a final tidy before she called it a day.

Ian had already gone to bed, and Evie was also finally asleep – there had been a bit of a scene. She'd been delighted with her new leggings and T-shirt, but when she'd tried them on, they'd turned out to be a bit too small. Evie had decided she wanted to wear them as pyjamas and had refused to go to bed without them on. Eventually, after a full-blown tantrum, she'd been convinced to give them back with the promise that Ben would swap them for a new pair. Antony had headed to the snug to recover from the episode in peace, and Ben and Penny were sitting on the sofas in front of the wood-burner.

'You know you'll never hear the end of it if you don't get her a new set?' Penny said, frazzled by the battle of wills as much as her husband.

'It's okay, I can get in touch with the woman I bought them from. She said it would be fine to exchange them.' He took a sip of his hot chocolate. 'It was weird with Dad today.'

In response to his sister's questioning look, Ben told her about the conversation with their dad, and what he'd told him about their old house. 'He said he only moved because Mum wanted to.'

'That's right,' said Mary coming into the room, making them both jump guiltily. 'It's okay,' she said, seeing Ben's face. 'I've always known that's why he agreed to move. I thought the change would be good for both of us, though, that the old house had too many memories for him, but really it had too many memories for me. I couldn't bear to be there anymore ... finding him like that was the worst thing that has ever happened to me.'

'Oh, Mum,' said Penny standing to hug her. 'I can't imagine how you coped.'

'Well, you two were young, and I didn't want you to know what had happened, and we found him in time, so ...'

Mary lowered herself onto the sofa and Penny sat back down next to her. Ben's dad had said that he hadn't attempted to take his own life, but whatever the intent, a combination of whisky and painkillers had nearly had a fatal result. Fortunately, Mary had arrived home in time and called an ambulance.

It was the big family secret; no one spoke about it, but the shadow of it all had fallen over them for a long time, and Ben and Penny had only recently been told the truth. In fact, Ben's breakdown had been what prompted his mum to speak about it. She'd always said it wasn't her story to tell, but finally knowing what his dad had been through had made it easier for Ben to understand why his father had withdrawn from them, and he sorely wished he'd known sooner.

'That job was hard for him, and there wasn't any support back then; no one had even heard of mental health. I know it's hard for you too, Ben, but I'm glad you can talk about it.' She patted Ben's hand. 'Your dad's not a talker. He fixes a problem by doing something practical. I've had to accept that. He can't always say he loves me, but he'll show me, and that's why he agreed to move, to make me happy. And I am. I love it here.'

Penny smiled. 'You both deserve to be happy, Mum.' She squeezed Mary's hand. 'I don't remember the old house very well. Just the wallpaper in my room. Evie would have loved it – bright purple flowers, I can still picture them!'

Her mum laughed. 'I don't know what I was thinking, but you were determined to have it!' She turned to Ben. 'I'm glad you're letting your dad help with your project. He enjoyed it – he didn't say as much, but I can tell.'

'I had a good time too, actually. Didn't love being told off about my dovetail joints, but other than that it was nice to spend time together.'

Ben felt surprised to find it was true, he *had* enjoyed spending time with his dad.

'Evie wants to help you paint it tomorrow. She has some

suggestions. You might need to manage expectations, she can be quite . . . opinionated,' Penny warned him.

'She takes after her mother,' said Ben, ducking as Penny threw a cushion at him. Mary, rolling her eyes, decided now was a good time to head off to bed.

25

'So what are you going to do?' Amy asked as she and Jenni took another lap of the park. George and Tilly were asleep in the double pushchair and, knowing they'd both wake if Amy dared to stop, Jenni had run ahead and grabbed them a coffee from the café.

'I did wonder about sending a message on the street WhatsApp group.'

'Hmm, yes, that would work. Or how about following him?'

'Well, I'd have to be on twenty-four-hour alert, and he'd only need to hop over the fence and I'd lose sight of him. I can't start clambering through the neighbours' gardens.'

It was ten-thirty on bank holiday Monday and, although Jenni hadn't planned to meet Amy, when she'd texted to say she was heading out for a walk, Jenni decided the exercise would make up for spending Sunday eating chocolate and lying on the sofa.

The sun was still shining, much to Jenni's surprise given that bank holidays usually spelled rain, and as they did another circle of the park, she enjoyed the promise of summer days to come.

She turned her attention back to Amy, who was still suggesting ways to keep an eye on Oscar. He'd been disappearing for even longer periods of time, much to Jenni's alarm, and when he'd been so late home last night, despite her calling for him from the back door for over an hour, she'd begun to panic.

'Why don't you pretend he's lost and call the fire brigade? You can get that Ben guy out looking for him.'

'Will you stop going on about Ben. And besides, I don't think the fire brigade search for lost cats, just rescue them from trees.'

'You have to admit he's very good looking.'

'He is, but unless you want to set fire to your house again, I'm never going to see him. Sorry,' Jenni added, seeing Amy's face. 'That was a terrible thing to say.'

'It's okay, but yeah, I'm not ready to find it funny yet,' said Amy.

Seeing her stricken face, Jenni changed the subject. 'Anyway, the thought of going on a date fills me with horror – I don't trust anything anyone says on their profile anymore.'

'Doesn't Tim have good-looking mates?' Amy expertly manoeuvred the buggy around a small dog.

'Absolutely not. Unless I want to date Janice, a freedom-pass-carrying OAP, and spend my weekends stomping around with walking poles.'

'Well, we'll keep her in mind if things get desperate,' laughed Amy, 'Maybe Lucy has some eligible single friends?'

Jenni promised to ask Lucy at work tomorrow, and Amy started reminiscing about a disastrous date she'd gone on before she'd met Simon. Hearing Amy describe how her date kept flossing his teeth between courses was all Jenni needed to swear off ever dating again.

They paused by the railings, watching the red-headed moorhens and white-legged coots peck busily at the water, while pigeons swooped in circles hoping to steal a crust of bread.

Jenni's attention was caught by a kerfuffle in the centre of the pond, and she watched in horror as several drakes surrounded a hen, chasing her as she tried to escape across the water.

Inappropriate, mid-course flossing suddenly doesn't seem so bad, Jenni thought with a shudder.

26

Hello,

This is a bit of an odd note to write, but your cat
has been visiting me — he's very friendly! I wanted
to reassure you that I'm not trying to steal him and to
let you know he's safe so you don't worry if he comes
home late.

No. 66

It was Evie who had given him the idea.

As her mother had anticipated, Evie had had a lot of
thoughts about decorating Fred's house. The practical brown
wood stain left over from weatherproofing the fence had
been dismissed immediately, and Evie had sent her grand-
father back into his workshop to find something else. When
the duck-egg blue and the various shades of tasteful – or

'very boring', according to Evie — off-white had failed to pass muster, Ben had agreed to take Evie to the local DIY store to buy colours she approved of.

They'd finally found animal-friendly, child-friendly, non-toxic and goodness knows what else waterproof paint and, expecting Evie to pick pinks and lilacs, Ben had been surprised when she'd instead chosen lime green and a dark purple for the roof.

'Do you think a cat would like these colours, Evie?' Ben had asked tentatively.

'Yes, I do,' Evie had replied firmly, dropping the tins into the trolley.

'You don't think they're . . . um, too *bright*?'

'Cats don't see colour like we do, Uncle Ben. Everyone knows that,' Evie had informed him briskly. 'They don't see things clearly far away, either. So I've picked these colours so Fred will be able to find his new house easily.'

'Ah, right. I didn't know that, Evie. Thank you for explaining it to me.'

'That's okay.' Evie had patted his hand patiently. 'It's not your fault you didn't have the internet when you were growing up. Mummy doesn't know anything either.'

'Well, that's not quite right, we did know things, Evie, we just had to go to the library and—'

But Evie had disappeared into the next aisle.

When he'd caught up with her, she was busy loading up

the trolley. She'd found some toys and had decided Fred needed a water bowl too.

'I think that's enough now, Evie,' said Ben, prying his niece's hands from the trolley handle and taking charge. 'He's not even my cat, you know.'

'I know.' Evie had stood on the end of the trolley so that she could get a ride to the checkout. 'But he needs water while he's waiting for you, and if he gets bored he can play with his new mouse,' she'd reasoned.

Ben had agreed that made sense, and besides, he knew better than to argue with Evie.

*

The following few hours had been spent painting Fred's house. Ian had left them to it, so Ben had spent the rest of the morning being bossed about by his niece. Evie had had firm views on what should be purple and what should be green, and she was a harsh taskmaster – Ben had been royally told off for smudging the colours together.

When Evie had finally decided he could be trusted, she'd left him to get on with it while she'd started another project.

The paint had dried in a couple of hours and when they'd returned to the workshop, Evie revealed what she'd been working on: some dubious artwork, tastefully displayed in Fred's new abode. But there had been one final touch before Evie could feel satisfied that the job was complete: a letterbox.

'A letterbox? I don't think cats get post,' said Ben, washing the final streaks of lime green paint from his hands.

'All houses have a letterbox,' said Evie, firmly.

'Okay, let's give it a go. If I drill three little holes in a row, and then use a hacksaw to join them up, we can make a small letterbox. How does that sound?'

'Good.' Evie had smiled happily. 'Then I can write teeny tiny letters to him!'

This is what had got Ben thinking. His dad's cautionary tale yesterday had been playing on his mind – he didn't want Fred's owner to think he was luring their pet away, or to be worrying when Fred stayed out late, but he didn't know where the cat lived. He'd seen him hopping over the fence behind the communal gardens, but most of the time the cat was already waiting for him, staring in at him from the kitchen windowsill, so he had no idea what direction he'd arrived from.

So what if Ben wrote a note to Fred's owner, and – and here was the genius part – used Fred to deliver it?

It seemed such a good idea, and his enthusiasm for the plan had stayed with him on the journey back to London, the cat house balanced precariously on his knees.

Unloading his bags from the boot after Penny had dropped him off home, he'd dumped them on the kitchen floor before placing Fred's house outside his back door. Then he'd found a piece of paper and although, feeling rather silly,

186

had started to write a note, before being interrupted by a meow at the window.

'Ah, perfect timing, Fred, I've got something for you!' Ben pushed the window wider so Fred could come in. The cat rubbed his head against Ben's arm and then jumped down to the floor to stare at the cupboard.

'Okay, treat's first.'

Now, with the cat curled happily on the stool next to the counter, Ben seized his moment. Rolling up the note tightly into a small scroll, he took a piece of string and threaded it through Fred's new collar.

Fred opened one eye and twitched his ear in warning.

Ben soothed him with a tickle under his chin, and when Fred closed his eyes again, hastily tied the string in a tight bow.

Confident the note was securely attached, Ben retreated.

When Fred finally left to go home, he'd take the note with him.

27

The wood-panelled room was full of urgent whispering as the teams conferred in hissed undertones. In the corner sat a man at a microphone, a pint of beer next to him. He was frowning at the sheet of paper in his hand as he waited a few more minutes for everyone to jot down an answer to his last question.

Jenni, nodding in agreement as Solomon listed all the presidents of the United States before declaring the answer *had* to be Teddy Roosevelt, turned to Tim and pulled a face.

Tim rolled his eyes at her. 'Don't worry, the music round will be coming up soon. I'm sure that will be easier for you!'

Jenni could only hope, especially given history, geography and general knowledge had all proved to be very much *not* her specialist subjects.

She looked around the room, assessing the other teams huddled together, whispering, pointing, some disagreeing, some looking smug. Tim was wearing his lucky shirt, he'd told her earlier – a blue linen number he'd worn the year they'd bagged the trophy. Jenni caught the eye of someone sat at the table next to theirs. He seemed to be taking things slightly less competitively as well, and they shared a knowing smile of sympathy.

Tim caught her and gave her a menacing scowl for fraternising with the enemy.

Tim's monthly quiz night was held at The Anchor, a Victorian pub near where he lived in the East End. Paul and Tim had been regulars since they'd moved to the area, and they had joined forces with Solomon, a forty-something graphic designer with thick-black-framed glasses and baggy jeans, and his girlfriend Tina, a lawyer who worked for one of the major banks in the city. The four of them had initially met during Sunday morning brunch in the restaurant downstairs, which had once been a proper old-man's boozer before, a few years back, undergoing a makeover befitting of a rapidly gentrifying area of London.

The regulars had complained loudly about how the character had gone out of the old place, while quietly admitting that they didn't miss the dealers in the loo, and that the arrival of smashed avocado on sourdough, while a cliché, was actually quite nice.

The function room upstairs, which, as well as quiz night, hosted children's parties and the occasional wedding reception, had retained some of its original charms. The huge wooden sash windows framed by faded green velvet curtains looked out over the high street, and the ancient scuffed wooden floors still had an authentic stickiness. It was also very draughty, not helped by the high ceiling, and Jenni was glad she was wearing her thick green cardigan and had brought a scarf with her, which she now pulled more tightly around her.

The compere moved on to the final question – something involving a sealion and World War Two – which Paul answered with ease, and then the round was finished. The lights came up and Tina and Tim headed to the bar to buy another bottle of wine.

Paul pushed himself back in his chair and stretched out his arms with a sigh. 'Well, that was a tough round, but I'm confident we got at least eight out of the ten right. As long as we beat the Bastard Badgers I'll be happy.'

He glared in the direction of another team, who were giving each other congratulatory pats on the back.

'We've got everything to play for in the final round, though,' said Solomon. 'I think we were right to play our joker on the geography round.'

Paul nodded in agreement. 'It's not just the Badgers we need to watch, though. I bet Haven't Got a Fucking Clue are doing well with all the World War Two questions tonight.'

Their post-round analysis was broken up by the arrival of

Tina, who plonked a bottle of red down in front of them. Tim followed, tipping five packets of crisps into the centre of the table. As Tina refreshed everyone's glasses and filled Paul and Solomon in on what she'd overhead as she'd waited at the bar – apparently, the Badgers were worried about their answers in the general knowledge round – Tim ripped open the crisps and turned to Jenni, picking up on the conversation they'd been having before the quiz started.

'So, what are you going to do? Write back?' he asked, reaching for a handful of salt and vinegar.

Jenni had told him and Paul about the note she'd found attached to Oscar's collar earlier that week.

Mystified, she'd carefully opened the rolled-up piece of paper and had been surprised to find a note from the person Oscar had been spending all his time away from the house with.

'I don't know. I suppose I should, but it's a bit weird, isn't it?'

'I think it's sweet. There's something deliciously old-fashioned about it all,' declared Tim through a mouthful of crisps. 'What if sixty-six is a rich old man, or a hunky single stud? This could be your destiny.'

'All right, Mystic Meg, calm down.' Jenni took another crisp. 'What if they're the knife-wielding, psychopathic Cruella De Vil of the cat world, looking to make a fur coat out of Oscar?!'

'That's a bit dark, love,' said Tim, wrinkling his nose. 'And besides, if they did want to do that, I doubt they'd drop you a note first. I think you should write back. Something bright and breezy.'

'Is this about the cat corresponder?' Paul interrupted.

'What's that?' asked Tina. 'You've got a talking cat?'

Jenni laughed. 'No, my cat's been cheating on me with someone else, and the person wrote me a note.' She explained what had happened to the rest of the table.

'Oh, they're *definitely* trying to steal your cat,' said Tina. 'It's a double bluff. They're *saying* they're not, but they are. Do you want me to write a cease and desist letter? That'll put the fear of God into them.'

'I don't think I need to do that just yet,' chuckled Jenni, 'but thank you. It was a friendly note, but I do feel a bit odd about Oscar hanging out with a stranger. And they're obviously feeding him, he's getting quite pudgy. He's very greedy.'

'Well, let me know what you decide to do, but you definitely need to make it clear he's your cat.' Tina took a sip of her wine.

'I agree. Janice has a shocker of a story to tell about what her neighbour did to her cat, doesn't she, Paul?' Tim said.

Paul nodded in agreement. 'Water pistols were involved. And the police,' he added after a slight pause.

'Talking of Janice, it's not too late to join us for Nordic

walking tomorrow. Tina and Solomon can't make it, un-
fortunately' – Jenni glanced at the couple, who quickly
arranged their faces into suitably disappointed expressions –
'but you've got no excuses.'

'Um, yes, well that's very kind, but I need to get back to
Oscar. Before he's permanently abducted and—'

Thankfully, just then, the lights dimmed and the compere
announced that the next round was about the begin. Tim
grabbed a pen and pulled the answer sheet towards him, all
thoughts of tomorrow's walking forgotten.

Jenni breathed a sigh of relief – she really didn't want to
walk with sticks – and, as the intro of a well-known pop
song began to play, she settled in for the music section.

She would write back to 66, she decided, although, was
it a bit odd now she'd left it nearly a week? Her delibera-
tions were brought to a close with a sharp nudge in the ribs
from Tim.

Remembering again why she hated quiz nights, she nevertheless leant forward pretending to care.

It didn't look like the music round was going to be her
moment of glory either.

28

Ben laughed when he read the note.

It had been nearly a week since he'd got Fred to deliver the letter to his real owner and, after feeling silly and wishing he hadn't sent it, he'd resigned himself to not hearing back, dismissing it from his mind. So it was a surprise when, on a sunny Saturday afternoon, he'd discovered a reply attached to Fred's collar.

Ben had opened his back door to find the cat lying in a flowerbed soaking up the warmth. He hadn't seen him at first, Fred's dark striped fur blending in with the soil of the recently dug border. But when the cat noticed Ben, he stretched and rolled over, his white belly clearly on show.

'Hello, little fellow,' Ben said, crouching down to give his tummy a tickle. Fred twisted back around and stood up, shaking his paws daintily to get rid of the bits of dirt stuck to him, then stalked towards the back door.

As the cat led the way, Ben noticed a flash of bright pink against his neck and realised there was a note attached to his collar.

Carefully removing it between swipes of paw as Fred washed his face, Ben sat down gingerly on the rotting garden chair that a previous occupant had left behind and unfurled the fluorescent Post-it.

He felt apprehensive as he unfolded the small square of paper.

Dear 66,

Thank you for letting me know my cat is safe. He's been disappearing quite a lot lately. I've also noticed he's getting a bit podgy, he's very greedy,* so please don't feed him. Thank you!

Best wishes,

38

P.S. He can be very persuasive. Stay strong and do not look directly into his eyes. He has ways of making you obey ...

It was the last line that had made Ben laugh as, just at that minute, and true to form, Fred jumped off the roof of his new house and began rubbing against Ben's leg, looking at him with an expression that suggested if he didn't get fed soon he'd pass out. As if to prove the point, the cat dropped onto one side, meowing weakly.

Ben laughed again, pushing himself out of his chair. 'Oh no you don't, Fred. I know all about your cunning tricks now, so don't even try it.'

Fred stood and threaded between Ben's legs, perhaps trying to knock him off balance, and then led the way back indoors to sit staring pointedly at the snack cupboard.

With a sigh – he really shouldn't, but he wasn't made of stone – Ben retrieved some cat biscuits and shook a few into the bowl.

'That's your lot, mate. I'll get into trouble with your real owner if I give you more.'

Speculating on who the mysterious No. 38 might be, Ben's thoughts returned to the note.

In a world of WhatsApps and emails, there was something old-fashioned about seeing someone's handwriting that made you feel, in a weird way, more connected to them; like you could guess what they might be like by how hard they pressed on the paper or how rounded their letters were.

38 has very distinctive loops, he thought. And they obviously liked bright stationery. The handwriting was rounded and neat and, although he didn't want to stereotype, he thought it had been written by a woman.

He wanted to write back immediately, but didn't quite know what to say. Besides, he'd just remembered that he needed to do something about the outfit he'd bought for Evie. Now, where had he put that woman's business card?

Rifling through the drawer where he kept old batteries, takeaway menus and the screws that were always mysteriously leftover after putting together a flatpack piece of furniture, he finally found it. There was an illustrated cat jumping from one letter to the next on the front, while, on the back, as she'd mentioned, were her social media tags. He opened the Instagram app on his phone (he'd signed up so he could follow Penny but never posted anything himself), and tapped out a quick DM. Her profile pic was the same logo as the one on her business card, and he was scrolling through her grid of colourful clothes when a reply came back.

> Sure, no problem. Happy to swap for a bigger
> size although only have these colours left.
> Which set would you like instead?

Accompanying the text were three pictures showing different colour combinations.

Ben considered the pictures then replied:

> The orange and yellow look good. How best
> to return my set – shall I post?

He was going to say he was happy to go to her house to swap the sets, but then thought better of it. He didn't want to seem creepy. So he was relieved when a DM came back suggesting that, if it was okay for him, how about they meet at Scrambled, a café near the Green.

Confirming that tomorrow afternoon at three worked for him, he was pleased to get a thumbs up emoji response.

Ben glanced at his watch. He didn't have long before he had to report for the night shift, so he'd better have something to eat before he headed out.

Pulling pasta out of the cupboard, he whistled to himself as he gathered ingredients for a basic tomato sauce. Reaching to turn on the radio to fill the kitchen with music, he realised he had that same feeling of nervous anticipation he'd experienced earlier. He realised he was looking forward to tomorrow, to seeing the woman with the long curly hair again.

Calm down, he told himself, but he couldn't stop turning up the volume as one of his favourite songs started playing, and, singing along, he started chopping an onion in time to the beat.

Fred watched unimpressed, ears flattened against his head in protest.

29

'Yes, Mum. I'm meeting him in a public place, he's a fire fighter and we're only in touch via Instagram, so he can't stalk me in real life!' Jenni rolled her eyes. She knew it was sweet that her mum worried, but *really*. 'I mean, yes, I could text a friend to tell them where, but I really don't think I need to. We are *literally* just exchanging clothes!'

Her mum persisted. 'I know you think I'm being over the top, but after spending time with Alan's daughter, my eyes have been opened. All this spiking business – which reminds me, if you have a coffee, don't leave it unattended if you nip to the loo or something. I'm so glad I didn't know any of this when you left home.'

Jenni's mum had returned from New Zealand after a wonderful few weeks away, even if her time with Alan's daughter – who was enjoying an ex-pat life working hard and partying even harder – had given Annie an insight into what a daughter released from parental supervision might get up to. She'd even managed to quit smoking – 'it's so draconian over there, thank goodness I had the nicotine patches. I'd never have got through it otherwise' – and her relationship with Alan had not only survived, but thrived.

They'd returned to their separate homes, but there was talk of living together. Jenni wasn't sure what this meant yet – buying a new home together or Alan moving in with her mum or vice versa – but she very much hoped the middle option. Even if it would be weird to have a man there instead of her dad, the thought of losing her childhood home altogether filled her with a selfish dread.

Whatever happened in her own life, she knew that her room, with her striped wallpaper and her floral curtains, holding all her memories, was always there, and the thought that it might disappear was too much to contemplate.

But for now, there was no talk of selling the house, as her mum was delighted to be home with her garden, although her friend Jane's tending of it in her absence had been sadly lacking.

'Honestly, Mum, it will be fine.'

'I don't know, darling, those sweet pea seedlings needed hardening off before being put out. Jane should have known better.'

'What?' Jenni asked, momentarily confused. 'Oh. I meant about tomorrow. It's a very busy café, and I know the woman who works there, too. I can text you when I get back if you really want me to?'

Appeased, Jenni's mum moved on, and for the next ten minutes Jenni was brought up to speed with all the village gossip, before Annie realised that she'd left the oven on and hung up abruptly.

Jenni rolled her eyes affectionately. Her mum was a one-off and Jenni felt lucky to have her. She remembered how Alex had always tutted at Annie's absent-mindedness, and had once muttered darkly about how the daughter always turns into the mother, as if that was a bad thing.

Another excellent reason why she was better off without him, Jenni reminded herself.

And if the same was true of sons and fathers, then she was most definitely better off without Alex. She'd never liked how dismissive Frank, Alex's dad, had been of his wife, Rebecca.

Jenni headed into the kitchen and opened the back door, letting the last sun of the day spread across the floor, highlighting the muddy, raspberry-shaped paw prints tracking from the cat flap to the food bowl.

Ignoring the desire to get the mop out and tackle the dirt, and channelling one of her mother's motivational fridge magnets – only dull women have immaculate houses – Jenni slipped on the old trainers she kept by the door and stepped into the garden. It was approaching the time of year when everything looked it's best – plants in fresh full leaf, flowers coming out, roses in tight bloom, everything perfect before the heat of the summer caused tall stems to flop, petals to brown and even the most reliable perennials to sprawl and sag.

She was particularly proud of the marigolds that were coming up in the tub – their orange petals would be perfect to use for dye, and she was looking forward to experimenting with some of the vegetables she'd grown from seed.

Jenni took a minute to enjoy the birdsong before a loud yowl heralded Oscar's return, as he clamoured over the fence before dropping down onto the paving slabs. For a small cat, his landing made quite a thud, and he trotted over to her, picking his paws up high as he hopped over the longer tufts of grass.

She stroked him under the chin, clocking that the note she'd finally plucked up the courage to write was gone, and the string she'd used to secure it no longer attached to his collar.

Oscar had successfully delivered his letter.

Now she just had to wait and see if 66 wrote back.

30

Ben reached into his locker and pulled out his backpack.

It had been a quiet night, which could often be hard as the hours dragged on, but they'd had a session in the gym – all firefighters had to maintain a certain level of physical fitness, and so working out was part of the job – as well as time for some revising. Ben was studying for his category C driving licence that would allow him to drive the engine, so he'd spent a few hours going through notes and preparing for the upcoming theory exam.

After an hour of studying, he'd decided he needed a coffee. Vick and Taz were already sitting at one of the tables, so he'd joined them, landing heavily on the seat with a grunt, his muscles sore from the workout.

'Only another two hours and then we're done,' Vick said with a yawn. 'How's the studying going?'

Ben had pulled a face and Vick had laughed. 'I know right? It's a lot to remember.'

'The problem is, I'll forget it all by the time I have the exam.'

'You'll be fine!' Taz said. 'Don't spend all weekend studying, though, it'll just stress you out more. How about we go for a drink this afternoon?'

'Sorry, mate. I've already got plans,' Ben said, explaining that he was meeting up with the woman from the fair to swap Evie's present

'I knew it!' said Vick triumphantly. 'I said you should ask her out!'

'Yeah, about time you got your act together,' agreed Taz, giving Ben a playful shove that nearly made him spill the coffee he was holding.

'Hang on,' Ben said. 'Firstly, I haven't asked her out, it's a business transaction—'

He'd broken off to glare as Vick had sniggered.

'Okay, wait, that sounded bad.' He'd tried again, 'I'm only meeting her to swap clothes.'

Vick and Taz had dissolved into laughter, and Ben, shaking his head, had given up trying to explain and instead had finished weakly, 'Yeah, well, anyway, I'm meeting her later.'

The teasing had continued for the rest of the shift, only stopping when Ben threatened to leave Taz stranded at the top of the practice tower. But now, as they were getting ready to go home, Taz tried again to get Ben talking.

'So what time are you meeting your date then?'

Ben lifted a hand to wave goodbye to the other crew members as he and Taz stepped out into the morning light.

'I told you, it's not a date!' he said indignantly, before adding sheepishly, 'Three o'clock.'

'Well, whatever it is, have a good time, okay?' Taz raised a questioning eyebrow at him.

Ben nodded. 'I'll let you know how it goes. But I'm off to get some sleep first.'

31

Scrambled, a local favourite on the café scene, was a hive of activity. Jenni stood in line and ordered a flat white with oat milk.

'You're not normally in at the weekend,' shouted Ana, as she fought to be heard over the hiss of steam as she heated the milk, swirling it around in the stainless steel jug. She ran the place with a cool, unflustered manner, no matter how busy it got.

'I know. I'm meeting someone who bought some clothes off me at the fair, but got the wrong size, so we're doing an exchange.'

'Your stall looked really great. I popped by in the afternoon, but you'd slipped away to grab some lunch, I think,' Ana said, wiping the nozzle of the steamer with a cloth before pouring the hot milk over the shot of espresso waiting in the cup.

Behind her in the queue, Jenni could hear a mother telling off her child for grabbing a chocolate bar from the counter, before hastily giving it back, just in time to avoid the start of a tantrum.

Thank goodness for that, thought Jenni. The café was too busy for a full-on meltdown today.

'Ah, thanks, Ana. I wasn't sure what to expect, to be honest, but it was a fun day, wasn't it?'

Ana had been manning The Scrambler, the café's mobile coffee van, that day, and she could often be found at other events, serving their speciality teas and coffees to a grateful crowd.

'It was great – manic though. I was shattered by the end. Here you go, love.'

Jenni tapped her card on the machine, inwardly baulking at the price. But Ana made an excellent coffee, so it was worth it.

She dropped an extra pound into the tip jar before rushing to grab a recently vacated table at the back of the café, before anyone else could sit down.

Congratulating herself on securing the much-coveted corner table, Jenni settled herself in the seat facing the door and large bay window that looked out onto the Green.

The pretty yellow gingham curtains were pulled back to let the light in, and she looked out on the view as she placed her coffee carefully down on the table. Taking off her coat, she draped it on the wooden chair opposite, just to make it clear that she'd claimed it and no, it couldn't be taken, then she took out the replacement clothes from her bag.

She tucked a long curl of hair behind her ear and lifted her cup to take a sip. It was ridiculous, but she felt really nervous.

She gave herself a talking to: there was absolutely no reason to have butterflies, she just had to swap the clothes and then, job done, go home. But her stomach kept flipping when she remembered how intense he'd looked while browsing through the items on her stall, sunlight highlighting the fair hair on his forearms, and the way his T-shirt fitted so snuggly against his obvious six-pack . . .

Urgh, what's wrong with me? she wondered.

To distract herself, she picked up her phone to check Instagram. She'd been adding more photos of her clothing to her grid, and several people had tagged her in their posts. She'd even had a few DMs asking where they could buy her stock.

She was wondering if she should set up a website, and, although she hardly dared voice the ambition, a tiny part of her dreamed of packing in the day job and making House of Oscar a full-time business. Perhaps she should think about setting up an Etsy shop first.

She was just about to like one of Tim's post – a picture of him walking in the park with Janice – when she sensed someone striding through the café and looked up to see a tall curly-haired man navigating his way past the pushchairs and organic cotton tote bags overflowing with equally organic fruit and vegetables.

He looked around, spotting her and raising his hand in greeting, just as he tripped on a Dachshund that was napping, snoring gently in the middle of the floor. Jenni couldn't help but laugh as he stumbled towards her, coming to an ungainly halt in front of her.

'Well, that was quite the entrance.'

He gave a rueful grin. 'Well, firefighters are highly skilled professionals trained to navigate even the most dangerous terrain.'

'But not handbag-sized dogs and pesticide-free fruit?' she teased. 'Don't underestimate them, you know. Small canines and killer apples are the bane of my life.'

Ben ran a hand through his hair, making it stick up on one side. 'Is it okay to grab this chair?'

'Oh yes, of course. I saved it for you. Here, hand me that coat, I just hung all my things on it to keep it safe.'

Ben handed her the rucksack and jacket hanging off the back of the chair, and shuffled closer to the table to allow someone to pass behind him, gently knocking knees with Jenni.

'Sorry about that,' he said, as Jenni pulled her leg away.

'It's fine, don't worry, it's a small table,' she replied, flustered, rearranging her feet. Though she was curious to know if the jolt of electricity she'd felt was down to him or a dodgy plug socket.

There was an awkward pause as they looked at each other, uncertain who should speak.

Ben got in first. 'Thanks for meeting so we can swap clothes. I mean, not *our* clothes, obviously,' he hastily amended, reddening slightly, wondering what the hell was wrong with him.

Jenni laughed. 'I'm sorry the other ones didn't fit. I hope your niece wasn't too disappointed?'

'She loved them,' he said. 'And wanted to wear them straight away. I don't know how I got the size so wrong, to be honest!'

His smile turned to a wince as he remembered the subsequent tantrum.

'Oh dear! It's hard to guess, I suppose, kids grow so quickly. My friend, Amy – you know, the one whose house caught fire? – I'm constantly shocked by how much bigger her two are every time I see them. I've turned into that annoying adult who always goes on about how they've got so big. Like, duh, of course you've grown!'

Ben nodded in agreement. 'I'm the same. But Evie is very bossy, she's always telling me off.' He told Jenni about the time Evie had had a meltdown when he wouldn't stop singing along to a song she loved. 'She certainly knows her own mind!' Ben finished.

'She sounds a bit scary. In a lovely way, of course,' Jenni added hastily, not wanting to offend, but Ben nodded in agreement.

'Delightful, but definitely terrifying, just like her mother, my sister, to be honest.'

There was a pause in the conversation before Jenni handed over the new outfit. 'Here. I hope this fits.'

'Thank you. I think she'll love it, she's into bold colours at the moment. And here are the originals back.' He passed Jenni a bag with the clothes carefully folded inside and made to stand, pushing back his chair.

With a pang of disappointment, Jenni realised he was about to leave. But then Ben asked, 'I, um, I don't suppose you fancy another coffee, do you?'

The surprise must have shown on her face, as he hastily continued, 'I'm sure you're busy, I just thought, well, I—'

'I'd like that,' Jenni interrupted with a smile. 'I'm not in a rush to get back; another coffee would be nice.'

'Okay, great. What would you like?'

She gave him her order and watched as he made his way to the counter. The café was less crowded now – no trip hazards in the aisles – and he ordered their drinks from Ana with a smile.

As he looked through his wallet for cash, Ana glanced over at Jenni with raised eyebrows and a grin.

Jenni felt herself blush.

Now they'd agreed to stay for a bit longer, she was feeling a bit anxious. What if they had absolutely nothing to talk about?

But as he returned to the table, hot coffees in hand and a warm smile on his face, she was pleased that she didn't need to say goodbye just yet.

32

'His name is Ben, and yes, he was very nice, and yes, we are meeting up again, but no it's not a date, it's an afternoon pursuing our, um, shared professional interests.'

Jenni took a sip from her freshly made coffee, her second of the day already, and moved out of the way so that Tim could use the machine. She'd arrived at the office early today and was already suffering because of the early morning start.

'Uh-huh,' Tim replied, eyebrows raised. 'Sounds like a date to me but—' He held up a hand before she could interrupt. 'Whatever you need to tell yourself. You have an excellent time pursuing your – what was it? – "professional interests".' He added air quotes to the last couple of words.

Jenni rolled her eyes. She didn't care what Tim said. It really *wasn't* a date.

Ben had been so easy to talk to. He'd told her about his job, although he'd brushed over the more harrowing parts, and she'd told him about the snow shoot and he'd laughed when she'd described the horror of finding out her photo had appeared in the subsequent campaign. 'And then Clive put photos up all around the office. I have flashbacks if I see an orange bobble hat now.'

'I hate to tell you, but now you've mentioned it, I actually remember that advert. I thought you looked vaguely familiar! It was on the side of buses.' Jenni had winced. 'Okay, okay, enough! I can't bear to even talk about it anymore. Tell me your most embarrassing work story.'

'Well, there was an incident involving gas masks, when I passed out playing table tennis,' he'd begun, and Jenni had leaned in.

One more coffee had turned into three, but, as they were getting up to leave at closing time, Ben had spotted a flyer pinned to the noticeboard behind the counter. It was for an exhibition in a gallery housed in a decommissioned fire station. The artist exhibiting was a local woman that Jenni followed on Instagram, whose work she loved. Her intricate collages made from tiny pieces of torn paper were delicate, but powerful, and Jenni was in awe of the designs.

Ben, meanwhile, had been interested as the building was where some his crew had been based before it had closed down and they were relocated to their current station.

Now, telling Tim, Jenni was feeling nervous again. Was it a date, despite her insistence otherwise?

'Oh my God, do you think *he* thinks it's a date?' she asked Tim in alarm. 'Maybe I should have been clearer that it wasn't when I suggested we go together and—'

'Just relax, for God's sake, Jenni. What's wrong with you?' Tim asked, a confused frown wrinkling his forehead. 'He sounds like a nice guy, you had a nice time, just see what happens.'

Seeing Jenni on the verge of panic, Tim hastily added. 'It's fine – he probably just wants to see if the old fire pole is still there or something, or take a look at the vintage signs or helmets or whatever on the walls. That's all. And you're just going to look at, what did you say they were? Torn-up bits of paper? All perfectly normal and not at all date-like. Anyway, come on, we need to get going. Clive is giving a shout-out to my walking range this morning.'

Cup in hand, Jenni followed Tim to the Monday Motivational, her mind whirring.

It was going to be fine. It wasn't a date. There was no need to panic at all.

Not. At. All.

33

The letterbox snapped shut and from his front room, Ben heard the thud of a package land on the mat. Making sure he put the latch on to stop his door slamming shut behind him, he went out and scooped up all the post lying on the floor. Sorting through it, he tucked the letter addressed to him under his arm, leaving the rest of the mail on the shelf for his neighbours, before returning to his flat.

He recognised his sister's handwriting on the front of the cream envelope and, opening it, he pulled out a note inviting him for Sunday lunch again soon, and a smaller letter addressed to Fred with a Post-it note attached that read:

Uncle Ben, please give this letter to Fred. I've made it very small so it will fit through his letterbox. Do not open it. It is for Fred only. Mummy says you'll just

pretend to do it, so please send a photo of Fred
reading his letter. See you soon. Love from Evie xxx

Ben put the letter to one side with a groan. He really didn't want to spend his day trying to get a photo of Fred appearing to read a letter. Instead, he decided a picture of him posting it through the letterbox would do, so feeling rather foolish, but nevertheless not wanting to disappoint his niece, he slotted the envelope through the opening and sent Penny the photo.

He took a moment to admire his handiwork. The house really did look good, although he still hadn't seen Fred use it. He wondered if it might be damp, and crouched down to feel inside, his fingers catching on something soft and furry. With a squeal that became a manly shout in later retellings, he whipped out his hand, terrified – again, later adjusted to merely concerned – that there was a mouse, or worse, a rat, in there.

Cautiously, using the torch on his phone, he shone the light into the interior. The purple walls glowed and Ben could see Evie's pictures – he really hoped Fred liked *Frozen* – that adorned the walls, together with, tucked away in the furthest corners, several fabric mice in various states of destruction, one with its stuffing spilling out, a bald tennis ball, a plastic ball with a bell inside, a Lego man, several foam bullets from a Nerf gun and, somewhat randomly, a KitKat wrapper.

Ben withdrew his phone and straightened up. Where had all these things come from? Were they Fred's, or was the cat using his house to hide stolen goods?

*

The bar was quiet, as was often the case on a weekday, and Ben very much preferred it to the hectic surge on a Friday or Saturday night. Sometimes he missed the buzz – the DJ playing in the corner, partygoers talking loudly and drinking too fast, the press of bodies at the bar – but tonight he was glad that there was a more peaceful vibe.

There were enough people, so the pub didn't feel completely empty, but he didn't have to shout to be heard, and, after wrestling with Fred to attach the new note to his collar, he was pleased to just hang out at his local with Taz, chewing the fat over a drink or two.

'So, how did it go yesterday? Did you "exchange clothing"?' asked Taz, taking a last sip from his pint and signalling to the barmaid for two more.

Ben nodded. 'Yeah. It was good. We ended up chatting for ages.'

He told Taz how he and Jenni had completely lost track of time and had stayed till closing time, eventually being bustled out by the owner.

'So you're going to meet up with her again, then?'

'Yeah, we're going to go to our old station, actually. It's

a gallery now, all looks very swanky apparently, and I fancy having a look around. There's a small exhibition about the history of the fire station. You should come.'

'Of course I'm not going to come, you weirdo. I don't fancy playing gooseberry!'

'It's not a date,' Ben said, seriously.

'Sounds like one to me,' the barmaid with blue hair said, as she placed a couple more beers down in front of them before stomping off back to the bar.

'It's not a date!' Ben called out to her retreating back. He turned back to Taz. 'It's not! She just wants to see the work of this artist, and I fancied having a look at the old fire station. It made sense to go together. We're just going to meet up first and get a quick—*oh my God*, she's going to think it's a date! I've asked her on a date and I didn't even realise! What have I *done*?' Ben reached over for his glass in a panic and took a long gulp of beer.

'So what if it is a date?' asked Taz, as Ben spluttered into his drink. 'Okay, okay, not a real date,' Taz hastily amended 'but whatever it is, she said yes, so what's the big deal?'

Ben opened his mouth to reply. Where to begin?

'Look, if you're that worried, just tell her you can't make it?' suggested Taz.

Ben thought about it. *Yes, that could work.* But ... but, if he was being honest, he was looking forward to seeing Jenni again.

Taz watched his friend as this realisation played out on his face.

'Don't overthink it. Just go. Nerd out over the history, whatever. You might even have a good time.'

Ben nodded, trying to calm his anxiety. Or was it excitement?

The conversation moved on to work, but Ben's mind was still on the date-not-date.

He'd enjoyed chatting to Jenni once they'd got over the initial awkwardness, and the conversation had flowed. She was funny and interesting; he'd enjoyed making her laugh, and the passion she'd shown when talking about art, and the gentle banter that they'd slipped into. And she was interested in him, too; had seemed genuinely curious to find out about his job and how he coped with the stress of saving lives. He'd told her about Penny, and Evie. And while he'd told her that some call-outs were harder than others, he hadn't gone into details. Hadn't told her about some of the more harrowing scenes he'd attended.

He also hadn't mentioned Luisa. He hadn't felt ready for that conversation yet. And he certainly hadn't told her about what had happened to him when she'd left him. But there was something about Jenni that made him feel he could trust her, something Ben hadn't felt for a long time.

34

Jenni stood waiting outside The Old Station Gallery, nervously checking her watch. Tables and chairs under large black umbrellas were set on the wide pavement outside the large red doors – a reminder of the building's heritage. The doors were opened wide and the bar inside was already busy, background music spilling out onto the street. Festoon lights, their amber filaments glowing, were strung from hooks, even though the evening wasn't yet dark, and the LED tealights placed on each table flickered. It looked delightful – pity she wasn't in a state to appreciate it.

They'd agreed to meet at seven-thirty, and Jenni had spent most of the day composing an apologetic DM cancelling, deleting it, then writing it again.

When a message confirming that he was looking forward to seeing her later came through, the alert made her jump. She'd replied with a thumbs up emoji and then had to go and have a little lie down. Thank goodness she'd been working from home today.

Lying on the bed, she'd shut her eyes and indulged in some deep breathing, before being jolted out of her mediative state by the arrival of Oscar, who was in a very affectionate mood.

'Oh, Oscar, I don't know what's wrong with me!' she'd said, stroking the cat as he'd purred loudly, headbutting her gently.

Pulling back the covers, she'd crawled under the duvet, making space for Oscar to curl up on the pillow next to her. Listening to him rumble gently, she'd run a hand over his little head, giving him an extra tickle beneath his ear. Blissed out, he'd rolled over, tummy on display, with his back legs in the air.

'Okay, I get the message, belly rubs, is it?' said Jenni laughing. Oscar had given a little mew in reply, before curling up with his back to her and settling down for a sleep.

Straightening the pillow to make him more comfortable, she'd found a piece of paper tied with pink ribbon attached to his collar.

She'd unfolded the note carefully, smoothing out the creases so she could read the tiny writing more easily. It really was quite exciting to get messages delivered via the cat.

Dear 38,
  I've found a bunch of stuff in Fred's house. I'm
worried he's a hoarder, a burglar or perhaps a serial
killer, and these are his trophies. Let me know if
they're yours and I can return them to you?
  Best wishes,
  66

There was a lot to untangle here and she was already feeling stressed enough without worrying about her cat being a thief. Turning the scrap of paper over and grabbing a pencil, she'd written:

What house and who the hell is Fred? And why do
you think any of his stolen goods belong to me?

Taking the opportunity to reattach the note to Oscar's collar while he was sleeping, she'd quickly tied the Barbie pink ribbon into a bow and then, with a rising wave of panic, decided she'd better get ready for her non-date with Ben before she changed her mind again and called the whole thing off.

Now, waiting outside the gallery, she decided to give it another five minutes and if he'd not arrived by then, she'd slope off, and never leave the house again.

But then she saw him heading towards her, long strides

crossing the width of pavement between them, in turned-up jeans and an open-necked, checked flannel shirt over a faded black T-shirt, a frown of apology on his face.

'Hello, I'm so sorry I'm late, I saw my sister and niece this afternoon and Evie gave me a makeover. It look me ages to get the glitter off.'

He decided not to add that Evie had said that he needed to look good for "his date", and that Penny had arched a knowing eyebrow at his denials that it was no such thing.

Jenni wasn't quite sure how to reply.

'Um, well, you do still have some eyeshadow.' She pointed to his left eye where there was a very obvious smear of blue streaking towards his hairline.

Ben tutted, pulled a tissue from his pocket and began wiping his eye.

'I told her not to use the face paint, it's a bugger to get off.' He continued to scrub away at his temple. 'How's that? Better?' He turned his face so Jenni could look.

Jenni took a moment to study the line of his nose, the stubble on his chin, his lips – rosy from the lipstick, which, she assumed, was left over from the makeover – that she suddenly wanted to kiss, before realising he was waiting for an answer.

'Um. Yes, all gone now, all, erm . . . good.'

'Great,' Ben smiled, grinning at her in a way that did nothing to cool her rising temperature.

'Fortunately, Penny stepped in before Evie could get at my hair. I had a green streak for months last time.'

'You're a good man to commit to such an extensive beauty regime.'

'Oh, you have no idea! You should see my fingernails. I've got different coloured polish on each one at the moment – I didn't have time to take it off.' He held out his hands to show Jenni, who let out a bark of laughter.

Ben lowered his hands with a grin. 'Come on, l need a beer. Shall we get a drink?' he asked, the anxiety he had felt before arriving slipping away.

'Yes, I'd like that,' Jenni said, smiling, the knots of tension she'd felt in her shoulders all day easing.

And she realised, as she felt the light pressure of his palm in the small of her back as they walked towards the warm glow of the bar, that she wasn't lying.

*

The evening turned out to be much more fun than she expected. After a drink they'd headed upstairs to the gallery to look around the exhibition, and while Jenni browsed in the gift shop afterwards, Ben chatted to Larry, the owner. Jenni had just finished paying for two postcards when Ben tugged on her arm.

'I've got us backstage access. Come on!'

Larry led them downstairs to a door in the far corner of

the bar. Unlocking it, he pushed it wide to allow Ben and Jenni into a narrow stairwell.

'We could only afford to do the bar and the exhibition space, so the rest of the building is still pretty much how we found it,' he explained. 'We've made it safe, so it's fine to take a look if you're interested. The bar's where the engines used to be parked up, but if you go upstairs you can see where the dorms were, and if you go right up the top, it opens up onto the roof. They used to fire-watch up there during the war.'

Larry clicked the latch on the door so it didn't lock behind them. 'I've got to get back to the bar, but take your time and come and find me when you're done.'

'Okay, thanks, mate, will do.' Ben was already heading excitedly up the rusty wrought-iron stairs.

'This is amazing,' Jenni said, following him up the steep steps. They stopped at the next floor up, but the large room showed no evidence of its earlier life, apart from a couple of signs urging caution, and another saying Fire Station – the old-fashioned font and rusty edges the only things giving away their age.

'This is amazing,' said Jenni again, walking around the high-ceilinged room, leaving dusty footprints on the lino-covered floor. 'I'd love a place like this to work in; all this space to spread out.'

She was imagining where she'd put her vats of dye, and

where she'd have a proper packing area, instead of folding things on her bed. She'd string a line between the two high windows so that the clothes could dry above her as she worked. She was just mapping out if there'd be room for a screen-printing table, and perhaps a corner for her sewing machine, when Ben called her over.

'It's strange to imagine it as it must have been, back in the old days,' he said, trying to picture what it would have been like without any of the mod cons he was used to now.

He could almost hear the alarms, the roar of the engines, the banter between the teams.

He turned to look for Jenni. 'Shall we go up to the next floor?'

She nodded, and as Ben held open the door for her to step through, she felt his warmth as she brushed past him. Aware of him behind her, they climbed the stairs until they reached a door on the top landing that seemed to be locked.

'Here, let me try.' Ben reached over, gave the door a shove and Jenni gasped as it opened to reveal what felt like all of London spread out in front of them: the Walkie Talkie, the Shard, the Gherkin, the smaller dome of St Paul's.

'Wow, this is incredible,' breathed Jenni in awe, taking in the lights of the familiar skyline.

'Definitely wow,' agreed Ben, stepping forwards and placing his hand on the railings in front of them. 'However long you've lived here, that view never gets old, does it?'

Jenni shook her head. 'It feels so peaceful. All the noise and drama down there, but up here it's so calm.'

'It makes you feel small; like none of it matters,' said Ben quietly.

Jenni glanced at him. There was something in his voice that made her wonder what "it" was for him.

She hesitated before replying. 'But also that there's lots of good things, too; that we can still be surprised and see something in a different way, like this view.'

Ben didn't answer, but a feeling of contentment washed over him as they stood together in silence. Although, it was an effort to ignore the urge to move his hand closer to Jenni's as she grasped the rail next to him.

Jenni leant forward slightly to glance over the side. Instantly regretting it, she lurched back with a stumble. 'Urgh, we're much higher up than I realised.'

Ben grabbed her arm to steady her.

'Don't worry, you're okay. Take a breath and focus on the horizon.'

Jenni did as instructed, distracted by the feeling of his hand on her upper arm, his grip firm, but gentle.

'Sorry. I don't know what happened, I suddenly felt dizzy and disorientated, like I could have just fallen. Do you ever get that feeling?'

'You need a really good head for heights to do my job,' Ben said, chuckling. 'We have to practise climbing a lot of ladders, so you get used to it. Although, the first time I did it, my knees just went to jelly halfway up, and Taz, my mate, had to come and get me. Not my finest hour.'

'Well, I don't think I'll be retraining as a firefighter any-time soon. I find taking the stairs to the first floor of my office enough of a challenge.'

Ben laughed. 'Your work comes with its own occupa-tional hazards, though. I've never broken a leg in the line of duty.'

'Yes, well, that's not technically part of the job descrip-tion,' said Jenni ruefully.

'Okay now?' asked Ben, realising he still held her arm and letting go.

Jenni nodded, feeling the cool air on her skin now the warmth of his hand had gone. Ben's easy chat had distracted her from the rush of vertigo, and she felt fine now.

'I've never had that before, I suddenly felt like I might just fall over the edge. Glad we weren't up there.' She pointed at the Shard, towering over London like the illuminated spire of an enormous cathedral.

They stood together for another moment until, reluc-tantly, Ben said, 'We'd better go back down. One for the road?'

Jenni took out her phone to check the time – Oscar would be expecting dinner about now but he could manage for a bit longer, he had plenty of biscuits to keep him going. 'Yes, sounds good,' she said with a smile. 'I'm not expected home for a while yet, so another drink sounds an excellent idea.'

Ben, holding open the door, let Jenni pass him and then carefully closed it behind them before heading down the stairs after her. He realised the feeling of happiness he'd been enjoying just moments before had lessened.

Who was waiting for her at home?

35

The phone buzzed next to him and Ben picked it up to see a message from Penny.

How was the date?

It was NOT a date.

Tetchy. I'm simply asking if you had a nice evening. And Evie wants to know if her makeover worked. So, how did it go????

I couldn't get rid of the eyeshadow so had to rub it off with a tissue.

Don't make me come over . . .

It was fine.

😳

Okay, it was nice. I had fun. We had a drink.
Satisfied?

Are you going to see her again?

I don't know.

????????

I think she's got a boyfriend.

What do you mean *think*?

She said someone wouldn't be expecting her
home till later.

Flatmate?

I don't know. She didn't mention sharing with
anyone.

Just ask her out again. If she does have a

boyfriend then she can say no, or it might be
a flatmate and she'll say yes and you can go
another date.

For the last time, it wasn't a date.

Whatevs

Knowing it was pointless trying to have the last word with
Penny, Ben turned off his phone and threw it on the sofa.

He leant back, his hands behind his head.

He'd had fun last night. Jenni was good company, and as
they'd stood on the roof, he'd felt a moment of pure calm
that he hadn't felt for years. When they'd gone back to the
bar, she'd made him laugh, telling him stories of her boss.
He thought she'd enjoyed it too. But her comment on the
roof had thrown him.

If she had a boyfriend, why hadn't she mentioned it when
they'd met at the café?

He turned his phone back on and glanced at the time.
He needed to get a move on, he had to be at the station in
half an hour.

He may not have all the facts, but one thing he knew
for certain, if Jenni was in a relationship he couldn't get
involved.

Grabbing his backpack, he headed to work.

36

Jenni stared out of the window, watching her bit of London change as the bus edged its way closer to the city centre.

Jenni liked taking the bus. It gave her time to think.

It had been over a week since she'd gone to the gallery with Ben and, she had to admit, she was disappointed she'd not heard from him since.

It was annoying, not because he hadn't been in touch, but because she realised she wished he had. And she didn't want to feel like that.

It had been difficult adjusting to being single after being with someone for a long time, and she didn't want to go through the exhaustion of dating, only to find herself on her own, *again*.

She tried to convince herself she definitely didn't want Ben to get in touch and she absolutely wasn't just a tiny bit gutted that he hadn't.

She hadn't heard back from 66 either, although, given the last message she'd sent, that might not be a bad thing.

*

'What are you doing after work?' Lucy asked, as Jenni caught up with her overflowing inbox. 'I need a drink – it's two-for-one cocktails at the Red Lion.'

'I'm doing absolutely nothing and that sounds like an excellent idea. Although, it is only 11am.' Jenni looked up from her email.

'Yes, sorry, a bit desperate, but Clive is driving me to distraction.' Lucy pulled her hair back and twisted it into a bun, something Jenni had noticed she did when stressed.

'Why, what's he done now?'

'It's this walking-wear idea that Tim suggested to him. The research team has come back with a report.' Lucy dropped her hands, letting her hair fall free again to lift up a huge ring-bound folder. 'It says that walking is the new running, and Clive is now super keen to launch a new range as soon as possible.'

She dropped the folder onto her desk with a thud.

'Tim has gone on a "research" walking holiday in the Alps,' the sarcasm of the air quotes was not lost on Jenni, 'on expenses. I *hate* him. And Clive wants me to present "some vibes" to the board tomorrow. Tim left no notes on what "vibes" pair well with putting one foot in front of another, and I've absolutely run out of ideas, so I think alcohol is the only answer.'

Jenni pushed her chair away from her desk and moved around to sit next to Lucy.

'Let's see what you've got.'

Lucy sighed and tapped at her keyboard, pulling up a PowerPoint presentation.

'Well, the heading is nice,' Jenni said, trying to sound positive.

'Oh my God, it's awful!' Lucy pitched forward facedown onto her keyboard in despair.

'Okay, don't panic. What did Tim say about the holiday? Perhaps that will give us some inspiration.'

'He kept droning on about fresh air and simplicity, after that I stopped listening.'

'Simplicity, that's good. How about wholesome as a vibe?'

'How about *boring*.' Will appeared with a cup of tea and sat down opposite them.

'That's really not helpful.' Jenni glared at him.

'Sorry.' Will shrugged. 'It's just walking takes ages, it's so basic. I prefer to cycle and whizz by everyone at speed!'

'Maybe we could reframe walking as being natural, and that when you're walking outdoors, you're at one with nature,' pondered Jenni.

'Yes, I like that, go with that,' said a voice behind them.

Jenni yelped in surprise and turned to find Clive looming over them in an acidic, lime-green cardigan.

'And I like that.' He pointed to the sweatshirt Jenni had slung over the back of her chair. It was one of her own creations and a bit more casual than she'd usually wear to work, but she'd been in a rush and it had been the nearest thing to grab on her way out.

'Where's it from?' he asked.

'It's one of my designs, actually,' Jenni said, feeling flustered. She had a sudden panic that Clive might see her side hustle as disloyalty to the company somehow. 'I customise the clothes using natural dyes.'

Clive didn't reply – was he about to sack her?

Jenni felt compelled to fill the silence and babbled on. 'I, um, did this one using beetroot first, then a second dip of turmeric.'

'Interesting,' said Clive finally, taking the sweatshirt off Jenni's chair and peering at the colours more closely. 'Can you do other colours?'

'Yes, of course. Natural dyes are quite subtle and muted, but you can get greens, reds, purples, oranges and yellows, depending on what you use.'

'And how do you stop the colours from running?'

'Salt and cold water.'

'No chemicals?'

'No, you don't need them. Salt is a natural fixative.'

'And what fabrics do you use?'

'Cotton, usually, although linen, flax or hemp all work well. Natural fibres take the dye best.'

Clive was quiet for a moment, seemingly lost in thought. From experience, Jenni knew it was best not to interrupt him when he was 'mulling', so she sat and waited in silence.

'Jenni, bring in some natural dye samples for the meeting tomorrow, and be prepared to talk the board through your process,' he instructed, before turning to Lucy.

'I'm thinking Natural in Nature – when we walk in nature, the clothes we wear should be made from natural materials. That's the vibe.'

With that, Clive disappeared down the corridor to his office at speed, and Jenni made a mental note to see if lime peel might produce a softer coloured dye than the hideous neon green of his cardigan.

Lucy started frantically typing the second slide of her presentation. 'I'm going to need pictures and details of the things you've dyed, Jenni, could you send them to me?'

Jenni nodded weakly, relieved she still had a job, as she started scrolling through the photos on her phone to find suitable pictures to send to Lucy.

Cocktails would have to wait, now that she had to spend the evening preparing for tomorrow's presentation.

Oh well, she thought, *if Ben does get in touch, I'm far too busy to see him now anyway.*

37

Ben pulled out his ear buds, chucking them on the counter before bending over with his hands on his thighs, panting. After finishing work, he'd headed home, but his mind had felt as fidgety as his body and he knew going for a run was the best cure for his current mood. He'd done two loops around the park, joining the early-evening joggers and double-lapping the end-of-day strollers, enjoying watching the sky turn stunning shades of pink, apricot and red.

Returning home, he felt much better. Tired in a good way, rather than exhausted. And his mood lifted even more when Fred appeared at the window, although that reminded him that he hadn't replied to the last note he'd received. He'd obviously scared 38 with his talk of serial killers, and he wasn't quite sure how to respond to their reply.

Letting Fred in, he headed for the shower, enjoying the feeling of washing away the day.

It had been a difficult shift. He'd been called out to a domestic fire, only to find a woman and her two children trapped inside a first-floor flat. They'd inhaled a lot of smoke before being rescued, and all three were in intensive care at the local hospital.

What had stayed with Ben was the husband's reaction. He'd arrived home just as his wife and children were being pulled out, and the shock and distress on his face was clear to see. When he'd left his family that morning, all had been well, but then his world had been turned upside down.

Ben always found that change in circumstance so upsetting to see. One minute you're fine, the next you're not. Life offered no certainties.

He turned the temperature to cold and plunged himself under the freezing water, attempting to blast away the last lingering thoughts of the rescue, and then stepped out of the shower to get dressed.

Ten minutes later, feeling much better, he strode into the kitchen and laughed when he saw Fred's cross-looking face glaring at him. If he could have drummed his fingers impatiently on the countertop where he was sitting, then that's what he'd be doing. Instead, his angry meow made it very clear that Ben had taken far too long.

Ben tickled the cat behind the ears and Fred closed his eyes in ecstasy, all forgiven, until they were interrupted by the phone ringing. Ben reached to answer it as Fred jumped down from the counter and hopped onto a stool, where he curled up and settled into sleep.

Ben glanced at the phone's display to see who was calling.

'Hi, Mum.'

There was a pause. Then the sound of his dad clearing his throat.

'Dad? What's happened? Is Mum okay?' Ben practically shouted, gripped with fear.

'Yes, yes she's fine, everything's fine. I just, er, I thought I'd give you a call.'

'Oh!' Ben frowned, puzzled.

'How are you?' his dad continued.

'I'm okay . . . ?' Ben was confused. What was going on? His dad never rang him. If he answered the phone when Ben called, he'd mutter a hello and then say put his mum on. He never asked Ben how he was or stayed on the line to chat.

'Good, good.'

Ben steeled himself for bad news. Were his parents getting divorced? Perhaps something had happened to Penny. Or worse still, Evie. Before panic set in, his dad spoke.

'I wondered if you'd like to help me with a summerhouse for the garden?'

'A summerhouse?' Ben repeated, confused.

'It doesn't matter. I just thought we'd done a good job with your cat house thing and your mum's been asking for somewhere shady to sit in the garden. I thought maybe you fancied having a go at something bigger, but if you're busy—'

'I think it's a great idea, Dad,' Ben interrupted. 'You just caught me by surprise, that's all. I thought something bad had happened. You don't normally ring.'

He hoped he didn't sound argumentative.

There was another pregnant pause before his dad asked, 'So what do you think? About the summerhouse?'

'I think it's a great idea. What do you have in mind?'

Ben listened, his panic subsiding, as his dad described the sort of thing he wanted: a medium-sized structure to fit in the corner of the garden, a bit of decking so they could sit outside on a sunny day, with a storage cupboard for deckchairs.

Ben grabbed a pen and started to make notes on the back of an envelope. They agreed Ben would draw up some proper plans and then they could go over his design before ordering all the materials they'd need.

'That sounds great, Dad. I'll get started when I have a couple of days off.'

'Okay. Thanks, Ben. Bye.'

Before Ben could say goodbye there was a click and the phone went dead. Ben rolled his eyes. Typical.

But then he remembered what his mum had said about his dad *doing* not *saying*.

Perhaps this was his way of trying to make things better between them.

38

Jenni pulled off her coat, hung it up on the back of the door, kicked off her shoes and then dumped her bag on the kitchen table.

Her head was still spinning.

The board had *loved* her samples. Lucy's presentation had been creative and impressive, and they'd been given the go ahead to proceed to the next stage.

Jenni, Lucy and Tim had been assigned to the project, working with designers and manufacturers, but, most exciting of all, Jenni had been appointed creative director, in charge of producing all the different colourways, before the team would jointly decide the final range.

It would be a lot of work, but Jenni couldn't wait to get started. She hoped she could persuade Amy to join her on the team as a consultant. She was on the last couple of months of maternity leave from Go Big, and HR had agreed that Amy could use her keeping-in-touch days to work on the project before her official return.

Jenni trusted Amy's instincts and knew her friend's marketing expertise was just what they needed. She couldn't wait to tell her about the exciting turn of events, and just hoped she'd be up for the idea. She'd wanted to call her immediately, but instead had sent a text asking her to call when she was free, before nipping in to M&S, throwing delicious meals from the Dining for Two range into her basket with wild abandon to add to the couple of cocktails in a tin she'd grabbed from the fridge.

Now, back home, she poured herself a cocktail before stepping out into the garden.

Sitting down at the rickety table, she took a long sip, relaxing back into the chair as the fruity – one of her five a day, surely? – drink worked it's magic.

She couldn't believe what had happened today. For the Go Big board to ask her to work on the new range was huge, and she knew it was the opportunity of a lifetime. But looking at her shed, she began to feel doubt creep in.

Cramped didn't even begin to describe her work space, and there was no room for anyone else in there – even Oscar had to perch on a pile of boxes if he ever joined her.

She'd have to take a much more structured approach to colour mixing, too. She couldn't just fling a few onion skins in a bucket and hope for the best. Clive and the Go Big team would demand consistency, so she'd need to record all her ingredients and quantities.

She took another sip of drink. There was no way her shed could cope. She needed somewhere bigger. She needed a proper studio.

*

'So let me get this straight. You want me to leave my children for a few hours each week to get paid to hang out with you and look at bits of fabric?' Amy asked after Jenni had filled her in on her new work venture. It was nine in the evening and Amy had finally had a chance to call her back after a rather fraught bath and bedtime.

'Yes, sorry, you're right, it's selfish of me. I shouldn't have asked. Spending time with your kids is much more important—'

'Of *course* I want to do it, you fool,' interrupted Amy. 'It sounds *amazing*. Simon and I have already talked about childcare for when I go back to work, and his mum has said she'll do a day looking after the kids. I'd love to do it.'

'Oh, that's wonderful, thank you. When you've sorted your hours with HR we can create a proper job spec for you.'

'Yes, I'll come up with a title suitably nature-based so we're on brand with the whole vibe as well. I think you're right about finding somewhere larger, by the way. We need a nice, big open-plan space to work in.'

'Good idea. I'll ask Clive if there's somewhere at the office we can use—'

The piercing squeal of a disgruntled toddler from Amy's end of the phone broke up the conversation. 'Sorry, Jen, I'm going to have to go, but let me know how you get on with Clive, and I'll speak to you soon.'

A nudge at her ankle made her jump, and Jenni looked down to see Oscar rubbing against her leg, purring now he had her attention.

'Do you want your dinner?' Jenni asked, before spotting the bright ribbon tied to his collar.

'Oh, another note. Let's see what number sixty-six has to say this time.'

Hi,

Sorry. I think I freaked you out with my last note. Fred is what I've been calling your cat as I don't know his real name. I was trying for humour, but I can see how I might have got it very wrong. Sorry about that. I promise there are no bodies buried under my patio, I actually save lives for a living!

I looked in the house I made him to shelter in if I was late getting home and it's full of toys. I'm not sure if they're his or if he's 'borrowed' them from another cat. Anyway, if they're his, do you want them back again? If not, I'll get rid of them.

66

Jenni laughed. She liked the tone of the note and, obviously, it was reassuring to know 66 wasn't quite the crazy neighbour she'd imagined.

Or so they said, she thought darkly.

She read the note again, looking for clues to their identity. Saving lives for a living was interesting. Perhaps they were an A&E doctor? Intriguing.

39

I gather today's talk went well. Lots of
excellent questions, Evie tells me 😂

Ben read Penny's text and grimaced.

He usually enjoyed the outreach work the service insisted all personnel took part in. They often went to schools to give talks on fire safety and tell kids what it was like to be a firefighter. Ostensibly, schools invited them in to 'inspire a new generation', but Ben had noticed that they were often scheduled towards the end of term, so he suspected that the invitation was less to do with inspiration and more about giving the teachers a chance to catch up on their marking while the children were occupied.

Whatever the reason, it was something he loved doing, as it had been one such talk that had set him on his own career path in the fire service. He still remembered the awe he'd felt when the firemen – as they were still called when he was a boy – had talked about battling fires and driving engines, sirens blazing, at high speed, and dragging people from the jaws of death. He'd known immediately this was the sort of job he wanted to do, although the reality included a lot more paperwork than he'd been led to believe.

He'd been particularly looking forward to that day's visit to St Mary's Primary – Evie's school.

The talk had gone well. The demonstration – putting out a small, controlled fire with a damp tea towel – had elicited lots of 'oohs' and 'ahhs', and had been sufficiently dramatic to make Ms Jones, the headteacher, rush from the staff room to check what was going on.

After everyone had quietened down, Ben and Vick had sat at the front of the class, ready to answer questions.

'So,' said Vick, ignoring the squirming coming from Patrick's direction, 'who would like to ask a question?'

Several hands were raised, waving for attention, and she and Ben took it in turns to reply to the usual queries: yes, the engine did go fast; no, they didn't rescue cats that often, really.

'You've asked some excellent questions today, everyone,' said Vick with a smile. 'Does anyone have anything else they want to ask?'

One hand shot up.

'I've got a question for my Uncle Ben – I mean Crew Manager Walker,' said Evie, sweetly.

'Yes, Evie, what do you want to know?' Ben asked, already sensing danger.

'How was your date with Jenni? Is she your girlfriend now?'

'Did you kiss her?' shouted one of the boys from the back, and the class erupted into laughter.

Just then, the door opened, and Ms Jones reappeared with a stern look on her face.

Thank goodness, thought Ben, smiling gratefully as she brought order back to the classroom.

'Topaz Class, is this how we behave when we have guests?' Ms Jones asked sternly, looking at the upturned faces in front of her.

'No, Miss Jones,' the children sing-songed in reply. You could hear the proverbial pin drop, it was so quiet.

'How do you do that?' Vick asked in awe. 'I can't even get my own two to sit quietly.'

'Years of practice,' said Ms Jones with a smile, as Ben gathered up their equipment and said goodbye to the class.

Evie rushed over to give Ben a hug before he left. 'Sorry, Uncle Ben. I just wanted to know if you'd had a nice time.'

'You could have waited to ask me when I come around for lunch. But I did have a nice time, thank you, Evie.'

Evie smiled. 'Good. I'll see you at the weekend. I've got another letter for Fred.'

40

'Of course you won't find foxgloves under 'F', they're under D, for Digitalis.' Jenni's mother rolled her eyes before disappearing between two rows of fruit trees.

Jenni sighed. A trip to the garden centre with her mother was always a triggering experience. The rotting smell of fresh compost, the unbearable heat of the greenhouses and the endless rows of plants that her mum moved slowly through, examining what felt like every single leaf. It reminded her of childhood weekends, being reluctantly dragged through the perennial section with only the vague promise of a slice of cake in the café afterwards to look forward to.

Sulkily, she headed off to find the right section, eventually locating the foxgloves. She texted her mother and her phone beeped immediately with a reply.

I'll come and find you when I've finished
with the peonies. Find Pam's choice. It's an
unusual variety and I want to get one for the
bed at the back of the garden.

Jenni gave another sigh. She was going to have to look at the label stuck in every pot to find 'Pam's Choice'.

Rolling up her sleeves – and feeling very strongly that this had better be followed by a trip to The Potting Shed for a coffee and chocolate brownie – she leant forward and started working her way through the rows of black plastic containers. The foxgloves were stunning but, she noted, poisonous for cats so not a plant for her garden. Thinking about Oscar reminded her that she hadn't heard back from 66 yet – she'd told them about not hearing back from Ben after their 'not a date' and hoped she hadn't scared them off with too much information.

Distracted, she didn't at first register the couple on the opposite side of the table, obscured by a sign dividing the digitalis from the euphorbias. It was only when the woman's voice rose in volume and became slightly agitated that Jenni started to pay attention.

'Of course we can't have those ones! Look, the sign says they're toxic. Do you want to poison the baby?'

'Don't be silly, of course I don't. I'm just saying that we

can't worry about every little thing. And, besides, the baby won't be crawling for ages, it's not even been born yet,' the man said, reasonably, with a note of humour in his voice.

Jenni froze. She recognised that voice.

Surely not? It couldn't be, could it? Here of all places?

She slowly looked up to peer through the foliage, and her worst fears were confirmed: it was Alex.

With a very pretty woman – a very pretty and very *pregnant* woman – standing next to him. A pretty pregnant woman with a wedding band on her finger.

Pushing her hair out of her face with a soil-covered hand, Jenni stood up, hastily brushed herself down and plastered a smile on her face.

Damn it, she'd hoped in the intervening years since they'd broken up he'd let himself go, but – and she hated to admit it – he looked great. Better, in fact, than when they were together.

'Alex! Hello. Hi!'

'Jenni! What on earth are you doing here?'

Jenni wasn't quite sure how to answer. It was a garden centre – what did he think she was doing?

'Um, I'm here with Mum. She's got a shady border that needs filling' – why, *why* was she speaking like Miranda Hart all of a sudden? – 'I, um, promised I'd help while I'm down for the weekend.'

'Your mum always did like her garden,' Alex said with a smile. 'We're visiting my mum and dad for the weekend too.' He paused, suddenly awkward. 'Sorry, I, um . . . This is Jelly.' Alex put an arm around the woman standing next to him, who smiled and stretched out her hand.

'Hi. Angelina – Jelly is just a nickname – nice to meet you. I've heard a lot about you.'

The last remark was said kindly, but made Jenni instantly want to run screaming to the hills. No one wanted their ex's girlfriend – *wife*, Jenni amended, noting the gold band again as Angelina tucked a strand of long auburn hair behind her ear – to say they'd 'heard lots about you'.

Jenni smiled back and shook Angelina's hand.

'Nice to meet you too. I haven't heard anything about you, but then again, why would I?' She attempted a laugh.

God, this was awkward. 'Er, anyway, congratulations on the baby,' she said, flicking her eyes down towards Angelina's stomach, and having a sudden, heart-stopping moment of doubt – perhaps she'd misheard and had now committed the greatest faux pas known to womanhood.

But both Alex and Angelina glowed and looked at each other with gentle smiles. Jenni would have found it nauseating if she wasn't experiencing massive relief over the fact she *hadn't* just implied that Angelina was looking a bit chubby.

'Thank you, we're so excited. We're due in December – just

in time for Christmas. A new baby in our new home, we can't wait!' Angelina said.

'New home?' Jenni looked at Alex.

'Yes, we decided we didn't want to bring up the baby in the city, so we've moving down here to be by the sea and near Mum and Dad. We're completing in a couple of weeks' time.'

Jenni's stomach flipped. She thought she detected a slightly sheepish look in his expression. It had always been *their* dream to move back nearer to where they grew up; be near the sea, deep in the rolling green hills that had been the backdrop to their childhoods. And now he'd taken the vision of the future they'd imagined together and given it to this woman smiling next to him.

There was a house they'd always loved – brick and flint, with wisteria growing around the door – that they'd decided was where they'd want to bring up their children. He'd played along, saying it was perfect and that, when the time came, they'd move. And she just knew, with a horrible feeling, that this was now the house that belonged to Alex and Angelina, and it would be *their* family playing in that beautiful garden, not hers.

Jenni couldn't speak, and the silence seemed to stretch, becoming harder to fill.

To Jenni's relief, her mother suddenly reappeared, dragging a flatbed trolley full of plants behind her.

'Ah, there you are. How are you getting on? Did you find 'Pam's Choice'? What's happened?' Taking in the stricken look on her daughter's face, she turned to see Alex and Angelina.

'Alex!'

'Hi, Annie, lovely to see you again.' Alex gave her his most charming smile. 'I'm afraid we've got to go, but nice to bump into you again, Jenni.'

'And good luck with that shady border!' Angelina added, before threading her fingers through her husband's and slowly walking away.

Jenni watched them leave, blinking fiercely, refusing to give in to the tears she felt burning her eyes.

'Oh, Jenni, love.' Her mum put an arm around her shoulders. 'Are you okay?'

Jenni nodded. Then shook her head. 'No, I don't think I am, actually. Did you know he'd got married?'

'No, I didn't. But I can understand you being so upset, love. You were together for a long time, it must be hard to see him with someone else.'

Jenni shook her head again. 'It's not that, I don't care about that. Well, I do, but I'm not upset. I'm mad that he's been able to just move on, find someone else and walk into the future that we'd imagined together, while I'm stuck. I can't go through all that again, knowing it might fall apart; that I might fall in love and be left again. I'm furious that . . .

that he's moved into *my* house with a woman called Jelly!' Jenni broke off, and bit the inside of her cheek. She was absolutely not going to cry.

Annie wrapped her arms tighter around her daughter, not entirely understanding what she was going on about, and gave her a long hug.

'You're going to be fine. Your dream is still waiting for you, you know.'

Jenni gave a tight smile and squeezed her mum back. They stood there for a moment more until her mum said, 'Come on, I think it's time for a cup of tea, and you can tell me why on earth he calls his wife Jelly.'

But before Jenni could explain, Annie yelped, 'Oooh, there's "Pam's Choice"! Quick, grab a couple before that woman takes them all!'

Jenni did as instructed, grateful for the distraction as she relived the shock of hearing Alex's voice; of seeing him again after all this time.

Loading the plants onto the trolley, she followed her mum towards the café. Why did she suddenly feel so very alone?

41

Ben had constructed a makeshift desk out of an old door, balanced on stacks of breeze blocks salvaged – with permission – from a building site on the neighbouring street. Spread across the desk haphazardly were sheets of A1 paper, sketchbooks and pencil drawings, fighting for space with an open laptop where Ben was working on the design for his parents' summerhouse.

Although he loved using pencil and paper, he was teaching himself how to draw using new software he'd recently invested in especially for the project. He'd taken a few of the initial drawings to Penny's to show his dad over lunch, and had now carefully flattened them out and used a couple of books to stop the sides curling back together, while he tried to recreate the designs using CAD.

Lunch at Penny's had been surprisingly relaxed. Arriving at eleven, Evie had greeted him at the door.

'Hello, Uncle Ben. I've been waiting for you,' she'd said in her best Bond-villain-style voice before leading him to the kitchen where the rest of the family were gathered.

As he'd walked in, he'd caught Penny mid-conversation with their parents, 'And now Ms Jones keeps asking me how his date went! Although, I think she might have more than a professional interest—Oh, hello, Ben, sorry, I didn't see you there. Would you like a glass of wine?' she'd asked innocently.

Before Ben could answer, Antony had charged into the house through the back door. 'It's ready, I need it now!' he'd demanded, striding towards the fridge.

Flinging open the door, he'd dragged a large joint of meat from the shelf, dumped it onto a waiting baking tray and then hurried back into the garden.

'He's using the Egg,' Penny had explained, shutting the fridge door. 'He's not done beef in it before, so it's all a bit fraught. I did say it would be much easier if I used the oven, but apparently Jeff at work did it and it was delicious, so there you have it.'

'Men and their barbecues,' said their mum. 'I remember your dad set fire to the shed one summer. I *did* say not to use lighter fluid.' She'd looked pointedly at her husband.

'And I've told you, there was a design fault. Argos recalled that make, if you remember.'

'Well, that is true, but I still think the lighter fluid was a mistake. Especially during a heatwave.'

Ben, having heard it all before, had decided to interrupt the thirty-year argument before it, inevitably, moved on to whose fault it was that the washing had been left out, which had only added to the blaze, and had turned to his dad.

'Here, Dad, have a look at these and tell me what you think,' he'd said, unrolling the drawings.

While the beef cooked in the Egg, they'd talked through the design and had decided what materials they'd need. And with his dad's notes in mind, Ben had started to look forward to making the revisions so that they could move on to the build phase of the project.

Their conversation had been interrupted by the arrival of Antony's barbecued beef, which had been just as tasty as promised.

Watching his mum and sister chat, Ben had realised that he didn't have the usual feeling of panic at being left alone with his dad, and was surprised to discover he actually felt relaxed during their family lunch for once.

After pudding, his dad had announced it was time for them to head off.

Penny and Ben had shared a knowing look. It was a family joke that his dad needed to allow a minimum of three hours for any journey.

'Okay, Dad, drive carefully.' Penny had given her dad a hug goodbye. 'Thank you for coming.'

'Bye, Dad, I'll make those changes to the designs and you can see what you think,' said Ben.

'Okay, sounds good. I'll find out what the builders' merchant has in stock next week and order up what we need.'

Ben had been shocked when his dad had given him a pat on the shoulder as he headed to the front door. It was the most physical contact they'd had in years.

'Bye, Grandma, bye, Gramps!' shouted Evie from the doorstep, waving goodbye.

'Well, that went well, I think,' said Penny, leading the way back to the kitchen. 'Shall we have another drink? Or would you prefer a *coffee*?' Penny had put a strange emphasis on the last word, staring at Ben pointedly.

'Oh, er, yes, I'd love a coffee actually,' said Ben.

He knew Antony was itching to demonstrate his new coffee machine and had promised Penny he would let him show it off without judgement.

'Excellent. Let me get that for you, sir,' said Antony, leaping towards the machine.

Ben preferred an Americano, but he hadn't had the heart to ask for something so simple, so he had requested a caramel macchiato instead.

What felt like two hours later, Anthony had set down a tall glass mug in front of him and had watched anxiously as Ben took a sip.

'Mmm, delicious, much better than Starbucks,' said Ben, trying not to wince as the hot coffee burnt his throat.

Anthony clapped him on the back in delight.

'I know right! And it's no trouble at all. I don't know why we all spend a fortune on takeaway coffee when we could just make it ourselves.'

Ben had thought he could get quite a few takeaway coffees before coming anywhere close to how much it would cost to buy a similar coffee machine, but he'd bitten his somewhat burnt tongue and smiled instead.

'Right, I promised I'd take Evie to the park so she can ride her bike. I'll see you in a bit, love.' He gave Penny a kiss and, calling to Evie, grabbed his wallet. 'I might pop to the café while I'm there,' he'd muttered as he'd headed to the front door.

'Did I hear that right?' Ben said. 'I've had to wait ages for a coffee I didn't even want, and now he's going to go the café?'

'You know what he's like. He loves a shiny, new toy, uses it twice and then gets bored with it. Don't worry, I'll put it on eBay next month and he'll forget he ever had it.' Penny gave a resigned shrug as Evie had run back into the room.

'Uncle Ben, Daddy said you might have gone by the time we get back, so please can you give this to Fred for me?' She'd thrust a tiny envelope at Ben, who had taken it carefully and put it in his pocket.

'Of course. I'll make sure he gets it when I see him next.'

'Thank you. See you soon!' Evie had given him a hug before running back to her dad. The front door had closed behind them as they'd left for the park.

'Talking of the cat, there's something I wanted you to look at,' Ben said, reaching into the back pocket of his jeans.

'Show me,' demanded Penny, taking a sip of her coffee.

'So, this cat that's been visiting me – you remember I told you I was worried its owner would think I was trying to steal it?'

Penny had nodded.

'Well, Evie's idea of writing to Fred inspired me, and I decided to contact the cat's owner by tying a note to his collar so I could reassure them I'm not a catnapper. Anyway, we've exchanged several letters and I got this one back a few days ago, and I'm not quite sure what to make of it.'

He'd passed the note to Penny, who'd started to read it out loud.

'*Dear sixty-six.*' She'd paused. 'Sixty-six?'

'That's me – we use our house numbers,' Ben said.

'Ah, okay.' She started again. '*Dear Sixty-six, thanks for the reassurance – didn't mean to accuse you of fencing stolen goods!*' Penny looked questioningly at Ben before continuing. '*For context, I was rushing out the door to meet someone, and to be honest, I got a bit stressed out by it all. Good thing it wasn't a date as they haven't been in touch since, which is a shame as I thought we'd had a good time and it would have been nice to meet up again.*'

Anyway, am relieved to know there are no bodies under your patio, but I'm ashamed to say Oscar (that's his actual name, not Fred!) is a bit of a thief. He has a habit of "borrowing" stuff from people, and he brings home random bits of litter so watch out. Better than mice, I suppose.'

'Well?' Ben asked.

Penny, ignoring him, read the note again before handing it back.

'Well what?'

'Well, apart from the fact that Fred is actually called Oscar' – Ben had been finding it hard to adjust to the new name – 'who do think wrote it? I've been looking for clues.'

Penny had looked thoughtful. 'I think it's a woman, maybe in her late thirties. She's obviously single and might have been for a while,' she declared.

'How could you *possibly* know that?' asked Ben, torn between awe and disbelief.

'Well, it's simple – you just have to read between the lines.'

'How?'

'Well, are the notes usually like this?'

'No, we don't normally write anything personal.'

'My point exactly.'

'Of what?'

'The date – or non-date – stressed her out, so it's not something she's in the habit of doing.' Penny had studied the

264

note again. 'And,' she'd added, 'I get the feeling she might have been in a relationship before, so a proper grown-up.' She sat back in her chair, satisfied with her appraisal.

'What do you think I should do?' he'd asked, impressed.

'I suggest you write back, but you also need to find yourself a girlfriend in the meantime, otherwise *this* could end up being your most significant relationship.'

Ben had glared at his sister.

Partly because she'd deserved it, but mainly to distract himself from the fact that, when she'd said 'find yourself a girlfriend', his mind had immediately conjured up an image of Jenni.

42

'They should call this place Pissheads,' declared Tim, laughing as he tore a chunk of baguette from the sharing plate and glanced around the underground space critically.

Back after his 'research' trip, he'd suggested they go for a drink after work at Magpie's, their usual haunt near the office, but Jenni wasn't in the mood for somewhere quite so noisy, and had instead suggested a recently opened bar situated in a renovated public convenience, which was actually much nicer than Tim was making out.

Jenni loved the old, glazed Victorian tiles, some slightly cracked, the stripped pine framework that marked the original toilet stalls, now fitted out with tables and benches, and the cosy lighting that, although now powered by electricity, used the original gas fittings.

Jenni was finding the cosy corner where the washbasins had once been, very soothing.

'So, tell me what happened, then,' Tim said, through

another mouthful of bread, as Jenni told him about bumping into her ex and his wife at the garden centre.

'And then he introduced Jelly—'

'I'm sorry, what now?' Tim interrupted, practically spitting out an olive. 'Jelly?'

'His wife.'

'His wife is named after a children's dessert?'

'No, her name is actually Angelina – Jelly's her nickname. Apparently.'

Tim mimed a dry retch. 'I think it's very infantilising. A worrying sign, if you ask me.'

'She was actually very nice. She said she'd heard lots about me,' said Jenni.

'That's not being nice, love. That's a power play.' Tim waved a breadstick at her. 'She's telling you to back off because she knows enough about you to take you down if the situation requires.'

'Hmm, I suppose it *was* a bit sinister, now that I think about it. But—' Jenni smacked Tim's hand out the way of the cheese board before he finished the lot, 'that wasn't the worst of it. Alex told me they're moving back home and I just know it's into *my* house.'

Seeing Tim's look of confusion, Jenni described the house she'd had her heart set on living in with Alex.

'The bastard,' hissed Tim, looking suitably outraged. 'Stealing your dream house from under your feet.'

'I know, right,' Jenni agreed, rearing back to avoid the cocktail stick Tim was now jabbing aggressively in her direction.

'Hang on, I've got an idea,' said Tim, wiping his hands on a napkin before picking up his phone. 'Well, for an IT expert, his social media privacy settings are terrible,' he mused, as he scrolled through Instagram.

'What have you found?' Jenni asked, taking a big gulp of her G&T, grateful that Tim was spying on her behalf.

'Evidence,' he said far too loudly, before leaning back triumphantly in his seat.

Jenni studied the photo: there was Alex, his floppy hair falling over his eyes, next to a glowing Angelina – she refused to use the J word, even in her head – and in the background was what Jenni assumed was their new house, if the estate agent's 'sold' board was anything to go by.

Jenni gave a squeak of joy. It wasn't her beautiful old wisteria-clad house with the picturesque garden of her dreams. It was a much more modern-looking house built from red brick. In front of the house was a square of bare grass, with an empty border running alongside a paved path, which explained why they were at the garden centre looking for non-toxic, baby-friendly plants.

Jenni felt her shoulders relax. She didn't know why it had bothered her so much, but knowing Alex hadn't stepped into their imagined future, and instead was carving out his own with someone new, made her feel better. She tried to explain how she felt to Tim.

'But you don't want to move to the country anyway, do you?' he asked, still puzzled.

'No, and if Alex and I had stayed together we might not have wanted to move either, but it was something we'd talked about, and so it upset me when it looked like he'd taken the future *we'd* planned together and had found it with someone else.'

Tim still looked puzzled, so Jenni tried again.

'I guess it's like how, when you break up with someone, you also break up with the future you'd imagined having with them. So you don't just lose the person, but the things you thought you were going to do together. And it just sort of hit me that Alex still has that future we'd planned, whereas I've spent all this time just ... I don't know ... *existing* in the present, and I don't feel like I've got a new vision of my life to look forward to. Does that make sense?' Jenni screwed up her face, hoping Tim understood.

'No. Well, a bit, maybe,' he amended, seeing her face fall. 'Now Paul and I are married, I expect to grow old with him. I don't know where or what we'll be doing, but if that suddenly changed and we weren't together, I'd have to say goodbye to all of that, not just him. And start drawing my future map again.'

Jenni nodded. 'Exactly! Seeing Alex made me feel sad and

lonely but also a bit annoyed that I haven't been thinking about what my new future looks like without him.'

Tim stared at her over the rim of his martini glass. He hesitated. 'I know I've been teasing you about it, but why don't you contact that fireperson again?'

'What, the one who ghosted me? I can't just randomly DM him and ask him out!'

Tim put up a hand. 'But why not? Perhaps he's just waiting for you to get in touch first.'

'Because . . . ' Jenni started, just as the waitress called last orders.

Tim ordered one last round before Jenni could argue.

'This is bad, I'm going to be a complete mess tomorrow,' she said, gulping down the last of her G&T before the new one arrived.

'You're at home tomorrow doing your tie-dye dunking business, though, right?' Tim asked with a barely contained hiccough.

'It's not *dunking*, it's a very precise process, actually,' said Jenni, indignantly.

'Soz, love.' Tim took their last two drinks from the waitress with a smile. 'Have you thought any more about where this "very precise process" is going to take place now you're the big-shot "creative director" of the Natural in Nature range?' he asked, performing quotation marks around her new title at Go Big.

After a frustrating email exchange with the facilities manager, the Go Big premises had failed to reveal a room that Jenni could use for the colour testing she needed to do for the new walking range, so it was looking like her shed was going to have to double-up as her research lab after all. Unless . . . talking about Ben had reminded her of their visit to the art gallery, and the memory of the large room in the unused part of the building they'd explored together suddenly came to mind. She remembered how she'd thought, at the time, that it could be perfect for an upscaled House of Oscar studio.

Excitedly, she told Tim.

'Genius! We should go and look. And . . .' he paused with a triumphant gleam in his eye, 'this is the perfect excuse to get in touch with the fireman again. Ask him to introduce you to the owner.'

Jenni's stomach flipped in excitement.

Only because she might have just found the perfect space for her business to grow into, she told herself sternly, and nothing to do with seeing Ben again.

'Okay, I'll do it right now. I need to start planning my new future and embracing possibilities and . . . whatever you said.' Jenni fumbled in her bag for her phone.

'Um, hold on, madam. I don't think four G&Ts down is the best time to message. I'm staging an intervention.' Tim plucked Jenni's phone from her hand. 'But I *am* holding you to this tomorrow, in the cold light of a sober dawn,' he continued.

'Urgh, you're probably right.'

'In the meantime, tell me again about when Alex appeared in front of you at the garden centre. I love that bit. I can't wait to tell Paul.'

'It's not funny, you know. I had a mud on my face, for goodness' sake,' Jenni said crossly, throwing the last olive at Tim who began to hoot with laughter.

*

It was pitch-black when Jenni arrived home. She'd had to take the night bus home – and it had felt like the journey had taken forever as they'd had to wait for ages at Elephant and Castle for a change of drivers, but finally she was back in the safety of her flat. Her first instinct had been to go straight to bed, but seized with an overwhelming need for food (to soak up all the alcohol, she could hear her mother lecturing) she headed to the kitchen and popped a couple of slices of bread into the toaster.

She was enjoying her toast with lashings of butter and Marmite with a cup of tea when the scrabble of paws against the back door announced Oscar's arrival. Finishing the last bit of her toast, Jenni put down her plate and pushed herself up from her seat to open the back door for him. She was too tired to go through the charade of trying to persuade him to use the cat flap.

'Honestly, Oscar, what would you do if I wasn't here to let you in?'

Oscar rewarded Jenni with some vigorous purring and rubbed against her legs, pleased to see her. She bent down to stroke him, immediately regretting it as, still worse for wear, she nearly lost her balance.

Cursing Tim, and her own weakness for being unable to resist that final G&T, she straightened up carefully, but not before she felt the scratch of paper against her hand. Plucking a note from Oscar's collar, she collapsed inelegantly back into her chair. Finally. A reply from 66!

She carefully unfurled the Post-it, squinting in an effort to focus.

Hi 38,

Pleased to report no more stolen toys.

I know it's hard, if you've been let down before, to summon up the strength to put yourself through it again. I don't really talk about it, but when my last relationship ended I was in a really bad place. I had other stuff going on, but finding out my ex had been cheating on me kind of tipped me over the edge. Sorry, that's a bit heavy! For what it's worth, I think you should give whoever it was you went out with another chance. In fact, I might need to take my own advice ...

Be brave and good luck!
66

She was struck by 66's honesty, and the last line about being brave really struck a chord – that's exactly what Tim had been saying too. Sliding a notebook she'd left lying on the table towards her, she grabbed a pen and started writing. There was no time like the present, she thought, to let 66 know she intended to take his advice.

*

Jenni dragged the spare pillow over her eyes and laid there, enjoying the feel of the cool fabric on her pounding head. This was all Tim's fault.

Now, she was paying the price.

But, hangover aside, that adrift feeling in the pit of her stomach that she'd been carrying around since her encounter with Alex had gone.

She felt . . . peaceful.

Her mind roved through her evening with Tim: laughing about Jelly, the relief that Alex wasn't in *her* house, the decision to message Ben again.

She stopped. Why had she agreed to do that?

Her phone buzzed and, lifting the corner of the pillow, she cranked open one eye and squinted at the four WhatsApp messages from Tim that had arrived in quick succession.

It's *not* a bad idea.

Do it.

Take a paracetamol first.

Love you!

Jenni eased herself up from the bed and walked gingerly down the corridor to the bathroom to wash away the excesses of the night's indulgence, and feeling the power shower massage her head and shoulders, she began to feel better.

After slowly getting dressed in leggings and matching tie-dye sweatshirt, she headed for the kitchen, put the kettle on and checked Oscar's food bowl, which was empty. In fact, now she thought about it, he'd appeared at the back door after she'd got home last night and, she suddenly recalled, he'd had a note tied to his collar.

Oh no! She remembered with a groan how she'd felt compelled, despite barely being able to focus, to write back immediately, telling 66 all about Alex and future mapping and – God help her – she might have even mentioned something about manifesting.

Panic shot through her – please say she hadn't put the note inside Oscar's collar?

Jenni sank her head into her hands, reminding herself that nothing could be as humiliating as the time she'd meant to email just Amy but had instead accidently replied-all to a company-wide memo about suitable work attire – fortunately, Clive had taken her comment about the tightness of his cycling shorts as a compliment.

A muffled meow at the back door alerted her to Oscar's presence and she rushed to open the door to let him in.

Her stomach flipped. He had a note attached to his collar.

She could only hope it was her drunken rambling letter from last night, undelivered.

With trembling hands, she leant down, released the string holding the piece of paper and flattened it out.

Bracing herself, she read the now-familiar spiky handwriting.

Oscar came over earlier this morning with a bit of string tied to his collar, but nothing attached. Perhaps he dropped it? Thought I'd better check in case it's urgent. Here's my number by the way.

A jolt went through Jenni. Oh, thank GOD.

Might be easier to text rather than use him as a postman!

The relief! Whatever she'd written last night hadn't made it to 66. Jenni sank back in her chair in gratitude, her knees weak.

After a few moments, she pulled herself together and stood up. Leaning back against the work surface, she gazed out of the window and took a sip of what was left of her tea. There, in the middle of the grass, was a rolled-up sheaf of A4 paper. No wonder Oscar had failed to deliver it to 66 – he would barely have been able to lift his head with the weight of the paper!

She heard a ping on her phone, alerting her to a new message – Tim checking in, no doubt, to make sure she'd contacted Ben.

She thought again about the previous note from 66. What had he signed off with? That was it: be brave and good luck.

Before she could chicken out, Jenni plonked down her mug, picked up her phone, opened Instagram, began typing and pressed send.

She'd done it, she'd messaged Ben.

43

'Ben's heard from that girl he bought the clothes from,' said Taz, through a mouthful of cheese and pickle sandwich.

Several of his workmates looked up from their lunch and *ooohed* as Ben looked at Taz crossly. 'I told you not to say anything. And anyway, we're not going on a date.'

'Oh dear God, here we go again,' said Vick, rolling her eyes and leaning over to grab the salt. 'This is all feeling very déjà vu.'

'Seriously, it's not a date – she's messaged me to ask if I'll introduce her to the owner of the gallery.'

'What, the time you went out for a date that wasn't a date?' Taz teased.

'And didn't contact her afterwards,' said Vick, less teasing, more accusing.

'I've told you, she's got a boyfriend.' Ben was really quite bored of having to go through all this again.

'That you don't actually know is her boyfriend,' Dean pointed out, much to Ben's surprise, as he could normally rely on Dean not to get involved.

'She said this person wasn't expecting her home till later!'

'They could be anyone, mate,' said Taz. 'And you told us you didn't even hear her properly.'

'And then you didn't get in touch to say you'd had a good time. You could have asked her if she a boyfriend outright. But no, you just ignored her. So rude!' Vick was getting into her stride now. 'And now she's been in touch – despite you ghosting her – and has suggested a valid reason to see each other so you don't freak out. It obvious.'

Ben opened his mouth to say something about it not being at all obvious, but before he could mount a defence, Taz had waded in.

'She messaged you this morning. Have you replied yet?'

Ben looked sheepish.

'Oh my days, man – she's had the guts to message you and you haven't even bothered to reply! No wonder you're single.' Taz shook his head, disappointed.

'You've got ten minutes before we have to be back on parade. Do it now,' Vick said in a gentler voice.

She and Taz were really working the good firefighter/ bad firefighter routine today, thought Ben ruefully. But they were right.

Or were they?

'What if . . .' he hesitated.

But Vick fixed him with a firm stare. 'Go. Now. Be brave.'

Her words struck a chord. It was what he'd written in his last note to 38. And he'd also said he should take his own advice.

He stood up to a round of applause and headed to the lockers to find his phone. Five minutes later he was back at the table.

'Well?' Vick asked.

'Done.' Ben smiled. 'Eight-thirty on Friday, same place as before.'

Taz clapped him on the back. 'See. How easy was that? Now let's go. Parade then the gym, and I'll race you on the treadmill!'

'Ah, it's so sweet watching you two compete for second place.' Vick threw them a condescending smile as she walked out of the mess. 'Come on, Dean, you can hold my towel.'

44

'Explain to me again why I'm here,' grumbled Tim, as he pulled out a metal chair beneath one of the large black parasols and sat down grumpily.

'Because Amy couldn't make it,' said Jenni, placing their drinks on the table and sitting down.

'Oh, great, that's nice, I'm not even first choice.' Tim pulled a face before taking a sip of his drink.

'How do I look?' Jenni asked, straightening her top nervously.

Tim turned to look her up and down. 'Hmm. Jeans, but your favourite ones that fit nicely rather than the baggy ones, top with a low v but not too much cleavage, hair washed *and* straightened, no make-up make-up. You look good, but without looking like you made an effort.'

Jenni sighed with relief. 'Perfect, just what I was going for! Thank you for noticing.' She smiled gratefully. 'I really appreciate you coming. I know you're missing quiz night.'

Tim sniffed, slightly mollified. 'Well, I couldn't abandon you, even if that means coming south of the river. I'm curious to get a look at this Ben, anyway, and I want to see the potential House of Oscar headquarters, too, of course.'

'I think you're going to love it, I really do. And you know what? I've been thinking that if the walking range does well, there might be other opportunities for us to work together.'

As they made plans that quickly escalated into both of them leaving Go Big to set up as joint directors of House of Oscar, the bar filled up and the noise increased. The DJ in the booth turned up the volume and people started spilling out onto the pavements, leaning against the large planters, nursing their drinks, desperately searching for a seat.

It wasn't until a woman in a tight silver jumpsuit and sky-high heels leant over to ask if she could take the vacant chair opposite them that Tim and Jenni looked up and noticed how busy it was.

'What time is it?' Jenni asked.

Tim glanced at his phone. 'Just gone nine. What time did you say you were meeting him?'

'I think we said eight-thirty,' said Jenni, trying to sound casual, as if the fact he was half an hour late wasn't a biggie.

She didn't *think* they'd said eight-thirty, she *knew* they had. God knows she'd checked his message about a million times. She picked up her phone to show Tim the message.

'Hmm, that's not good,' said Tim. 'But I'm sure there's a perfectly good reason why he's late,' he added hastily, seeing Jenni's face crumple.

'I should have known he wasn't interested when he didn't reply after the first time, shouldn't I?' she said.

'Perhaps we should fake an incident and call 999, and then he might show up,' laughed Tim.

Jenni glared at him. 'This is your fault, you know.'

'My fault? How is it my fault?' Tim replied, surprised.

'You made me contact him. I was quite happy—'

'Oh, please, you weren't happy at all. You'd just bumped into your ex with a jelly and you were covered in mud. There's nothing happy about that, love!'

Jenni was about to protest that she absolutely was happy when her phone buzzed. 'I'm too scared. You look,' she said, panic in her eyes.

Tim reached for the phone. There was a tense silence.

'Oh God. Just tell me, get it over with. What's he said?' she pleaded.

'Well, nothing, actually.' Tim paused dramatically before looking up. 'It's from your mum. The sweet peas didn't survive the frost. She thought you'd want to know.'

'For fuck's sake.' She looked dejectedly at Tim. 'Should

I DM him?' she asked just as her phone buzzed again. Tim read the message.

'Don't tell me. Mum again. Disaster with the dahlias? Foul play in the foxgloves?' Jenni took a swig of her drink.

Tim looked up. 'Ben's not coming.'

45

Ben ran along the platform and jumped on the train just as the doors started to close. He grabbed the pole to steady himself as the train slid away from the station, before falling gratefully into the seat nearest the glass partition. He dumped his backpack between his feet and leant back wearily, his head resting against the window.

Typical. Why today, of all days, had his watch been called out on a job just as their shift was about to end.

These things could happen at any time, but he hadn't been able to message Jenni until 9pm – half an hour after he was due to meet her – when he'd finally been stood down. A suspect package had been called in and all nearby divisions had been scrambled to attend. After the initial burst of adrenaline had passed, they'd spent hours waiting outside the pub where the alert had been raised, preparing for the worst, hoping for the best. Eventually, confirmation had come through on the radio – nothing to see here – so they could head back to the station. He'd showered as quickly as he could and ran for the train like a maniac.

The driver announced the next stop and he realised he was closer to the Fire Station Gallery than he was to home. He'd planned to go home first and get changed, but what if he just jumped off the train here and went to meet her now? Perhaps she'd still be there talking to Larry.

He was conscious of his outfit – a plain grey tracksuit that had seen better days, and his beaten-up old trainers, but so what? He sat frozen for a moment as the train shuddered to a halt at the station, not knowing what to do for the best. Should he stay on the train, go home to get changed and hope that Jenni might still there,? Or should he jump off the train now?

As the pre-recorded voice announced that passengers should stand clear of the closing doors, he grabbed his bag and leapt to his feet, dashing off the carriage, making it just in time before the doors clamped shut.

He sprinted down the platform and took the steps two at a time until he reached street level. If he ran, perhaps he'd make it before she left.

Not standing Jenni up suddenly felt urgent, necessary. And if he let her down, he suspected she wouldn't give him another chance.

Thankful that the gallery was only a short distance from the station, Ben weaved his way through the delivery drivers on bikes and the too-fast idiots on electric scooters. The pavement widened and Ben saw the tables under their black parasols and slowed his pace, scanning the crowd outside the bar.

He remembered the first time they'd met here, arriving to find Jenni waiting for him. He remembered seeing her looking down at her phone before she spotted him, the smile she'd given him making his stomach flip.

He ran a hand through his dishevelled hair, desperately trying to flatten the front where it had spiked after washing it, and took a steadying breath.

And then he saw her.

She was sitting with her back to him, but he recognised the long, curled hair that fell to her waist, almost reaching the seat of the chair, and when she turned her head slightly, the corners of her lips lifted in a smile.

And then he stopped in his tracks.

A man, blond hair teased into a quiff at the front, blue linen shirt highlighting a tan, was walking towards her table, and it was clear that Jenni was smiling at him.

Ben watched as the man slid down into the chair next to her, putting an arm around her and pulling her in for a hug. They stayed leaning against each other, the affection between them obvious.

Ben took a step back as he heard the man say, 'One more for the road, love. Then let's head home.'

*

Ben was relieved that the quiet, residential streets were empty as he made his way home. Every step that bought him closer to his flat only served to remind him of the night he'd discovered Luisa was seeing someone else.

She'd never liked that he worked shifts, but when she'd stopped complaining that he was never around and that she was fed up going out on her own, he'd thought she'd finally accepted that erratic hours came with the job he loved.

But he'd been wrong.

She'd just found someone else who could be there for the romantic dinners, or when she woke up in the early hours of the morning craving affection. He'd discovered by accident, although he often wondered if she had actually wanted to be caught out, too ashamed or too much of a coward to confess the affair to his face.

The day it had happened, a major fire on an industrial estate outside of London had started and crews from surrounding stations had been called in for support as they battled around the clock for several days to bring it under control. It was one of those jobs that affected everyone, no matter how long you'd been in the service.

The despair and the guilt you felt when you hadn't been

able to rescue everyone stayed with you, and left a mark that was impossible to get over, no matter how much counselling and support the service offered.

Ben had never forgotten the desperate voices of those trapped in one of the buildings, their plea for help piercing through the smoke and flames, until, eventually, they had been silenced by an explosion that had ripped the roof off the factory.

It had been the worst day he'd ever experienced on the job, and when they finally managed to put the fire out, days later, he'd returned home a shadow of his former self, the reality of what had happened already lodged in his brain.

He'd wearily caught the tube home, anticipating Luisa would be home by the time he got back. He hadn't had an opportunity to message her to let her know he was on his way, but as he'd passed by the off-licence next to the station, he'd picked up a bottle of wine, hoping the alcohol would numb the pain and sadness rippling through him. He'd smiled weakly at the girl behind the till, thanking her, before turning to leave the shop.

And that's when he'd spotted Luisa, framed in the huge window of the pub opposite, with a man Ben didn't recognise, but knew immediately wasn't a work colleague or a friend. There was something about the way they were sitting slightly too close together, seemingly unaware of everyone around them. And then the man had leant forward and Ben had watched as this stranger kissed her tenderly.

Even now, Ben could remember every second that had followed: when Luisa had finally got home, the shouting, the accusations, the recriminations, the sound of her crying from behind the bedroom door as she threw her clothes into a suitcase.

He remembered how the darkness had descended as the front door had slammed behind her.

Penny had found him three days later, in bed, the curtains closed, his phone turned off. He hadn't argued when she'd packed a bag for him and told him he was coming home with her.

Seeing Jenni with another man tonight just confirmed that he couldn't face going through all that again. He was better off alone.

He pulled the key from his pocket and let himself into his flat. Walking into the kitchen, he flicked on the light, hoping to see Fred waiting for him at the window, but there was no sign of him.

Frustration and disappointment coursed through him, but life would go on. He'd be fine.

Tomorrow, he'd be back at work, and he'd take a twisted delight in telling Taz and Vick that he'd been right, Jenni did have a boyfriend, and they should drop it once and for all.

46

As it turned out, the evening hadn't been a complete disaster, Jenni reflected. Even though Ben had been a no-show, they'd found Lenny and he had let them have another look at the second floor and had been open to the idea of letting the space out. They'd left it that she'd be in touch to arrange a follow-up meeting with Clive.

After reading Ben's message saying he wouldn't be able to make it, she'd been disappointed, but Tim had persuaded her – after a couple more G&Ts – to reply, suggesting a breezy 'no worries, another time'. But as the minutes turned to hours, her disappointment turned to anger as he failed to respond.

The bastard.

'Are you dwelling?' Tim walked into the kitchen resplendent in a bright yellow and purple tie-dye T-shirt with matching shorts. He'd missed the last train home and had stayed over at Jenni's. Refusing to put yesterday's clothes back on, declaring the linen shirt far too rumpled – 'I look like a rhinoceros's arse', were his exact words – Jenni had dug out some of her samples for him to wear instead.

'I just think it's bloody rude that he couldn't even be bothered to reply, that's all.' Jenni banged two mugs down on the counter and flicked the kettle on. 'And he's not even messaged this morning to say sorry about last night,' she continued. 'It's just plain, old bad-manners. Oh God, I sound like my mother.'

'Here, eat a croissant. Carbs make everything better,' said Tim sympathetically.

Jenni tore a corner off the pastry, shoving it in her mouth, chewing crossly. 'You're right, it does. I feel a bit sad now, though,' she added glumly.

'Maybe he isn't the one, but that doesn't mean the one isn't still out there waiting for you to find them.'

Jenni sighed. 'I suppose so. But I think, from now on, I'll just dedicate my time to the one man who *is* in my life: Oscar. Although, speaking of the devil, I haven't seen him yet this morning.'

'Perhaps he's with the mysterious Sixty-six,' said Tim, spreading jam and more butter on his croissant. 'I think that last note suggested someone younger than I'd imagined,' he mumbled. 'Perhaps you should find out and call them now you've got their number.'

'I'm not going to call a complete stranger, and besides, I told you, I'm never dating again.'

'So dramatic, but I love it.'

Jenni rolled her eyes. 'What time are you going home? Maybe we could see if Amy's around for a coffee in the park before you have to go?'

'Paul's out, so that sounds perfect. You can show me your current dunking headquarters, in the meantime.'

'I've told you before, I don't just dunk. It's a highly scientific process. But fine, let me find Oscar first. He's normally here when I get up, and never misses breakfast . . .'

*

Jenni gave the Dreamies another rattle and called for Oscar even louder than last time. She'd been standing in the garden for half an hour, shaking treats and shouting his name, but so far, no luck. He hadn't come home before she and Tim had left to meet Amy after breakfast, there'd been no sign of him when she'd got back from the park or at bedtime, and even though she was convinced he'd finally come home overnight, the kitchen was empty when she'd got up the next morning.

She thought back to the last time she'd seen him, on Friday morning. She remembered the noise from the builders working on the house up the road had already started, even though it had just turned eight. He'd been his normal self, demanding more food even though she'd just put down a fresh bowl of biscuits, curling around her ankles until she caved in and poured out more. He'd reluctantly allowed her ten minutes of tummy rubs before heading to the sofa for a nap. She'd given him a final stroke behind the ears, then she'd left for work.

That meant she hadn't seen him for over forty-eight hours, and now she was worried something might have actually happened to him.

Picking up her phone, she called her mum, letting it ring for several seconds.

She was about to hang up when a man answered, taking her by surprise before she realised it was Alan.

'Hi . . . it's Jenni, is Mum there?'

'She's out in the garden, she'll be back in a sec. Are you okay? You sound a bit flustered.'

Alan answering the phone had thrown her. Her dad had always picked up the landline, and even after all this time, she still expected his to be the voice she heard first when she rang home. The memory of his comforting tone, combined with the worry about Oscar, bought tears to her eyes.

'Jenni, are you still there?' Alan's anxious voice cut through the silence.

'Sorry, yes. I'm worried about Oscar, my cat. He's been missing for two days and I'm not sure what to do.' Jenni's voice broke, saying the word 'missing' out loud made her realise how scared she was that something terrible might have happened to him.

'I'm sure he's fine, probably hiding somewhere, but I understand why you're worried,' Alan said soothingly. 'Did he have a tag on his collar or anything like that?'

'No, I've been meaning to get it done, but just didn't get around to it.'

'Listen, here's your mum. I'm sure he'll be home soon.'

'Hello, darling, when did you last see him?' Her mum got straight to the point.

'Friday morning. It's been nearly forty-eight hours now, Mum, it's just not like him.' Jenni bit her lip.

'Have you tried calling him?'

'Of course I have! I've been outside shaking a box of bloody biscuits for hours. Upstairs must think I've gone mad!'

'Well, have you asked the neighbours if they've seen him?' asked her mum. 'You remember when Helly, our old cat, went missing? She'd got locked in Jon's tool shed.'

Jenni did remember. It had been a wet Sunday evening, but she'd been so frantic that eventually her dad had agreed to knock on the door of every house in the village with a picture of Helly, asking if anyone had seen her.

She remembered the relief she'd felt when they'd finally got a call saying Helly had been found safe and well, curled up under the potting table in an open bag of peat-free compost, snoring like she didn't have a care in the world.

'I haven't, but that's a good idea.' She would post a photo of Oscar on the street WhatsApp, asking if people could check their sheds as well.

'And is there anywhere else he might go?' asked her mum. 'Has he been making a nuisance of himself in anyone's garden or anything?'

Jenni paused. Why hadn't she thought of that? He was probably just at 66's house.

'Actually, there is somewhere he's been going – they've even built him his own little house in their garden. We've been writing notes to each other attached to Oscar's collar, but I've got their number as well, now. I could send them a text to see if he's there.'

'I think that would be a good place to start, darling. I'm sure he's absolutely fine.'

'Thanks, Mum. I really hope so.'

'Let me know how you get on. I'll call you later. Bye, love.'

Jenni ended the call, her worry turning to annoyance. If Sixty-six thought they could just keep Oscar, they had another think coming!

She was sure she had kept the note with their phone number on it, but it wasn't in the drawer where all the other random things like rubber bands and bits of string ended up, and it wasn't hiding in the pile of takeaway menus.

Then she remembered: she'd pinned it to the corkboard next to the fridge to keep it safe.

Grabbing her phone she quickly typed, *Hi, it's 38, I can't find Oscar, is he with you?*, entered 66's number and pressed send.

47

Jenni had been so certain that 66 would say Oscar was with them that when they didn't immediately reply, she'd felt poleaxed all over again.

The street WhatsApp group were lovely, sending replies to her post promising to keep an eye out, but no one could remember seeing Oscar over the past few weeks, let alone days, which did nothing to quell Jenni's growing concern.

Her imagination was running wild, filled with awful thoughts of Oscar being hit by a car, hiding wounded in a nearby garden. Or even worse, what if . . .

Thankfully, at that moment, Amy rang.

'Any news?' she asked in reply to the frantic text message Jenni had sent her.

'No, nothing. I'm getting really scared now.'

'What about this person at number sixty-six he's been visiting?'

'I texted the number, but I haven't heard back from them yet,' Jenni replied, emotion making her voice crack a little.

'Have you checked if the message was delivered?' asked Amy.

'No, but . . .'

'Well, check now, then. Perhaps you put the wrong number in, or they haven't received it yet?' Amy urged.

Jenni looked. 'It's the right number, but I can see they've not read it.'

'You know, you could just go to number 66 and see if they're in? It's literally just down the road from you.'

'Oh. Yes. That's a good idea. I'll go now,' Jenni said, brightening. 'I don't know why I didn't think of it sooner.'

'You're in shock and not thinking straight,' said Amy. 'Go now. I bet Oscar's been there all along.'

Telling Amy she'd be in touch later, Jenni ended the call and checked her messages again in case there had been a reply while she'd been talking. Still nothing. But never mind, she couldn't wait any longer, she'd just pop along to 66 Copestone Road now. At least she'd be doing something practical rather than just worrying.

Hurrying from her flat, she turned right at her front gate and, checking the numbers as she passed, she walked briskly to number 66, her heart burning with hope that Oscar would be there.

Number 66 Copestone Road was a smart-looking

semi-detached house with a pink front door at the end of a short black and white checkerboard path. Jenni stood on the doorstep and rang the bell, encouraged to hear voices within, but when the door finally opened the woman who answered just looked at her blankly. She obviously had no idea what Jenni was talking about and she certainly hadn't seen a tabby cat, let alone been feeding one and tying notes to its collar.

'I'm sorry, love, he's not been coming to our house. If I see him I'll let you know.!'

As the door shut in her face, Jenni felt even more despondent than before – she'd been so certain she'd find Oscar there.

But it did confirm one thing, if 66 didn't live on the same street as her, Oscar had obviously been roaming further away. Texting as she walked back up the street to her flat, Jenni sent another message to 66.

> Hello, sorry, it's 38 again. Please could you
> tell me your address? I thought you lived on
> the same road as me (Copestone) but I've just
> visited 66 and it's not you!

*

Ben lent back in his chair and stretched. He'd caught up on his sleep, had enjoyed a leisurely late breakfast and then spent the rest of the day absorbed in the plans for the summer-house. He'd sent the revised version to his dad and had been chuffed by the reply – Ian had asked for a few final tweaks, but otherwise he'd been full of enthusiasm and was keen to get the project underway, so Ben had spent the day making the changes his dad (and mum) had requested. Keeping in touch was so much easier now than the awkward phone calls of the past, and the shared project made Ben feel closer to his dad than he had for a long time.

Satisfied with the changes he'd made, he emailed the plans to his dad and then stood up. Time for a break.

In the kitchen, a drink in hand, he picked up his phone, which he'd left lying on the table. Realising it was still on silent from when he'd been at work, he saw loads of notifications, texts and WhatsApp messages flash up on screen – Penny was getting increasingly annoyed at his lack of response; he'd deal with that later. He scrolled through the texts, stopping at one from a number he didn't recognise.

Hi, it's 38, I can't find Oscar, is he with you?

Followed by a request for his address. With a lurch, Ben realised he hadn't seen Fred, or rather Oscar, for a few days now and it was unusual to have gone so long without seeing him. Poor 38, they must be frantic.

He quickly tapped out a reply, giving his address and

saying he was home now if they wanted to come round, and pressed send thinking it would be strange to finally meet Oscar's owner.

*

Spotting the number 66 etched into the glass panel, Jenni made her way down the path to the communal front door. As soon she'd got 66's reply with their address, she'd rushed straight round to Henfast Road, which backed on to her road, passing the house on the corner and nearly tripping over the huge pile of sand their builders had left on the pavement outside. Her mind frantic with worry, she reflected that the one teeny tiny positive about the whole horrible situation was that she had been so busy stressing about Oscar that she hadn't thought about Ben once.

Now, standing outside the building marked with the number 66, she saw the numerous buzzers for the flats and wasn't sure which one to press. Taking a few deep breaths, she tried to think logically. If Oscar normally waited for 66 outside that had to mean their flat had direct access to the garden. She paused for moment and then pressed down on the buzzer labelled 'ground floor flat'.

She heard footsteps approaching and, a few seconds later, the door opened.

*

Jenni?'

'*Ben?*'

They stared at one another, puzzled.

'What are you doing here? I mean . . . it's just . . . how did you get my address?' Ben trailed off.

'I'm . . . I've lost my cat, I . . . Oh—' Jenni paused as, suddenly, the penny dropped.

Ben stared at her.

'You're number thirty-eight, aren't you?' he asked, his voice so quiet Jenni could barely hear him.

'Yes,' she whispered. 'And you're number sixty-six?' she said, her heart in her mouth. 'Have you seen my cat?'

48

Jenni looked around the tidy room, with its white walls and Ikea furniture, and felt sad that Ben lived in such a bland home, without the colour and clutter she loved to surround herself with. She glanced at the makeshift desk in the corner, paper scattered over its surface, and wondered if he'd written the notes to her there, imagining him hunched over, considering every word.

It had been obvious from his reaction that he had had no idea she was number thirty-eight while they'd been corresponding via Oscar, but that wouldn't stop her picking over the bones of their more recent, more personal letters with a fresh perspective. And she definitely had a few things to say about him no-showing and then ghosting her again. But right now her focus was on Oscar.

After the shock of discovering who each other was, Ben had invited her in so they could search for Oscar together.

'So, have you seen him?' she asked as soon as Ben closed the door behind them.

'No. I don't think I've seen him since Thursday.'

He saw the hope disappear from Jenni's eyes and quickly added, 'But he might be in the house I made for him. I haven't checked in there yet.'

'Does he use it?' she asked, as Ben unlocked the back door and they stepped out into the communal garden together.

'I've never seen him go in,' Ben confessed. 'But he does sit on top of it, and that was where he was hiding all those toys I mentioned.'

Jenni crouched down to look inside the box. 'Empty.' She looked up at Ben. 'Where is he, if he isn't here?'

'We'll find him,' Ben said, gently. 'Let's go back in and come up with a plan.'

Jenni blinked back tears.

'Come on,' he repeated, touching her arm fleetingly. 'It will be okay. We'll find him.'

Jenni could only nod mutely and pray he was right.

49

Jenni stopped abruptly outside her flat and turned to Ben. 'This is me,' she said, pushing open the metal gate.

'Thank you. For helping and everything. I really appreciate it.'

'It's okay,' said Ben. 'Try and get some sleep. I'll come over in the morning and we can blitz the neighbourhood with the posters.'

Jenni nodded. 'I'll call my boss first thing and take a day's holiday. I'm owed loads of leave.'

It was far later than Jenni realised. After the initial search of the cat house, behind the bins and at the very end of Ben's garden, he'd made them both a cup of tea and they'd talked about the bizarre set of circumstances they found themselves in. And it *was* bizarre, they both agreed.

Ben had explained how he had turned up at the gallery that night, but had left quickly when he saw Jenni with another man, and Jenni had reassured him that Tim was not only her work friend, but also happily married. If it wasn't all so ludicrous, it would have been funny.

But with Oscar missing, nothing was funny to Jenni, and while she was – she had to admit – relieved she hadn't been stood up by Ben, *again*, she couldn't imagine how they might be able to move past all the confusion and coincidence.

Jenni watched Ben walk away, fighting the urge to call out to him and invite him in, not wanting to be on her own, or, if she was honest, not wanting the evening to end. They still had so much to unpick.

But instead of calling him back, Jenni pushed open her front door, hope flaring that Oscar might be there waiting for her.

But the flat was empty and Oscar still wasn't home.

Jenni pulled on her pyjamas and sat despondently on the sofa. She thought of Oscar hiding somewhere, injured and scared, all alone and in pain. Her heart broke to think of him so vulnerable and confused, not knowing how to get home, wondering why she hadn't rescued him.

A ping on her phone made her jump. She picked it up to see a text from Ben.

> I know you're worried but we're going to find
> him, I promise.

And for some reason she couldn't explain, she believed him.

*

Exhausted, Jenni sat slumped at the kitchen table, covering her face with her hands. They'd been out since ten that morning. Now, nine hours later, posters of Oscar covered every lamppost, fence, tree, sign and wall in the neighbourhood. They'd also knocked on every door, but no one they'd spoken to had seen him.

Ben sat down opposite her, reaching for her hands, and pulled them away from her face. Despair was making her brown eyes muddy and her skin was pale and ghostly.

'Listen, we've done everything we can for now,' he said. 'Oscar's photo is circulating on every WhatsApp group in a five-mile radius, we've put posters up and dropped leaflets at every house on every street. Everyone will be looking out for him. We just have to cross our fingers and wait.'

Jenni nodded. 'I know. Thank you. It's just now we've done everything we can, I feel like there's nothing left I can do. And ... just ... what if ... '

Tears filled her eyes and Ben squeezed her hands tight, praying he'd be able to keep his promise and bring Oscar home to her.

50

The next morning, bleary-eyed and shattered, Jenni stepped into the reception of Go Big, now redecorated to reflect Clive's latest cycling obsession, and tried to quell the sick feeling in the pit of her stomach. She felt awful coming into work. What if Oscar came home while she was out and she wasn't there? Ben had said that he'd check her garden during the day in case he turned up, and that went some way to help her feel a little calmer.

After living on her own for so long, relying solely on herself, it felt strange to have someone be there for her again, and she was wary of getting too used to it. But, for now, it was nice to have someone who cared.

Approaching her desk, Tim, already sitting at his computer, looked up and, upon seeing her face, jumped to his feet to give her a hug.

'Oh come here, love. It's good to see you.' He pulled away to look at her properly. 'You look bloody awful!'

'Cheers, Tim, that's made me feel loads better.' Jenni dumped her bag on the floor and pulled out her chair. 'But you're right. I look and feel terrible.'

'Listen, I know you're worried, but you need to look after yourself,' he said gently, taking her hand.

'Tell me what's been going on.'

'Well, he's been missing for a week now, and I'm going out of my mind,' she said, wearily.

'And what about Ben?'

Jenni gave him a hard stare. 'What about Ben? He's just been helping me, that's all.'

'Sorry, I didn't mean to be insensitive. It's just, whenever I've called you, you've been with him. I just wondered if anything had happened between you, I mean.' He leant forward, giving her hand a squeeze.

'No, nothing has happened, but . . .' she hesitated. 'Well. I do like him. He's been so kind and . . . I suppose under different circumstances . . .' She trailed off, a shadow of regret passing over her face.

'I know you're really worried about Oscar, and Ben does sound like a nice guy, which is why he's helping you, but are you sure there's not something more there? I just can't believe he'd be putting so much effort into finding Oscar if he didn't maybe have feelings for you too.' Tim raised a hand to stop her interrupting. 'Look, I get it. You're scared of getting hurt again, but for what it's worth, I don't think it's just about a missing cat. I think he likes you too. And I think you need to take a chance, just like I did when I met Paul.'

'Maybe, but you know, it's so hard. What am I going to do if we don't find Oscar? How can I even be thinking about anything with Ben right now? And anyway, what about everything we said to one another in the notes, before we knew one another? It's so complicated, Tim . . .' She put her head in her hands.

'Oh Jenni. Listen. I'm only saying this because I want you to be happy.'

She looked up as he continued.

'It's only as complicated as you want to make it. You've met someone you like. He seems to like you too. Okay, so the anonymous notes thing is a bit weird, perhaps, or maybe it's just the most unusual meet-cute story you've ever heard. Either way, you do have a choice. To be *brave*. To look to your future and paint a different picture for yourself – maybe one with your dream house *and* Ben in it.'

Jenni smiled. 'That's one of the most profoundly moving and emotionally intelligent things I've ever heard you say.'

'I'm touched, but don't try and change the subject.'

Jenni took a deep breath before repeating tentatively, and so quietly Tim almost didn't hear her, 'Okay. I'll be brave.'

51

Evie crouched down to look inside Oscar's house.

'Nope, he's not here.' She looked up at Ben. 'Do you think he'll ever come back?'

'I really hope so,' Ben replied. 'We've done everything we can to try and find him.'

Evie nodded solemnly. 'I saw the posters on the trees. Poor Oscar.'

'We'll keep looking. Jenni, his owner, thinks we should put up some new posters at the weekend, so you could help me design them if you like?' Ben suggested.

'Okay,' said Evie, looking pleased to be asked to help. 'I'll get my glitter pens from my bag.'

Penny had rung that morning in a flap. She'd been called into court unexpectedly and needed him to pick up Evie from school. Quite frankly, he'd been pleased to have a distraction from the endless worry about Oscar. And Jenni.

Something had definitely shifted between them. The boundaries had moved and he couldn't stop thinking about her. He could see the pain she was in, how worried she was about Oscar, and he was finding it increasingly difficult to resist gathering her up in his arms.

He took Evie the long way through the park, stopping at Scrambled on the way home.

As Evie worked her way through the squirted cream piled high on the 'don't tell your Mum' hot chocolate, Ben looked around the café, quieter now after the rush of the post-school pick-up, and remembered sitting here with Jenni that very first time. How they'd ended up chatting for ages, how easy and comfortable it had been, the pulse of electricity that he'd felt when his leg had bumped hers under the table, and when he'd caught her looking at him, her dark eyes wide and beautiful.

Yes, it was – he searched for the right word – *odd*. Odd that she'd also been the person he'd been sending notes to, had told things to that he hadn't told anyone else, even before he'd realised it was her he was writing to. It felt awful to admit, especially while Oscar was missing, but he really liked her, really liked spending time with her, and couldn't help but worry that it all might stop when they did, finally, find the cat.

His thoughts were interrupted by the sound of his phone pinging with a new message, and he smiled, despite himself, to read a text from Jenni.

Thanks for checking for Oscar at mine earlier.
Felt terrible leaving for work today in case
he came home. I know you would have let
me know if you saw him, but just checking
anyway?

Ben quickly typed a response.

No, sorry, no sign of him, I'm afraid.

He paused before adding more.

But listen, do you want to come to mine
tonight? I've got my niece with me till her
mum picks her up later, but I could cook?

He waited nervously for a reply as the three dots appeared, indicating she was typing, then stopped, then appeared again.

That would be lovely, thank you.

52

Jenni, who hadn't been able to concentrate all day anyway, slipped out of work early and rushed home to grab a quick shower before heading to Ben's.

She kept her head down as she walked back from the station so she could avoid seeing the posters of Oscar's face, his pirate patch of black fur surrounding one eye, staring out at her from every lamppost she hurried past.

She was beginning to worry that she'd never even know what had happened to him, let alone see him again. She shook her head to dislodge the thought, and instead tried to focus on how she felt about having dinner with Ben. Talking to Tim had made her realise just how much she liked him, but she wasn't sure how, or even when, she'd feel brave enough to approach the subject with him.

Reaching the corner of her street, she turned into Copestone Road, tutting as she stepped around yet another huge pile of sand that had been left outside the vacant house being renovated. She'd nearly tripped over a cement mixer that had been set up by the builders on the side of the road the other night, and she hoped the work would be finished soon as she was fed up hearing the drilling that seemed to go on all day.

She showered quickly, threw on a pair of comfy jeans and a House of Oscar sweatshirt, and grabbed a bottle of wine from the fridge, before slamming the door behind her.

Standing by the front door at Ben's flat, she felt suddenly nervous. Dinner at his house, even with his niece in attendance, felt different. More intimate this time, somehow, and as she pressed the buzzer and waited, she felt something like butterflies in her stomach.

The front door finally opened, and a small girl in school uniform, with her hair in pigtails and covered in glitter, grinned a toothy smile at her.

'Hello. I'm Evie. And you're Jenni,' she said solemnly, before turning on her heels and heading back indoors.

'Come,' she commanded as Jenni shut the door behind them and followed Evie into Ben's flat.

'Jenni's here,' called Evie, leading her into the kitchen where Ben was sliding a baking tray full of fish fingers into the oven.

'Hey,' he said, slamming the over door shut. 'Sorry, dinner's a bit delayed, we got distracted drawing some pictures of Oscar. The new posters,' he explained sheepishly.

'That's okay,' Jenni said. 'And thank you for inviting me over,' she added. 'It's really kind of you.'

'Why don't you go and sit with Evie while I tidy up in here?'

'You can borrow my gel pens if you like,' offered Evie generously. 'But you have to put the lids back on or they dry out.'

'Right, okay, noted,' said Jenni, joining her at Ben's desk, which was covered in drawings of cats. 'I like that one,' she said, pointing at a particularly colourful picture. 'Why's he on an iceberg?'

'It's Elsa's castle, silly.'

'Oh, of course it is, sorry,' Jenni replied, chastened.

Sitting quietly with Evie while she drew, the smell of fish fingers cooking in the background made Jenni feel like a child again herself, when all she had to worry about was making sure she didn't lose the lids so her gel pens didn't dry out.

'Dinner's ready,' called Ben, and Evie jumped up, rushing to the kitchen, all thoughts of pen etiquette forgotten.

'Shall I get the squashy trays?' she asked her uncle. 'So we can have a sofa picnic?'

'A sofa picnic?' Jenni asked, confused.

'Yes, it's when we have dinner on our laps on the sofa and watch TV. Don't you have them?' Evie asked, her forehead creasing.

'Ah,' said Jenni. 'Every night's a sofa picnic for me. I'm so good at it, I don't even need a special tray,' she said with a smile.

They decided on a Pixar film to watch, and as they sat next to each other on the sofa, trays on laps, fish fingers bizarrely sticking out the top of a pile of spaghetti bolognese – an Evie special, apparently – Jenni felt herself relax for the first time in days.

She didn't feel the need to make polite chitchat or be on her best behaviour, she could just sit back and watch the movie. Or perhaps, more truthfully, watch Ben watching the movie, her stomach flipping when he glanced over at her and caught her looking, before giving her a smile that made her melt.

They had just finished eating another of Evie's favourites – jelly and rice pudding – when the buzzer went, and Ben got up to answer the door to his sister.

Jenni helped Evie collect all her pens and put them back into her pencil case while Evie gathered up her drawings of Oscar, handing one to Jenni.

'Here you go, this one's for your poster. I really hope you find him soon.'

'Thank you – this is a beautiful picture. I hope we find him soon too.'

Behind her, in the hallway, Jenni could just about hear Ben whispering, before his sister hissed back, 'Of course I won't embarrass you, I just want to see her for myself.' And she braced herself as the door was flung open with force.

Five foot four, with long blonde hair, wearing a smartly tailored trouser suit, Penny stepped forward with a friendly smile.

'Hello, I'm Ben's sister. I'm really sorry to hear about your cat,' she continued. 'You must feel bloody awful, I'm so sorry.'

Jenni, disarmed by Penny's kind directness, nodded. 'Thank you. I just feel so helpless, but Ben's been helping me try to find him, and Evie's drawn me a lovely picture for a new poster.'

She was about to show Penny the drawing, but Ben turned to his sister.

'Right, I think that's everything. I'm sure you're in a hurry and need to get home.' He quickly ushered a protesting Penny and Evie towards the door.

'Don't think I don't know you're trying to get rid of me,' Penny whispered loudly as Ben bundled her down the hallway. 'But thank you for picking up Evie. I'll ring you tomorrow.'

She hugged her brother briefly. 'She seems nice,' she said quietly.

'She *is* nice,' said Evie, hugging Ben goodbye. 'I like her.'

Ben found Jenni in the kitchen, washing up.

He stood in the doorway for a moment, watching her,

a curl of hair falling forward over her face as she bent over the sink, her sleeves rolled up to reveal slender wrists, the cut of her jeans accentuating the curve of her hips and slim waist.

He was seized with the sudden urge to wrap his arms round her, kiss the place where her jawline met her neck. Shaking his head to get rid of such thoughts, he picked up a tea towel and cleared his throat as he began to dry. 'You don't need to do this, but thank you,' he said. 'And sorry about that.'

'Don't worry, it's fine.' Jenni smiled. 'She's just protective of you. I can understand that.'

Ben winced. 'Yeah, she worries about me.' He paused. 'She was great after I split up with my ex and I don't think I could have got through it without her, or Evie, come to that. Especially the way my dad reacted.'

He paused, remembering how awful he had felt, the trauma of that terrible fire and then finding out about the affair so closely linked in his mind.

'It must be lovely to have a sibling. When my dad died, I only had my mum. We're really close, but she had her own grief to deal with. I know I'm really lucky to have friends like Tim and Amy, but I'm not sure it's quite the same as having a brother or sister.'

'I'm really sorry to hear about your dad,' Ben said, gently. 'Sounds like you've had some tough times with your dad?'

Jenni asked, rinsing the last fork under the cold tap. 'Sorry, you don't have to talk about it if you'd rather not.'

'It's okay,' Ben said, 'It's just not something I really talk about much. Dad didn't handle my breakdown very well, and our relationship suffered because of it. I think because he'd been through one too, and it was something he felt ashamed about – different times and all that. But, weirdly, it was Oscar who got us talking again. Dad helped me build his cat house and it gave us a way to communicate again. It's made me understand him a bit more, and as a result I feel less angry with him.'

'That sounds like a really difficult time for you. How are you feeling now?' Jenni asked.

Ben paused. How *did* he feel now? The breakdown was something in his past, but he still carried the fear that those feelings might come back one day.

'I have more good days than bad days, and I know how to handle the bad days now. I had a bunch of therapy sessions, so I know that it was a combination of things, not just one event that caused it.'

He took a breath, wanting to be honest with Jenni. It felt important, like if he didn't, then they might not have a chance. He needed to be brave, take a chance.

'It wasn't just splitting up with my girlfriend that was the problem. I discovered she was cheating on me on my way home from attending a fire, the worst I've ever seen.'

Standing by the sink, drying the final plate for much longer than needed, Ben told Jenni what had happened that day.

When he finished, Jenni turned towards him, she didn't speak but her eyes were full of emotion and Ben appreciated that more than any empty platitude. She reached for the tea towel he was holding to dry her hands, and as she did, she felt the world around them still. He moved closer, and she tilted her face up to him. His breath brushed her cheek as he slid his arms around her waist, pulling her against him.

The shrill sound of her phone caused her to jump back, knocking a bowl still draining by the sink and watching it crash to floor.

'Oh my God.'

'Bloody hell.'

The moment broken, Jenni hastily apologised and dashed to grab her phone from the table, glancing at the display.

'It's not a number I recognise,' she said, frantically answering the call and stepping out into the hall.

Ben took a dustpan and brush from the cupboard under the sink and began sweeping up the broken bowl, trying not to listen.

'Hello?'

'*Yes.*'

'Oh my God. Where?'

'*Yes.*'

'Okay.'

'Thank you. Thank you so much. I will. Thank you.'

It was only after Ben had dropped the broken shards wrapped in newspaper into the recycling bin that he realised that Jenni was still in the hall. He found her sitting in silence on floor. Her face was pale and she was still holding her phone to ear.

'Are you okay?' he asked, crouching down to her.

She opened her mouth to reply, but nothing came out.

'Jenni, tell me. What's wrong? What's happened?' Ben took her phone from her and could feel her hands trembling.

'They've found Oscar.'

53

Jenni had been up, washed and dressed since six-thirty.

She still couldn't quite believe Oscar had been found, and she was dazed and confused, even after a fitful night's sleep.

She'd answered her phone impatiently, ready to give the caller the brush off for ruining the moment with Ben, but when the woman on the end of the line asked if she was speaking to the owner of a missing cat, Jenni had felt her veins run cold and her knees buckle beneath her as she braced to the hear the news she had been dreading for the past week.

But instead, the woman said she was calling from a veterinary practice in Kent and that Oscar had been found alive and well, a bit hungry and tired, but absolutely fine.

She'd been barely coherent as she'd struggled to understand how on earth he'd ended up so many miles from home.

Jenni listened as the vet explained that he'd been found in a storage shed at a builders yard in the Isle of Sheppey.

He'd put up a bit of a fight, but the man that found him had managed to scoop him up and take him to the vet to be checked for a microchip. The yard turned out to be the office site for the building firm who had been working on the huge house renovation on the corner of Jenni's road, and they thought Oscar must have jumped into one of their vans for a snooze at some point and ended up being driven all the way back to Kent.

Jenni felt giddy with relief and completely overwhelmed with gratitude when the vet said that the builder who found him, Dave, had offered to bring Oscar back with him when he travelled up for work the next day.

Now, the following morning, Jenni was waiting anxiously for Oscar's safe return, and trying not to think about what might have happened with Ben had the phone call not interrupted them.

Her phone pinged and she was startled to see a message from Ben.

> Let me know when he's home. Hope
> he's okay.

What? Her heart sank at the tone of his message. There was none of the warmth she'd come to expect from him. No reference to what had happened, or nearly happened between them. Nothing.

She was trying to think how best to reply when the doorbell rang.

She dashed to answer it, and through the glass panes of the front door she could see the outline of a man holding a big square box.

Oscar.

Her heart raced as she wrenched open the door and asked breathlessly, 'Are you Dave?'

'Yep, and you must be Jenni?'

When Jenni nodded, he continued. 'This is one feisty cat you've got here! He's been shouting at me the whole way!'

As if he knew he was being talked about, a loud and pro-longed yowl of protest came from the box as Dave handed it carefully to Jenni.

'Thank you so much for bringing him back, I've been so worried about him. I can't believe he ended up in Kent of all places!' Jenni said, overwhelmed to finally have him back home.

'No problem, love. Just glad to see him back home, safe and sound.'

And with that, Dave sauntered back down the path, his paint-splattered overalls straining uncomfortably around his middle.

'Come on, you,' Jenni said, stepping back in her flat and closing the door behind her. 'Let's get you out.'

She lowered the box onto the kitchen floor, flipping the

lid open as Oscar's purrs filled the room. He pushed his head into her hand as Jenni tickled the magic spot behind his ears, making him purr even louder as relief flooded through her.

She couldn't believe it – Oscar had made it home again.

54

'You've got sixty seconds to clear the area, GET A MOVE ON,' the watch commander shouted, as Ben checked around him, looking for casualties, his vision obscured by smoke, his breathing loud in his ear as he sucked in oxygen through the mask he was wearing.

He could just about see Vick ahead of him, holding up two fingers to indicate two more rooms left to check, pointing to her right. Ben headed to the opposite side of the narrow hallway, pushing open the doors to lean inside.

All clear.

They burst through the double fire doors at the end of the corridor and into the stairwell, racing down the stairs to the ground floor before finally making it out of the building and into the open-air car park.

Even though it was just a training exercise, Ben's heart was pounding and the adrenaline was coursing through his veins as he pulled the mask from his face and sucked the cool, clean air deep into his lungs, shrugging off the straps of the tank from his shoulders.

'Good work everyone!' bellowed the commander. 'Successful evacuation, no casualties. All bodies accounted for.'

Packing up all the kit and readying the engine for departure, Ben's thoughts drifted, not for the first time that day, to Jenni. He'd texted her quickly before his shift, but had yet to receive a reply.

He hoped Oscar was home now, and he hoped ... What did he hope?

Obviously, he hoped that the cat was okay, but also that he'd still get to see him. He hoped, too, that he would still see Jenni. And he hoped Jenni would still *want* to see *him*. Not just see him, spend time with him. Spend *more* time with him.

He realised with a jolt that the time he'd spent with her over the last week had been the happiest he'd felt for a long time, despite being worried about Oscar.

'Ben, are you going to actually shut that door or are you just going to stare at it for another ten minutes?' Vick shouted out to him, interrupting his thoughts.

He slammed the compartment door shut and fastened it, before jumping up to take his seat in the engine.

'Come on, then, out with it. What's going on?' Vick asked, impatiently.

'Oh nothing. Just that the cat has been found,' said Ben glumly.

'Right, but that's good news, surely?' asked Vick, puzzled. 'So why do you look so miserable?'

'Yeah, it is. It's just that—'

'Now you don't have an excuse to hang out with Jenni anymore?' interrupted Vick with a shrewd glance.

'Yes. If you must know. What if he's the only reason she's been spending time with me and now it will go back to . . . *normal*. Me, on my own again.'

'Blimey, someone's having a pity party today,' said Vick, smiling. 'Just ask her out and get on with it, Ben, you're being silly. Either that or kidnap her cat. The choice is yours.'

As Ben took a shower at the end of his shift, he realised she was right. And when he got home, he knew exactly what he needed to do.

55

Jenni carefully rolled up the small rectangle of paper and, while Oscar was eating yet another treat – she was unable to deny him *anything* right now – she carefully attached the note to his collar. Tying it on securely with silver thread left over from Christmas – and all she could find – she checked that it was safely in place and stood back.

She'd spent the day pandering to Oscar's every need, relieved and emotional to see him back in his favourite spot, draped along the back of the sofa, with his legs in the air, seemingly unaware of the drama his trip to Kent had caused.

She'd sent text messages to Amy, her mum and Tim to let them know Oscar was safely back home, but something was holding her back from contacting Ben.

She knew she should have replied to him as soon as Dave had dropped Oscar off, but Ben's tone was so 'off' that she didn't know what to say, or how to say it. She worried that she'd imagined the connection she thought they'd shared. But no. She remembered the look on his face as she'd leaned against him; remembered how safe she felt in his arms and how close they'd become in the last week.

The thought of not seeing him again made her feel ... bereft.

Spending time with Ben had brought her a happiness that she'd never expected to find so close to home.

So, before she could talk herself out of it, she knew exactly what she had to do. She'd follow Ben's advice, be brave, and send one last message, via Oscar.

56

Throwing his kit bag down by the front door, Ben kicked off his trainers and headed for the kitchen. With a sigh, he put a pan of water on the hob to boil and grabbed a tin of budget tomatoes and a half-empty pack of pasta from the packet.

All day, he'd been hoping to hear from Jenni – was now the time to follow his own advice and be brave? He didn't want to lose what he thought they had between them without even trying.

Pulling the tin opener from the drawer next to the sink, he was hit by the sudden sensation of being watched, and glancing over to the window he noticed two bright eyes staring at him intently.

Oscar.

'Hello, mate,' Ben said, opening the catch to let him in. 'It's so good to see you! I hear you've been on holiday!'

Oscar was purring loudly, turning in circles on the kitchen counter and arching his back as Ben stroked him gently.

'Oh, Oscar,' Ben whispered. 'Am I glad to see you.'

Tears pricked behind his eyes as Oscar gave a timid meow, the sound touching Ben's heart in a way he didn't think possible.

'You poor thing, you must be starving.' Ben turned to reach into the cupboard for Oscar's favourite biscuits.

And that's when he saw it.

A note tied to Oscar's collar.

His heart racing, his fingers fumbled to loosen the knot, before taking a deep breath and unfurling the paper.

Dear Ben,

If you're reading this, you'll know that Oscar is home safely. I've fed him hundreds of times today, I'm surprised he's managed to jump over the fences and into your garden, but that's Oscar, I suppose. Where there's a biscuit, there's a way!

I've been so worried about him, but you made a horrible situation so much easier. Thank you for helping me. Thank you for being so kind and thoughtful, and for caring about Oscar as much as I do.

I'd got used to being on my own, but I realise

now that I've missed having someone to share my life with. Both the good bits and the really awful bits too.

A wise person once told me to Be Brave. (The capital letters seem necessary here.) So, would you like to go on a date with me? 8.30 tomorrow at the gallery?

Jenni x

57

'So, let me get this straight, instead of just texting him to let him know Oscar was back, like a normal person would, you sent him a note via the cat?'

'Tim! You're freaking me out. I thought it would be a cool, you know, gesture or whatever. And anyway, you're not focusing on the actual issue here. I asked him out on a date. Isn't that what you told me to do?'

She paused, waiting for Tim to reply.

'I did, yes,' he agreed eventually. 'But you could have just messaged him?'

'I know, but his text to me had been so … oh, I don't know … matter of fact.'

'Okay, but maybe he was just in a hurry or something? Anyway, I'm proud of you. I know it's taken a lot for you to put yourself back out there. And I'm sure you'll hear from him again. I've told you, no man would spend so much time looking for someone else's cat unless they were interested. Let me know how you get on. And it *was* a cool gesture,' he added, before hanging up.

Jenni felt herself relax a little. Now all she could do was wait until Oscar returned from his night-time adventure, and hope to God he brought a reply from Ben back with him.

*

A heavy object landing on her chest woke her with a jolt.

She opened her eyes and lifted her head from the pillow to see Oscar, inches from her face, staring intensely at her, kneading the rumpled duvet cover.

She'd missed this the most, she thought, reaching to stroke his soft fur, running her hand over the curve of his back, inching her fingers up to his neck to tickle him behind the ears.

And that's when she felt something catch against her wrist. A note.

Tugging gently, she released it, her heart beating fast, and she read the one word that she knew would change everything.

Yes. x

Epilogue

'Urgh, Oscar, not again?' Jenni reached out to flick the damp crisp packet off the bed. Since he was no longer delivering correspondence between Jenni and Ben, he'd taken to bringing home all manner of rubbish for her to deal with instead: discarded lottery tickets, empty sweet wrappers, their shiny foil weathered and faded, used stamps ripped from the corners of envelopes.

He'd definitely been a Womble in a previous life.

A glance at her phone told her that she still had an hour before she was due to meet Amy and Tim at the studio. She felt a thrill of excitement every time she thought about it.

After doing the deal with Larry, Go Big had agreed to rent the space at the gallery and fund all the renovation costs to create a studio. It was a dream come true to be finally in

338

a position to merge her side hustle with her new role as creative director at Go Big, working alongside Tim and Amy. And the fact that her studio was at the gallery, the location of their first not-a-date-date, second stood-up-but-still-not-actually-a-date-date and third absolutely-was-a-date-date, made it even more special.

Putting her phone back down, Jenni reached out to wrap her arms around Ben, and curled into his back.

'Hello, thirty-eight,' he whispered sleepily, rolling over to pull her in close, resting his chin on her forehead.

Jenni snuggled into his neck, breathing in the warm scent of him and sighing contentedly.

'Hello, sixty-six,' she murmured, feeling his smile as he did every time they used their private nicknames for each other.

They'd talked long into the night after their third date. Tentatively, at first, unpicking the doubts and fears they both felt had been holding them back, but sure in their hearts that the connection they had was too strong to ignore. They agreed to take it slow, to not put too much pressure on each other, or themselves, and to see where it went.

Be brave, Jenni had reminded him as she she'd taken Ben's hand, and he'd whispered 'good luck', echoing the words he'd written in his note to her, before finally pulling her towards him and kissing her. It had been totally worth the wait, Jenni had confided to Amy the next day.

Ben's phone buzzed on the bedside table and, reluctantly, he pulled away from Jenni to reach for it, hoping it wasn't a call from work. He wasn't due at the station till the weekend and he planned to visit his parents later that day to give the summerhouse a final lick of paint before the grand opening party that his mother was planning.

Ben let out an exasperated sigh.

'Is it work?'

'No. It's just my mother. *Again*. She wants to know if you have any allergies so she can decide what to cook for lunch when you visit.'

'Really?' Jenni laughed. 'It's still weeks away, she's got ages.'

'They're very excited about finally meeting you, and Mum wants to get everything ready, apparently. She's even roped Penny in to help set everything up.'

'Ah, that's so sweet,' Jenni snuggled into Ben again. 'Did she say anything about your dad helping you with the drying racks? I loved your suggestion of building something more sturdy in the studio than my washing line idea.'

'He messaged me last night actually. He wants to get started straight away. I think he's already bored now that the summerhouse is nearly finished. He also mentioned something about building a climbing frame for Oscar, so watch out!'

Text to his mum finished, Ben turned back to Jenni and

reached over to pull her close again, just as Oscar, who'd disappeared to the kitchen for biscuits, returned, jumping back onto the bed, nestling down between them.

'Oh Oscar,' they both groaned as he made himself comfortable before finally curling up, his tail tucked tightly around him. Satisfied, he settled down to sleep with a contented purr.

His work here was done.

Acknowledgements

I'd like to pay tribute to my mum's tireless, even obsessive, love of the written word. While pregnant with me, she was writing her first novel. During my early childhood, she was writing her second. Over the years, I would see her working on this novel or that play or attending some writing class or other. Despite several draining treatments for pancreatic cancer, she still had an unshakeable desire to finish this book, which she worked on for as long as she had the ability to do so. Since her passing, I realised I had only seen the tip of the iceberg: I've since discovered numerous notebooks full of beautifully handwritten stories dating back to her school days, Word documents and Google documents and USB drives full of short stories and scripts and fragments of novels. Writing was integral to who she was, and though I wish she could be here to see it, I'm deeply grateful to see this part of her out there in the world once more.
JAMIE PATEL